I0747176

Blood

MOTHER

JA HUSS

Copyright © 2025 by JA Huss
ISBN: 978-1-957277-34-9

Edited by RJ Locksley
Cover Design by JA Huss

ABOUT THE BOOK

Ryet

The hunger burns, the feeding soothes. I hate this curse, I hate the world, and most of all, I hate myself. Because I am chained to the blood of the only thing I truly want—the little Black witch called Syrsee.

Syrsee

I thought it would be simple: feed the scion, survive his transformation, forge some kind of new life together. But each drop I give Ryet brings the Darkness closer. Each drop he takes drags the demon out.

Paul

For thousands of years, the Darkness ignored me. But that monster was never my god, and Josep was never my salvation. It is Ryet who will deliver me from evil.

Josep

I alone hold the power to create a vampire. Not Paul. There is but one, and it is me. I am the monster. I am the king—unrivaled and invincible.

Little Baby

I was a mistake. From the moment I was born, I was unwanted. Discarded. And then he found me. Evil itself wanted me. But if I am damned to eternal Hell, I'm taking someone down with me.

1 - Little Baby

Before he made you, he made me

It's three forty-two am when I stumble through the back door of my house smelling of smoke and sex. I am so drunk I forget to take off my Docs and they clunk on every step as I make my way upstairs to my bedroom. On some nights this clunking would be enough to earn a beating from my father, but on this night, it's not. He's been drinking for three weeks straight. I haven't even seen him for days. Heard him, yes—he and my mother are always fighting—but seen him, no.

The basement is his man cave so that's where he likes to get his booze on. And when he's on a bender like this, he doesn't even come up to eat. Sleeps down there too.

I love his benders because while he's still dangerous when he's falling-down drunk, his aim is pretty bad. He still tries to hit me, but more often than not he breaks his knuckles on a wall instead of my face.

Sobriety, as far as I'm concerned, is my number one enemy. Both mine and my father's. When he's drunk, he's too busy thinking about himself to care about me. And when I'm stoned, I'm too immersed in my own self-delusions to care about the truth.

Which is that my life sucks and is going absolutely nowhere.

I flop into bed, not even bothering to take off my boots. The room is spinning, but I don't care. And since I decided to drop out of school so I can hang at Boyd's house every day, I can sleep in as long as I want.

I moan as I turn over onto my stomach, and then pass out, hoping that my father stays drunk forever.

* * *

When I wake, I find myself in a place of emptiness.

But as soon as I think that thought, there is a mist here. Purple, but some gold too. It's hard to see because there is nothing but darkness all around me, but I can feel it. It cools my burning hot body and feels good on my skin.

"Hello?" a voice says.

I don't startle. I'm not scared. But maybe I should be? I'm not sure.

"Are you awake now, Echo?"

Echo? I make a face. Though I don't think I'm really making a face because I don't think I actually have a body. "Who's Echo?" Then I'm even more confused. Because that's my voice and how could I have a voice if I don't have a body?

"Oh." The other voice is calm, and low, and kind of seductive. "Oh, I see. You're…" She falters for words, then tries again. "What are you? I mean, *who?* Who are you?"

Who am I? I don't know. So I say, "I'm just me."

"I think you are Echo."

"I don't know about that."

"Well…" There's some hesitation here, like this woman is about to explain something to me but doesn't quite know how to start. "I think you are. In fact, I should just get to the point here, Echo. That's your name. I should know. I made you."

"*Made* me?" I scoff. "No. That's decidedly not true." These words come out automatically and they come out with such certainty, the woman goes silent for a few moments, allowing me to think. To ponder my… conviction. Because how the hell do I know she's not the one who made me? I have no memory of anything at the moment. I don't even have a body.

Which, again, is contradictory since I do have a mouth and a voice.

"OK," the woman finally says. "All right. Well, if it wasn't me, then who?"

I shrug my shoulders, surprised that I have shoulders to do this. And I'm just about to say I don't know, I just know it's not her, when a name comes to me. "Josep did."

"Josep?" Her response to my answer is filled with both surprise and delight. "Well. I guess I didn't see that one coming. But who am I kidding? I didn't see any of this coming. Well, the death. My own death, I mean. I knew that part."

"You're dead." I say these words flatly and with no emotion. "Does that mean I'm dead?"

"Well, death, as it pertains to witches, can sometimes be… subjective? Yes. That's a good word to describe it. You see, I no longer have a body but I live on in spirit. And isn't that the only thing that counts?"

"No." And again, I say this automatically and with a surety I don't actually feel. Then more words are spilling out. Words I don't seem to have any control over. "Spirit can't fuck, witch. Spirit can't eat, or drink, or feel things."

The woman scoffs. "That might be true, but a spirit knows that those things—these things that only physical bodies feel— they are…" Again, she struggles for a word.

"You need a thesaurus," I say, which makes her laugh. "You talk too slow. You come off as very indecisive."

"Is that so?"

"Finish your sentence. These things—fucking, and eating, and drinking, and feeling—they're *what*?" My words are angry. If they were a color, they'd be red.

"I was going to say they're inconsequential. Is that a big enough word for you?"

I open my eyes, realize I'm sitting in a pool of glowing

lavender water which is located inside some kind of cave, and look at the woman. She is very beautiful, but in an older way. She's not old, per se. I just know she's older than me and… well, youth is everything, isn't it?

She's wearing a tight red dress that is so low cut, her large, round breasts are spilling out of it. She doesn't have any wrinkles, her body is perfect, and her eyes are bright. So she doesn't *look* old. And now that I think of it, old is the wrong word. I seem to be fascinated with words right now, so I pause here to get it right.

Not old.

Wise.

Yes. She comes off as wise. Which is a good thing to be.

But she's not exactly… *here*. She's mostly intact from the torso up but her legs are a swirling mist of purple.

Witch, she called herself.

But I don't think so. Maybe, at one time, she was a witch. Just like maybe, at one time, I was a girl named Echo.

"My name is Little Baby." Once again, these words don't seem to be my own. "You will call me Little Baby."

The remnant of the witch smiles and her eyes twinkle. "Oh, that's adorable. Little Baby. I love it. It actually suits you."

I ignore her, turning my head to look around the cavern. It's clearly someone's home, even though living in a cave is typically a euphemism.

I blink and shake my head. Euphemism? Where the hell did that come from?

Anyway. There's a lot of furniture here in the cave—couches and chairs, a bed and a desk—so it's definitely a home.

Whose home? My home?

And then there's that name again. Josep. This is Josep's home.

I look down at my body and find that I was right. It's not all there. I'm in the pool, so for a moment I think that maybe it's an illusion because of the way the light refracts into the water. But it's not. I have no legs. I'm a torso, like the remnant witch, but instead of being made up of a swirling mist of purple, I'm made up of water.

Which is the same thing, actually, when you think about it.

A small chuckle forms and then there it is, coming out of my mouth in the form of color. Gold, to be precise.

I feel very smart right now. I mean, refraction? Where did that word come from? I'm not sure, but it does describe the bending of light so I used it appropriately. Anyway. Mist is nothing but water in droplet form.

The magic surrounding my lower body is a concentration of the magic surrounding hers.

Which means I have more power than she does.

Makes sense, since I'm younger and isn't youth everything?

"What are you, Little Baby?"

I sigh and look back at the woman. Then there it is. The name of what I am comes flowing past my lips, unbidden. "A remnant. Just like you."

She smiles. "Would you like help out of that pool?"

I look down at the water, then back up at her. "I don't seem to have any legs. So… no. I think I'll just stay here."

The witch laughs. "You can't stay there, Little Baby. Where's the fun in that?"

"Are you deaf? I just told you, I don't have any legs."

"Come now, of course you do! They're there. They're just

not actualized yet. You're in the middle of it. Well, I really think it's over now. You just don't know it's over."

"What the hell are you talking about?"

"The actualization. I don't know what happened to you, but I've been around the block, Little Baby. I can take a good guess. You were turned. You used to be a girl called Echo. She was Paul's favorite, so she must've been hanging about when Josep went upstairs. You can tell me all about it later, but for now let's get you out of that water."

Then she offers me her hand.

I don't take it. My mind is swirling with the words she just spoke. *You used to be a girl called Echo.* She's right. I know she's right. But I have no memory of that. Which bothers me. Greatly.

"Come now. Take my hand. I promise, you can get out of the water."

"Why should I believe your promises?" I'm irritated so these words come out as a sneer. "You don't have any legs either."

The witch bursts out laughing. Then looks down at the mist surrounding her lower body. I look at it too, and as I watch the mist fades and her legs appear. Well, not legs, per se, because she's in a long dress.

When I look back up at her, she's smiling at me. "There. Legs. Satisfied now? You're new, Little Baby. And while you do seem to have quite the command of the English language, the magic is something that must be learned. I can teach you." She pauses here, letting those words hang in the air for a few moments before continuing. "Would you like me to teach you?"

And once again, she offers her hand.

I take it. Because I would like to get out of the pool. I really, really want legs. And the moment our hands touch, there they are. Smooth, and pale, and made of flesh.

The water changes color. The lavender glow subsides. But at the same time, I feel it. Not all around me this time, but inside me.

"That's it," the witch says. "You've got it now. Stand up. You can do it."

"Stop talking to me like I'm a child."

"Your name is Little Baby. Of course you're a child."

Reluctantly, I admit she's right. I am a child. Not in body—I'm in my twenties, at least—but in spirit. So maybe she was onto something about that.

I hate being wrong. At least I think I do.

"Stand up. Baby steps for Little Baby."

I sneer at her, but she just laughs. Which feels… disrespectful, since clearly—

"Clearly," she says, cutting off my thoughts, "you are a powerful thing, Little Baby. But experience is everything, dear girl."

"Hmm." I stand up—my legs weak and wobbly, but very much there—and, with her help, step out of the pool. We face each other, nearly eye to eye, and I tip my chin up. "Youth," I say. "Youth is everything."

"Spoken like a true child."

I yank my hand out of hers and walk across the smooth rock towards a floor-length mirror propped up against the side of the cave wall. "You should be nicer to me."

"Why's that?"

"Because I'm more powerful than you."

"Power is only useful if one can wield it, dear girl."

I don't say anything back because I have reached the mirror and I'm looking at myself. There's a hazy mist around my body now, just like it was around hers. Only mine is still two colors instead of one. Lavender and gold.

I'm pale, pale white, and my skin kind of glows, making me almost appear silver. I'm thin, but shapely. My hips are wide and my breasts large. My hair is long and silver. Or maybe lavender, I can't really tell.

I'm…

"Gorgeous." The witch is right behind me and she coos this word into my ear. It sends a chill down my spine and my skin prickles up in response. I stare at her in the mirror, our eyes locked on each other's. Then she gently pulls a thick strand of wet hair off my shoulder and smooths it down my back.

Again, I get the chills.

She's making me feel weird and I don't like it, so I step away, out of her reach, and cross the room to put some distance between us. "Now what?" I ask.

Her eyebrows go up. "Now? Well, now, Little Baby, we make a plan."

"What kind of plan?"

"What kind of plan would you like to make?"

"I don't know," I say truthfully. "I don't really understand what's happening."

"You mean you don't understand what *happened*. Past tense."

I shrug up one shoulder. "Fine. I don't understand what happened so I don't know what to do next."

"Well, you're in luck. Because not only do I have a plan, but I know exactly what to do next." She says all these words as she takes herself across the room to a couch. Then she sits down, pulling her legs up and tucking them underneath her, getting comfortable. She pats the cushion next to her. "Come. Sit. I've been dying to tell someone everything I know about mirrors.

That someone"—she pauses to sigh—"is otherwise preoccupied. But you'll do, Little Baby. You'll do just fine."

"And then what?"

"Then…" She smiles at me. And in this smile I see something new in her. Something evil. Something devious. Something sinister. "Then," she says again, "we'll plot our revenge."

"Why would you assume I want revenge? You don't even know what happened to me."

"Oh, I can take a good guess, Little Baby. I am no ordinary witch, you see. I am one of *them* too. I drink the blood. Not anymore, of course. I'm dead. But I was you once. I was… Little Baby, though Josep never called me that."

"You know him."

"Of course I know him. Before he made you, he made me."

Drunk on blood and sex

My life: In bed with the man I love. Who is a monster. Who drinks blood to live.

My blood.

I am food.

And I love it.

It's all very dreamy (in a gore kind of way.) Living back at the Guild has been a nice reprieve, but more on that later. Right now, I've captured my man's attention and I'm intrigued to see where it leads.

Ryet turns over in bed, his hand slipping across my stomach. Then he's pulling me close, pushing his face into my neck. For a moment I think he's gonna drink, so I back out of the scene I'm reading—i.e. immersed in, since this is how one reads the books when you're magical—and pay closer attention to him. But he just kisses me instead, tempting me away from the book and trying his best to turn me on. "Where are you now?" He whispers this right into my ear.

I let out a little huff of air. "A harem."

"A harem?" He chuckles, then licks my earlobe. Which he knows drives me nuts. He's such a tease in the morning.

"It's a smutty romance about a sheikh."

"*Syrsee.*"

"What? It's… pleasure reading."

Ryet grabs the tattered paperback from my hands, chucks it across the room, then laughs into my neck and starts biting me. I forget all about the harem scene and how what's-her-name was refusing to sleep in Sheikh Whoever's bed and redirect all my thoughts to the man I very willingly share a bed with.

The pull. God, how I love the feeling of the blood being pulled out of me. It gets me so worked up, I nearly come undone. But Ryet knows this and uses it as part of his tease. He likes to make me want him. He likes to leave me wanting on occasion as well.

If any other man did this to me, I would call it insecurity. But Ryet is not insecure. Not about sex or blood. He knows how much I like the feeling of being fed on, not to mention the act of feeding on him. He's been there, of course. With Paul, not so much me. But it's the same thing. It's all so addictive. So Ryet knows he's got nothing to worry about. There isn't a man alive on this Earth who can satisfy me the way he can.

It's just him. Forever. That's my plan, anyway. Him forever.

My eyes close and my breathing picks up as Ryet's lips dance across my neck. He nips at the skin, pricking it with his sharp teeth. Then his tongue flicks out to lick up the tiny drops of blood. He's teasing himself as well as me and when I slip my hand under the covers and grip his hard shaft, he sucks in a breath, hissing at me. "You're always in such a rush."

"And you always want to take your time."

Now it's my turn to hiss because his response to my reproach is a bite, quick and stinging. Then his lips are there, pressing against my skin, and my hand automatically begins to jerk him off. The moment I begin doing this, his hand is on my knee, opening my leg and pressing it against the bed. Then his fingers are rubbing me, stroking back and forth across my pussy before entering me, pushing in and out in the same rhythm as his bloodsucking.

I'm done. Lost. Living inside bliss itself. But I make myself wait. I control my reaction for as long as possible because I like to come just as he's finishing. It's a little game we play because that final drink is better than sex itself, but in combination with an orgasm—my God, there's no other pleasure in the entire universe that can compete.

But I can only hold on so long, so it's usually me who ends his drink. I come and he pulls hard on my neck, drawing out as much blood as he can while my back arches and I bite my lip to keep from squealing.

A few moments later and I relax into his waiting arms. He holds me tight, whispering things in my ear. Very sweet things. How he will love me 'til the end of time. How I am his soulmate. How we will spend our cursed eternity together.

And I believe him.

I bask in the afterglow of my own bliss and believe him.

* * *

After a few moments, Ryet pulls back and a bit of blood drips down my neck, tickling me. He leans back in, kissing and licking the wound he just made until it heals.

When he's done, he flops back on the pillow, sighing. "Your turn."

Is it normal that I feed on him? Probably not, in the grand scheme of things. I'm not a vampire, after all. I'm a Black witch.

But my life went off the rails months ago now and, well, it is what it is.

I sit up a little, then dive under the covers. What's good for the goose is good for the gander, after all. If he can tease me, I can tease him and my tease doesn't start with his neck.

Since drinking has become a part of my life, I've learned to embrace it. It's just a part of who I am now. And I've discovered that I have *preferences*. I like to drink from Ryet's upper thigh. And trust me when I say this, there isn't a woman alive who can turn him on the way I do.

He's naked—we both are. There's no point in putting on pajamas when we spend just as much of our time at night feeding as we do sleeping. At the end of each day we get in bed and drink each other, then we sleep off the blood lust only to wake up a couple of hours later to do it all again. We do this on repeat all night long. If Ryet and I are physically together, the lust is always there. As is the hunger. It all has to be satisfied in some way.

To an outsider, this might sound exhausting, but to me? It's everything. The drink, the pull, the lust, the bliss—it's even better than reading a Guild book.

Though I hope it never comes to this, I would give up the books to feed and be fed on by the man in bed with me right now.

I'm addicted to *him*, not just his blood.

My hand is still wrapped around his hard shaft when I glide my lips up his inner thigh until I hear it. The pulsing of the blood. The call to drink. He lets out a moan and then his fingertips are sliding through my hair. A moment later he's gripping my head, pushing down on it as my mouth opens and my teeth nip at his skin.

Since I don't have fangs, this is how I open him up to drink. Tiny pinprick nips, but just at first. As soon as I get the blood flowing, I bite harder. I can't get to his artery, but that much blood at once is too much anyway, so I don't feel disappointed that I never quite get a gush from him the way he does from me.

"That's it," Ryet says, just as I get a small flow going. His hips start moving, his back arching. "Keep going."

I take the blood, pulling as much as I can out at once—not just for my benefit, though I do love the taste and how I can feel his blood as it makes its way through my body. I do it for him because I know how good it feels. I want him to feel the way I do when I'm being fed on.

He never will, of course. Not unless I grow fangs or cut him open with a knife or something. So when I feed I give him sexual favors as well. That's what my hand is doing as I drink. Sliding up and down his shaft in long, slow strokes.

I take one last long pull of blood, biting his thigh as I do it, and Ryet comes, spilling his seed all over my hand as his back arches up and he gnashes his teeth together, growling like an animal until the intensity of the orgasm subsides. Then he is spent and living in the bliss.

I'm still there as well so I rest my head on his thigh as he absently strokes my hair, and then... once again, we fall asleep. Drunk on blood and sex.

* * *

It takes a lot of effort to get up in the mornings. I mean, Ryet and I, we're always hungry. We can always use another drink and who doesn't want another orgasm?

But we both have roles to play here. I am learning how to navigate the books. Just simple ones still. Nothing magical yet. But I'm getting better at immersion. I won't be stuck at level one forever.

One day soon, I think, *I will get what I came for. Knowledge.*

This, and only this, is what drives me to get up the next time I wake.

It's eight-thirty in the morning, which is a little bit later than I usually wake up, but the Guild is very understanding about our needs. I am not expected to be at the library until nine-thirty and Ryet doesn't have to report to the lab until ten.

I always wake up before him. He just needs more sleep than I do. And this time I don't wake him, or wait for him to wake, either. I can't. If I do, we'll never get out of here because I'll just want to drink again.

It's an endless cycle and if we allow it, the blood lust would take over our lives.

Which sounds fun. But… at what cost?

I don't want to be a feeder, lying in bed in my old age covered in filth. Though I don't really think that will be my destiny—I don't really know if I can age, let alone die. But still, that image of my grandma dying in that disgusting room that smelled like death—it's very strong. It's burned into my memory.

I will not turn into her. I won't.

That's why I get up in the mornings and report to the library. That's why I leave Ryet in bed. And even though, in the back of my mind, I'm always thinking about the next time we'll be together and the next time we feed on each other, I can control it if I don't see him during the day.

When we first got here about eight weeks ago, we did meet up for lunch. I think we were both still… actualizing? That's as good a word as any to describe the transformation going on inside our bodies. So our blood lust, while very strong at night, wasn't an issue midday.

Until it was.

After a few weeks of settling in, Ryet and I found ourselves sneaking away after eating. The bushes, a bathroom, anywhere we could find a little privacy. All so we could feed. And then we would get tired, and pass out, and wake up, and do it again and... well, let's just say it was not a productive way to spend one's day.

We got sloppy and the Guild took notice. We were 'encouraged' to go our separate ways during the day. Not ordered. Not exactly. And what could they have done if we refused? Kicked us out? They need us more than we need them. But, since we're guests here, we took their advice seriously.

No more blood at lunch.

I do love my blood, but I don't miss it much during the day because when I get to the library, I go right into the level one reading room and from the moment I enter until the moment I leave, I live in the stories.

Stories that aren't as interesting and addictive as my real life, but even the simple ones I've been learning to read the past few weeks are definitely good enough to keep the blood lust at bay.

The trashy romance I was reading between feedings last night is just a little bonus. Definitely not on the Black Witch Reading 101 syllabus.

Myer, who is my archivist guide, has an approved reading list for me. But my powers to actualize a story don't stop when I leave the library building. I found the book about the sheikh in the little thrift store just down the mountain near the place Ryet and I sometimes have brunch on the weekends.

I'm sure Myer knows I'm reading on my own now, but so far, he hasn't said anything.

I dress, blow Ryet a kiss so I don't wake him, and then leave our little apartment.

Most of the Guild citizens start work much earlier than I do, so all the walking paths in our little mountain village are bustling with people doing whatever it is they do. Some wave to me, and I wave back. Some don't even look me in the eye as they pass. Not because I'm a Black witch, but because they are immersed in their tasks for the day. So far it's been a very friendly experience. Pleasant is probably the right word.

I don't feel like one of them—I definitely still feel like an outsider—but it doesn't bother me. In fact, I like it. I am something other than them and it's OK. At least with me. What the collective citizens of the Guild think of me, I don't really know. But I don't really care, either.

I think that is the biggest change I've noticed in myself so far. I'm… confident. And… I dunno. Maybe… proud? Of what I am? I mean, there are so few of my kind. And I'm even more rare than most Black witches because I have the blood of vampires inside me. Not just any vampires, either. Paul and Josep, and Ryet. The American Vampires.

Not to mention the Darkness.

My hand absently goes to my belly when that word appears in my head. There is a Darkness inside me, growing, and maturing, and becoming something new. Ryet put it there, so there must be a Darkness inside him too.

When I first got here, one of the first things the Guild doctors did was give me a physical. They said I wasn't pregnant and there were no signs that I could feel, so I let myself believe them.

It's not true. I feel this pregnancy deep inside.

But I don't want to think about that night when the four of us were all tangled up in the cabin bedroom, drinking each other and passing the Darkness between us through blood. Not because it's traumatizing. It's not. Ryet took me away from the actual act and we spent it flirting in a library so I don't even know what happened.

But I'm a good visualizer and even though in my head, at least, I understand that it was a horror show, *emotionally* it's actually erotic. And when I think about it, an almost overwhelming desire for sex takes over.

Not just for Ryet, either. But for Paul and Josep too.

I want to do it again.

That's why I don't think about it.

* * *

When I enter the level one reading room in the Guild library, Myer is sitting on a golden velvet-tufted couch that faces the door. In front of him is a wooden table with a massive tome of a book in the middle.

My heart skips when I see this book because this is not *Go, Dog. Go!* It's not a Dick and Jane reader, it's not Dr. Seuss, or the Baby-Sitters Club—which is what I was 'reading' yesterday.

This is a magic book. I can tell just by glancing at the ornate leather cover.

And it's *old*.

"Good morning, Syrsee."

"Good morning, Myer." But I don't look at him. I can't seem to take my eyes off this book.

"Have a seat. We've got a lot to discuss today."

I slip around the couch in front of me and sit down. The book on the table is facing my direction, not toward Myer, who is on the other side of the table.

I drop my bag to the floor, then finally meet Myer's gaze. "Today?" I ask. "I get to read this one today?"

He's just about to answer when someone knocks at the door.

"What is it?" Myer's tone is irritated, gruff, and unfamiliar. So far, he's been very friendly with me. We did know each other back in school, after all. He kissed me once. But almost immediately, my guard at the school interrupted us.

But his response to the knock on the door is anything but friendly.

My thoughts pause here for a moment because everything about the Guild campus feels… oh, I don't know. Precarious, I guess. And I'm always on the verge of thinking this happily-ever-after for now is about to vanish. So any small discrepancy makes me nervous.

I don't want to go back out into the real world. I want to stay here in this place where I don't really belong, but am tolerated nonetheless. Because I don't really belong anywhere and the past several months have been a bit of a horror show for me.

The door opens a crack and a young girl pokes her head in. "I'm sorry to disturb you, Archivist. But I have a message." Her eyes flit to me, then back to him, as if to say, 'A private message.'

Myer sighs. And again, he's not even trying to hide his irritation. "It needs to wait."

The girl is shaking her head, opening the door as if to say, 'Come out here and we'll talk about it.'

Myer reads between all the lines, gets up, and looks down at me. "Excuse me for one moment."

"Of course," I say. Then I watch him as he goes to the door, pushes the girl out, and blocks her from my view as they whisper back and forth.

He sighs again. Then turns to me. "I'm sorry, Syrsee. I'll be back in five minutes."

I'm confused at the one-eighty turn in his normally congenial personality. "Take your time. I'm not going anywhere." I smile at him. But he doesn't smile back. Just leaves, closing the door behind him.

I sit back, sinking into the comfy cushions of the couch, forcing myself to reign in my imagination. "Well, that wasn't weird."

But it's all fine, Syrsee.

It's fine.

And just as I'm thinking these words, my eyes track to the book on the table in front of me and I sit up again. Paying attention to what is right in front of me instead of the foreboding feeling floating around in my head.

Should I open the book?

I mean… the correct answer here is absolutely not. While no one ever said I wasn't allowed to read the books since I've gotten here, just the fact that Myer is my chaperone sends the vibe. He is my guide. There is no question about that.

But I can't help myself. So I look over my shoulder, just to make sure the door is closed, and then I lean forward and with a single fingertip I flip open the cover.

For a moment I'm confused because I'm looking… at myself.

But then I realize that this isn't a page in a book.

It's a *mirror.*

In the same moment that this word forms in my head, I fall forward. And the next thing I know, I'm falling into it.

3 - Ryet

Ryet doesn't live here anymore

When I wake up, I'm craving blood, my dick is hard, and Syrsee is gone.

It's like this every day and I'm sick of it. All I want is her. I want to drink her, and fuck her, and then sleep with her, only to wake up and do it all again.

Sometimes I feel a little guilty about all my carnal wants and needs, but it's not the worst way to waste a life. And anyway, I have a strong suspicion that this phase we're going through right now where all we crave is each other won't last.

I just want to make the most of it. I mean, for all I know there will come a time when she repulses me and never again will I lust for her the way I do now.

I don't want that to happen, but since when does anyone care about what I want?

Never. No one ever asked me if this is what I wanted. It would be nice to given a choice. But even if I did have a choice, what would I do?

I think about leaving. This whole mountain. This world. I think about digging a hole in the earth and burying us inside it, never to see the light of day again.

I'd do it. I would. But only if I could take Syrsee with me, and she likes what she does here. She's reading books. I can't take that away from her. It was my promise. *You will read the books.* That's what I told her. Well, actually, what I told her was... *You're gonna read the books and find us a cure.*

A cure. What a joke, not to mention a lie.

Not sure there is an actual cure for what I am, but more importantly, I don't want to be cured. There's nothing to cure. I am who I am. And Syrsee is who she is too.

This is us.

It took my whole life to get here. Ninety-three years, to be exact. That's the sum total of my first life, when I was born, and my second, when Paul began my transformation from scion to vampire.

No. I am not here to be cured. I'm here to let the Guild poke and prod me until Syrsee gets what she came for, which is those books and the knowledge contained within.

I'm certain that if I asked her to choose—me, and the blood, and sex, and the dirt, or those books—she would choose me. But I would never ask her to do that. To give up what she wants so I can have what I want. It needs to be mutual or it'll never work.

And I really, *really* want it to work.

So happy medium it is.

She doesn't tell me about what she does in the library, but I don't tell her what they do to me in the lab, so I guess we're even.

Suddenly, Paul is in bed next to me, his warm body pressing into mine. His *naked* body. He chuckles. "You miss me, don't you?"

I look at him, squinting, trying to decide—as I do every morning when he appears like this—if he's real or not. I've asked him, of course I've asked him. But he doesn't ever answer me. All he wants to do is touch me. And drink me. And feed me.

And, since Syrsee is never here when I wake up, I let him.

Mostly because I don't think it's real. It's some kind of

dreamwalk, which is kind of real, but not real enough for it to feel like cheating.

And anyway, Syrsee, and Paul, and I are connected whether we want to be or not. He's part of this—whatever *this* is. And maybe he's appearing to her the same way? Maybe she lets him touch her, and drink her, and feed her as well?

I wouldn't actually care if she did. I have no feelings of jealousy about Paul. This detachment isn't rational because he's handsome, powerful, seductive, and charming—in his own way. So I should be jealous. I'm just… not. Whatever relationship Syrsee has with Paul, it's not what she has with me. Same goes for him and I. I wouldn't want him to disappear, but I would choose Syrsee over him without hesitation.

So I don't think Syrsee would care that I'm spending my mornings with fake Paul after she leaves.

"I do miss you," I say, finally answering his question. He doesn't need to ask this question every time we meet up, he knows I miss him. He just likes to hear it.

And once the words come out of my mouth, his hand is sliding up my bare leg. It glides right over my hard cock and then up my chest. His palm comes to a rest on my cheek and then he turns my face towards him so we can look each other in the eyes.

"And all it took was ninety-three years and a little Black witch between us. It was worth the wait, Ryet. Don't you agree?"

I press my lips together and hum. "Mmm. I do."

This makes Paul smile so big, his eyes go bright. "It was always you, you know that, right? You have always been my reason."

It's not true. He's been trying to make a baby vampire for

hundreds of years. Much longer than I've been around. But I understand what he's saying.

He loves me. For whatever reason, he does.

"Do you want a drink, Ryet?"

"Always," I say back.

"Then help yourself." He turns his head away from me, exposing his neck, and even if I had denied my desire to drink him, that silent offer would be enough to change my mind.

My blood lust for Syrsee is constant but my blood lust for Paul is beyond that. It's insatiable.

At first all I do is lean over. But I can smell Paul's blood and before I know it, I'm crawling on top of him. His hands caress my body as I open my mouth and press down, breaking the skin, puncturing the artery, and then it's gushing. Blood fills my mouth faster than I can swallow it.

He never let me do this as a scion and I love every moment of it.

A moan escapes and for a moment, I think it's me. But the low rumble of a growl is actually coming from Paul. "That's it, Ryet. Take what you need." He's stroking me. My head, my leg, my back—I feel his touch everywhere. "Hell, take more than what you need. Take all you want, Ryet. You've earned it."

A flash of anger passes through me, then the reason. A memory of Jane and the kids.

But it's so quick, so fleeting, there isn't even enough time to get mad. There isn't even enough time to care.

Jane is gone.

The kids are gone.

I'm gone.

But Paul is still here. Even though I'm not really sure where 'here' is, he's here.

There is so much blood in my mouth now, I start to choke on it. I don't want it to end the drink. I don't feel full enough. I want more. But I pull back anyway because it's dripping out of my mouth. The moment I do this, the wound I made begins to close.

Paul is stroking my head like I'm a child. And since the drink is over, it annoys me. I push his hand off and roll over on my back, eyes closed, mind closed, body relaxed and approaching satisfaction. But, as always, I'm still hard. There is still more to *want*.

I feel like that's the only word on my mind these days. I want. All I do is want. Blood, and sex, and, if it were available right now, dirt.

"Don't worry," Paul says. "I'll take care of you. I'll always take care of you, Ryet."

And so he does. He strokes me. Slowly, with a firm grip. His body pressing into mine. His mouth at my neck.

"Drink me," I say. "Feed."

"You like it, don't you, Ryet?"

"Just do it."

"It was all worth it, wasn't it?" When I don't say anything, he keeps going. "Go ahead. Lie if you must. Tell me you hate it. Tell me you crave that little wife of yours. That pathetic past life of yours."

But I don't crave her, or have any use for that life, and he knows this. I've already told him that it was worth it, but it's never enough. He asks this question over and over again every time he appears to me. Like he needs constant reassurance. Or maybe he's worried I'll forget and start blaming him for something.

And let's face it, Paul is a hundred percent responsible for every evil thing that ever happened to me, so he deserves this insecurity. But I'm done fighting with him. There is no point. So again, I say, "It was worth it, Paul."

Paul chuckles. "I knew it. I knew you'd love it. I knew it from the moment you were born. When I was sitting in that forest looking down at you in my arms. I felt this. I felt all of it and I knew."

I think about that baby and that forest. I've seen him holding it in my dreamwalks before I knew it was me. And now that I have a clearer picture of what is happening and what it all means, I have questions. "Do you love them all like you love me?"

"Does it make you jealous that I have more scions?"

I shrug, not bothering to open my eyes. "Jealous of what? You've given me everything."

There is no chuckle now but I know he's smiling. "I did, didn't I?" He sounds different. Serious. His voice less musical than it usually is.

"Mmmhmm," I hum. Because I'm tired and I'm probably gonna fall asleep.

"Well, I love them all in different ways, Ryet. So I guess the answer is yes. But none of them will deliver the gift of Darkness. That's you. And Syrsee, of course. You are the best of me. And so I will always be there for you. Remember that when the time comes."

I hear the threat in these last words. Well, threat is probably not the right word. More like a warning, maybe. Because what he really said, and I know this because he's done it so many times now, is that things are going to get horribly bad for me. There's no way around it. And he wants me to know he'll be there when they do.

"Am I going to live through it?" My words come out sleepy and slow. My eyes remain closed.

Paul swipes some hair away from my face. Then he leans in, his mouth touching my neck, his sharp teeth ripping my skin. He licks up some blood before answering my question. "I certainly hope so. You and I, Ryet, are meant to spend eternity together. I'm counting on it."

And then he feeds. Pulling the blood out of me. Mixing us up once again.

I go somewhere else now. Some other realm, maybe. It's nothing but an empty place filled with gold and purple mist. But inside the mist there are specks of black.

The Darkness.

The mists, both colors, represent magic. Or a better way to put it, I think is that they represent what can be *done* with magic. They are like paint colors sitting in front of a canvas, waiting to be used.

Mostly, so far, at least, I've used them to dreamwalk.

"But you can do so much more, Ryet." Paul says this because he's standing next to me in the mists now, but still feeding on me at the same time.

"Where are you right now?"

He shrugs up one shoulder. "I'm right here."

"No. Where is your physical body?"

"In the dirt, back home in Montana."

"What are you doing there?"

"Waiting for you."

"Waiting for me to do what?"

"Come up out of the ground, of course. I'm waiting for your third life. I'm waiting for the new you."

"What about this me?" I point to myself.

"All things in good time, Ryet. We're not in a rush."

"I don't understand what will happen."

He turns and smiles at me. This version of him is wearing a suit. He looks very... *Paul*. Commanding, and arrogant, and fucking desirable. "You're going to Hell, Ryet. But don't worry, I'll be there too. I must have that final conversation with our Maker."

"Isn't the Darkness our maker?"

"It is."

"Isn't it... technology?"

"It's that too."

"But it's not like... I mean, does it talk?"

"Of course not."

"So how do you converse with it?"

Paul turns to smile at me. "What do you mean? We're talking to it right now."

I'm just about to ask him to explain when I hear a distant voice. "Ryet?"

"Syrsee?" I'm still looking at Paul and he shoots me a big smile. "Now what are you doing?"

"Just helping things along." He puts a hand on my shoulder, turning me around. "Come on. Let's go back. Syrsee doesn't have much time and there is blood to exchange."

I'm still trying to figure out what all that means when I wake up in bed. Syrsee is here now, climbing over my body to fit herself into a space that Paul has made between us.

"There you go, sweet Syrsee. Get comfortable," Paul says. "Let's all have a drink now, shall we?"

But what the three of us do next is not drinking. It's blood lust. It's all kinds of lust. I'm inside Syrsee as she drinks from

Paul, Paul's inside Syrsee as she drinks from me. And then she's between us as we both drink from her.

It's… sin.

That's the only word I have to describe what we do to, and with, each other in this bed. Which isn't even a bed. It's nothing but a bit of Darkness.

Just like us.

It is pure sin.

I wake.

And when I open my eyes it's just me, lying in our bed, with a hard-on and covered in blood. Which would be concerning if I hadn't been waking up this way for weeks now—the part with Paul, at least. Not Syrsee joining in.

I sit up, letting out a long sigh, and look at my body. Is it my blood? Is it his? I'm not sure. It shouldn't be possible to actually drink in a dreamwalk, but what the hell do I know about dreamwalking anyway? What the hell do I know about anything, actually? Paul never handed me a rule book. It was always just need-to-know. And, as far as I can tell, my name is the last one on the list of who needs to know. Pretty much everyone in Paul's life knows more about what's happening to me than I do.

I swing my legs out of bed and get up. There is blood all over this room, not just the sheets. But there's no way to tell how much of it is from Syrsee and me drinking all night and how much is from… well, whatever it was that just happened.

Housekeeping cleans up after us every morning after I leave, so I just go into the shower, wash off all the blood, and come out pretending that everything's fine as I put on my clothes, grab my phone, and leave, heading for the lab where I will spend my day.

And when I come home tonight the apartment will be clean, the sheets will be bright white again, and all I will be thinking about is the drink.

This is my life now.

I live, and eat, and breathe… *blood*.

* * *

The first week or so I was here, I would stop at this café near the research center and grab a cup of coffee. I would stand in line, and glance up at the trendy menu board that had everything written in liquid chalk, and I would smile at the Guild people all around me as they talked about their upcoming days or whatever else was on their minds.

It felt like a very Ryet thing to do. I'm not like a coffee fanatic or anything, but in my other life it was a morning habit. And it's not hard to blend in here. I'm living in my Ryet body. There are no wings. There's no bruise-colored skin. My eyes aren't glowing red. I look like every other human around here so I figured… well, carry on, ya know?

But right around week two, when I started to realize that the blood lust was taking over, I just stopped going in. This was also right about the time when the people in the lab stopped being coy about what it was they wanted from me.

The first few days I showed up in the lab they took blood samples. Lots of them. And it felt pretty normal. I mean, the blood is everything to a vampire. It feels like a logical first step. At the very least, it's something physical. Something scientific.

But they don't want my blood. It's dead outside of me anyway. One day—again, right around week two—they left the samples in the room I was in. The room is big, and open, and there are like half a dozen research stations and twice the number of researchers all sharing this one area. There's nothing private about it. Half walls made up of soapstone lab benches with open shelving above filled with glassware and other science shit.

Usually they hook me up to an EKG machine or whatever it's called. I might've just made that up because I heard it on TV, but it's the brainwave electrode thingies they put on your head. It's actually a helmet, but anyway. My point is, they didn't take the blood. The lab tech got called away and it was just forgotten about until the end of the day when someone finally noticed.

And the blood in the vials wasn't even liquid anymore. It looked like molasses, or maybe tar. Thick, and black, and gross. It looked like the Darkness, actually. It looked dead and it was tossed into the trash.

That's when I figured out that they don't care about my blood. They're after something else and that something else was far less tangible. That something else turned out to be the thoughts inside my head.

"Ryet," the lead researcher told me the next morning, "the magic is inside you, but it's not something physical. It's your brainwaves. It's your frequency. It's your..." Well, he went on and on about this and the words he used got progressively more and more technical. I vaguely remember him saying something about the Doppler effect, but that's only because everyone's heard that term. It's how they track rain.

What did it all mean? Well, he might've told me during that actual conversation, but all I heard was blah, blah, brainwaves. Blah, blah, frequency. Blah, blah, Doppler effect. It made no sense to me at all.

They stopped taking my blood that very day.

And ever since then, when I get to the lab, they wave at me. "Hi, Ryet!" they call out. "Get undressed and we'll meet you in there." And then they point to the little dark room made up of glass where my chair lives. It's a very special chair with a headset, and those electrode thingies that get stuck to various parts of my naked body, and cameras. Lots and lots of cameras.

Because even though nothing has happened so far, I get the feeling that they are expecting something very spectacular to happen very soon.

And they don't want to miss a moment of it.

They're gonna record it so all of humanity—or maybe just everyone in this room—will understand exactly who and what they are dealing with. Who and what I really am.

Because Ryet doesn't live here anymore.

I am the Darkness.

Sometimes cat, sometimes mouse

Being in the dirt is supposed to be restful. It's supposed to be like going home. It's supposed to be like being in the only place you've ever known, and once you're here, inside its soothing embrace, it should feel like you never left.

To be in the ground is to belong. To know oneself. To understand your place in the universe.

This has been true for all of my existence.

Right up until about… well… now.

Even though I know the transformation isn't finished—hell, it's so early in the process one might say it hasn't even started—I have the urge to breathe air.

Air.

This is it.

The end.

I have a few moments of mourning after this realization. A true sense of loss. Like one might feel if they had lost a father.

Which is a good analogy because the dirt is the place of Darkness and the Darkness is our father.

I want to move on. It feels right. Like the time has come. But even I have doubts.

I can hear Josep under the ground. He's breathing, though it's very slow. And every once in a while, he moans. But mostly he's quiet.

The scions, on the other hand, are very loud. They are screaming under the ground as the Darkness eats them alive. Not literally, of course, but that's what it feels like the first time it takes over all your cells. When it squirms its way inside each and every one of them like parasitic worms. Because, after all, it is the Darkness that makes us vampires, not the blood.

I try my best to go to back to sleep. I know I need to let the process continue. But every time I try, I get paranoid that I'll suffocate. The dirt feels like a heavy and great weight on my chest.

Which, when thinking logically, is how it *should* feel. It just never has before now.

Something has changed.

I push up out of the dirt and come out into the open air, thinking about this change. It's good. Change is good. Change is what I've been after all these centuries. I thought I had figured out what would happen to me once Ryet and Syrsee were fed and put in the ground and I became a 'father.'

I had grand visions of this new me. I might have imagined myself on a throne, in a throne room so opulent it bordered on disgusting. Which doesn't look anything like the rustic Montana lodge made of wood cut from the forest just a few dozen feet away. My vision had more of a *Game of Thrones* feel to it. The whole Jon Snow storyline, actually.

It's absurd. But that's what I was imagining.

Me, on a throne, wearing fur, with minions, in a massive room.

I look down at myself.

Nope. I'm just a demon.

I could still pull it off, though. I look over my shoulder at the lodge. I'm like a hundred percent sure that inside one of those rooms there's a bearskin rug. I could make this work.

The problem is, I'm not cold. I don't need a bearskin rug coat.

Oh, my God, Paul. What the fuck?

You're insane. These are stupid, stupid thoughts that have no bearing on anything. Think. Concentrate. Focus.

I take a deep breath, hold it for five seconds, and slowly let it out.

There. Better. Mind is clear and... nope. I'm still thinking about fur coats.

This is when it hits me that I'm not all here.

I cannot think straight.

Oh! That bearskin rug lives in the library!

Focus, Paul!

Something is not right.

Something is really, *really* wrong with me.

* * *

I wake up in the dirt. The heaviness is... absent. The sense of suffocation... gone. The idea of wearing a bearskin rug as a coat and sitting on the Iron Throne... ridiculous.

I really need to stop watching TV. It rots the mind, it truly does.

And then I am laughing. Dirt falls into my mouth, and it tastes like brownies. Which only makes me laugh harder and then it's filling up my throat and I'm clawing my way out of the ground and sitting on the hillside, looking at a full moon, and I'm pretty sure I'm a werewolf now.

I laugh again, hysterically, and I think... I think I'm stoned.

* * *

The next time I wake up, Ryet and Syrsee and I are in bed drinking and fucking as it should be. "Thank God," I say. Then I panic, because I don't thank God for anything. Ever. I believe in the idea of God, of course, but we don't have much of a relationship at the moment.

So I know it's not real.

None of this is real.

I'm fantasizing about becoming Jon Snow and wearing his amazing fur coat—which is so much better than a bearskin rug, there's just no comparison.

I'm not stoned out of my mind.

I'm just… insane.

Ryet stops his drinking of Syrsee and turns his head, blood dripping out of his mouth, eyes red as scarlet. "What did you say?"

I shake my head. "Nothing. I didn't say anything."

"Yes, you did. You said you're insane."

"Nope. I didn't. Never said that."

Ryet laughs. Then Syrsee is stirring. "Keep drinking," she moans. "Take more."

I let out a long breath, tired of the confusion. "Ryet," I say, and I use my stern Paul voice. "What is happening?"

"Come here," Ryet says. His voice is soothing and calm. He hand is reaching between my legs. "Come on, just come back to us. I'll take care of you, Paul." And then he's fisting my cock and—

* * *

I sit up. Straight up. Which takes a huge amount of effort because it displaces a lot of dirt.

Then I just stare into the darkness. Lowercase, not proper noun Darkness.

What is real?

Is this real?

Has anything ever been real?

I don't move. Don't turn my head. Just let my eyes look around a little. Then I listen. I hear the beating hearts of scions in the ground, and the voices of scions above—the ones who didn't partake in the ritual. They are looking for us. They have found the fresh dirt. They are thinking about digging us up because they want blood.

Josep says, "Don't go up there." His voice is calm, and low, and deep as it always is.

But it's not out loud, it's in my head. Which is how it should be, we're in the ground after all. But the veil of unreality is still mingling with my dreams and I'm not convinced this is real yet.

"You're fine," Josep says, again in my head. "It's the actualization." Then he lets out a breath. "I think."

"You *think*?"

"There's nothing to worry about. I'm having them too."

"The dreams?"

"Yes. I was in a candy store lusting after lollipops." He says these words in his typical monotone, unaffected way.

So I laugh. "I was Jon Snow."

"Who?"

"For fuck's sake, Josep. Why must you be so antiquated? You can't just ignore pop culture, OK? You have to keep up with the times!"

"You're insane."

I blow out a breath, which displaces the dirt and sends it back into my mouth. "I might be."

"Just kidding. You're not insane. You're just not actualized yet."

"Well, I don't like it. I'm tired of this and I'm going up top. Are you coming with me?"

"No. I'm going to eat that lollipop. It tastes like Little Baby."

"Who?"

But he's gone and I'm alone again.

Which is probably not a bad thing since he's no saner than I am. We're going through the same change and it's causing… hallucinations. Or something.

I start clawing my way up through the dirt, justifying my decision to pause my actualization because I need to give these leftover scions a job or they will start doing things that will piss me off later.

They begin talking excitedly as they realize the dirt is being displaced and someone is emerging from the ground. They don't know it's me yet, so they are blurting out things like, "This is fucked up!" "We got left behind!" and "We need to dig them all up and demand our share!"

Which is pretty ballsy.

I respect ballsy. It's a quality I look for in a minion. But it's disrespectful when directed *at* me.

I emerge from the dirt and since I'm covered in it and not in my beautiful Paul form, they don't know who it is and these complaints continue for a few more seconds.

But then I am out, and my wings are spreading, and they are gasping, and shocked, and then, in unison, they realize who I am and kneel with heads bowed. Together, like it was planned this way, they say, "My lord!"

It's a *very* Jon Snow moment.

I exhale. Tired of myself. Tired of the insanity and

confusion. And very tired of this Jon Snow thing. "Rise," I say, lifting a hand up for effect.

My scions all get to their feet, most still looking down with bowed heads, but more than a few taking peeks at me.

One, in particular, nearly looks me in the eyes. I point to him. "What is your name?"

He takes a moment. He doesn't swallow hard, like he's gulping down his fear, but he wants to. "Kael, my lord."

"Kael. That's right. I remember you." I smile here because Kael, in my memory, was quite fun in bed. Not as fun as Ryet. I like the chase and Ryet gave me the chase of a lifetime. But Kael put up a good fight too. It was more physical than mental, if I remember correctly.

I walk over to him, keeping my eyes locked with his. Then I place a hand on his cheek. "Are you mad, Kael? That you're not in the ground?"

"What do you think, *my lord?*"

Yes, the balls on this one are big. "I think you're misunderstanding what is happening here."

"Maybe you could enlighten us, Lord?" This doesn't come from Kael, but from a lesser scion I call Leo. He looks nervous when I look over at him. "I mean," he backpedals, "if you want to, that is. Only if you want to, my lord."

I smile at him, putting him at ease, then turn my attention back to Kael. "You're the control group, Kael. That's why you're not in the ground with the rest of them."

"So we're not being turned?" another scion asks.

I don't even bother to look at this one. "No."

They begin to mumble. These mumbles turn into grumbles. All the while Kael and I are staring at each other.

"Do you have something to say to me, Kael?"

"I want a drink."

I scoff. "That's it? Carnal desire? That's what you want? Don't you want to know what the hell is happening here?"

He shrugs up one shoulder. "Sure." His eyes flit down to my throat, then back up to meet my gaze. He smiles. "I do. But what I *really* want, my lord, is *you*."

I laugh. This one, he really likes to play the game. Not like Ryet, who is always so blunt and truthful. Always telling me exactly what's on his mind. Kael here, while loyal—I don't doubt his loyalty—isn't blunt at all. He's sneaky. He's deceptive. He's cunning. Sometimes cat, sometimes mouse.

Right now, he's pretending to be the mouse. Which is nice. I like being the cat.

I nod at him. "If that's true, you'll get it. But first"—I look back at the other scions—"I'm going to fill you all in. Because everyone has a purpose and you, my good men, are the control group."

There's some murmuring here. Intelligence isn't a trait I much care about when I make scions. I am a simple vampire, after all. I like blood and sex. So most of these men don't understand what I mean.

But it's OK. I don't mind providing details. "The control group," I continue, "gets the benefits of our mistakes. After all, we've never done this before." I pan a hand to the ground. "It's all very new. Mistakes *will* be made. Then we will learn, and adjust the protocol, and you, my dear leftovers, will be *better* than this first batch."

They look at each other, murmuring again, and they begin to understand and start nodding their heads.

Feeling satisfied that they've all been placated—with the possible exception of Kael, but if it's blood and sex he really wants, I will deal with him later—I turn back to the task at hand. Which is to give them a job to do. Idle hands are the Devil's workshop, after all. So I point to one of the dumber ones. "What kind of coat does Jon Snow wear?"

He looks confused. Maybe even a little bit startled. "My lord?"

"Jon Snow. That majestic black, fuzzy coat. What kind of animal is that? Is it a yak?"

The scion shrugs his shoulders. "Um... maybe?"

"No," another scion says. "It's some kind of sheep."

"Yeah." Another nods. "It's a black sheep."

"Sheep?" I'm not quite sure 'sheep' is the look I'm going for. "Well, do we have yaks around here?"

The scions all look at each other, mumbling a discussion until they come to a consensus. "No, my lord. There are no wild yaks in Montana, my lord."

"Maybe some ranchers have some?" another adds.

I sigh. "OK. Forget the yak. I need..." I pause to think. "Wolves. Pelts, actually. I need wolf pelts. A lot of them, I'd say." I point at the group, aside from Kael. "Your job is to secure me fifteen wolf pelts. Good ones. And then I'll need a coat."

Kael snickers, but I ignore him and point to a random scion in the group. "You. You will take those pelts and make me a coat."

He points to himself. "Me?"

"Yes, you. I'm sure there's a how-to video on YouTube. You'll figure it out. You'll do fine. Now go. All of you. Hunt me some wolves!" I raise a clenched fist into the air, turning this last bit into a proclamation.

And then I usher them off with a dramatic wave of my hand.

Which they do not respond to immediately. It takes a few

moments of confused mumbling before they actually turn away and start walking back to the various bunkhouses, but they do finally disperse.

Then I turn back to Kael and smile. "Come with me, blood lover. I have big plans for you."

5 - Josep

She is well and truly mine

I am licking Little Baby like a lollipop and she is tasty. In this dream she is still the tender, young, innocent, pink-haired Echo. Her thighs are creamy white and appear fragile under the grip of my large hands because she is a small, weak halfbreed girl.

Which I quite like because I am a big, muscular vampire man and the disparity in our size is a turn-on for me.

I am between her legs and she's writhing underneath me, her back arching, her mouth open and moaning, her eyes squeezed shut. My tongue must hit the sweet spot just right because suddenly her knees clamp against my head.

She comes.

Of course, she always comes. We've been in this dream for days, maybe even lifetimes, and her climax arrives every few minutes. It's in this moment when I hear Paul. Not his voice, but his hands. Clawing the dirt near me.

"He's not doing well."

I look up, gazing across the tight abs and perky tits of Little Baby. She's sitting up a little, eyes open and nothing but black pits. "What?"

"Paul," Little Baby's mouth says, though this is not Little Baby's sweet voice. "He's not handling it well. He doesn't love me best, Josep. That's why he was never my favorite."

This is not Little Baby. And the moment I think this, her body morphs beneath me. It becomes black sand. Shifting black sand. Which isn't sand at all, but those particles that the Darkness is made of.

Still, it retains the shape of a woman with her legs open.

"That's right," Little Baby Darkness says. "It's me you've been fucking, Josep."

My mouth drops open. My head is spinning. I cannot think straight. "*What?*"

Little Baby Darkness laughs. Then she reaches forward and her black sandy hand pats me on the head. "It's OK, love. I'm here now. I'm with you. We can be together. Me and you. Like it was always meant to be."

My eyes shift left. My eyes shift right. "This isn't real."

Little Baby Darkness smiles her black sandy smile, showing me black sandy fangs. "Oh, it's real, blood lover. It's real."

I wake up in the dirt gasping for breath. Which isn't normally something I do, so for a moment I'm certain that I'm still hallucinating. But then, up above, I hear Paul talking to the scions. Something about… something. Who cares?

Little Baby Darkness was right. He's not doing well. If I cared at all about Paul—I mean, if I cared about more than his blood and sex parts—I would claw my way up and we'd talk through it. But… I… just… really don't care about Paul. Other than eating him and fucking him.

"She's woken up, you know."

I look down at my chest and find Little Baby Darkness. Her cheek is pressed against my skin and the long tip of her fingernail is tracing down the middle of my stomach. I watch, willing her to grab me between the legs, but she doesn't.

And she doesn't look like the Darkness now, either. She looks like Echo. Young, and sweet, and sexy pink-haired Echo.

"Why are you here?" I ask her.

She looks up at me with wide, innocent blue eyes. "Because you're trying to kill me."

"That's not true." Even if it was true, I wouldn't admit it was true, but it's just really not true. "That's absolutely not what I'm trying to do. I just want your power, Little Baby Darkness. That's all."

She lifts her head up and begins crawling up my body, her knee easing in between my legs, her breasts flat on my chest. And then *her*, hovering above me. She places a hand on my cheek and smiles. "I've given you everything, haven't I?"

"Of course. And I am thankful."

"But you don't love me, Josep. Not as much as I love you."

I would like to point out here that this thing on top of me isn't human. Well, I'm not human, either, but at least I'm made of flesh. This thing is not flesh. It's technology. Something very advanced that I don't understand, which kind of makes it magic —or evil, depending on your interpretation of the world. So everything about this moment is a trick.

"I'm tricking you," she says.

I nod, matter-of-factly. "You are indeed. You're a lie, Little Baby Darkness. And even though I am made of you, which makes me a lie as well, I need more than the lie. I need…"

Well, what I need is a partner. Someone to love.

Which is exactly what the Darkness appears to need in me. But it's… different. It's too 'other.'

"Well," I continue, "I just don't see us together, Little Baby Darkness. I would like Real Little Baby." I shrug here, feeling good about my authenticity. "You just don't do it for me."

I'm expecting outrage. Hell, if I'm being honest, I'm expecting it to kill me. I would like to play the game and win. I would love to be as invested as Paul. That man, my God, he's driven. But I lost interest in life so long ago now that I can't even muster up the illusion of interest.

Little Baby is a tiny prize. If I have to be here, I would like her to be here with me.

But I don't actually *have* to be here.

Everything we're doing is a distraction. It's a game. I'm playing but I don't care about the finish line. It's just a way to prolong the inevitable.

The Darkness knows this. It knows I have a bottle of the Black blood in my bunker. It also knows that Little Baby is mine. Something all mine because I made her. So it took her form, not *just* to trick me, but to experience whatever it is I feel for this remnant of a girl.

Which is… nothing. It's not personal. I don't feel anything, ever. I'm gone. I've been gone for so long now, I doubt I was ever here.

Little Baby Darkness pets me and gazes into my eyes. "I can be anything you want, Josep. Anything at all." And then she morphs into Paul and strokes his hand down my cheek.

"Is it me you want?" These words come out of Dark Paul's mouth and in his voice.

Eating and fucking Paul, as basic as it sounds, has been enough to content me. He's bigger than life. He fills up every empty space when he's around. And he's energetic. He never gets tired of trying new things. He's always busy. He feeds this energy to me and I drink it up. The blood and the sex is enough to keep me interested. If it weren't for Paul, I'd have sipped the Black blood centuries ago.

But he's not enough to entice me into infinity.

I reach up and take Dark Paul's hand off my cheek—

surprised that it doesn't feel like sand—and hold it close to my chest. Not because I'm making some kind of gesture, but because it's just kinda sad that this thing—this powerful, all-knowing thing—is… *begging*.

For *me*, no less. Which is more than sad, it's pathetic.

"Listen," it says, morphing back into Little Baby Darkness, "if you don't at least try, Josep, then I'll just become her. I'll steal everything she is and just be her. And then you'll have no choice. This would not be a hard thing to do. I am, after all, inside her right now."

I shrug up one shoulder, kind of surprised at my indifference. Not about Little Baby, but the Darkness. It wants me. To be its lover, or slave, or confidant.

But it's a *lie*.

This has always been my problem with the Darkness. It's a lie and I've always known it. I can feel the lie. And the lie is so much worse than the truth because the truth is, I have no one. No one cares about me.

Paul pretends because he needs this, right here. This, what I'm doing with the Darkness. Which is being close to it, and understanding it, and being the object of its desire. Paul wants that, and that is *all* Paul wants.

The Darkness doesn't want *me*. The Darkness wants me to *do* something. This comes in the form of the power it puts into my blood. It fills me up with lies. And then, in turn, I give these lies to others.

If you really think about it, I'm nothing more than a transfusion. Except I'm not even that important. I am nothing more than the transfusion *bag*. I'm a bit of thick plastic hanging on a rack. That's it.

This is the crux of my relationship with the Darkness.

Little Baby Darkness kisses me. Right on the lips. And it's nice. If I were to allow myself to believe the lie, it would be so nice. To really have her as my own. A partner in this world. A lover. A friend.

"I can be that, Josep," the Little Baby Darkness whispers. "I can. I can do anything. I promise you."

"But you cannot be the real her, Little Baby Darkness."

She sits up, straddles me, then leans over my chest and places both hands on my cheeks as she stares at me with very blue eyes. "I can. I *can*."

I take her hands in mine and remove them from my face. "Why? Why do you want *me*?"

Her eyes flit down to my chest. Then come back up to my face. "Do you want the truth?"

This is not Little Baby's voice. It's a deep voice. One of a man, but of course, this thing on top of me isn't a man. And then, just as I think that, it morphs into one. A man who is me. Who looks just like me.

"The truth is the only thing that matters," I tell Dark Me.

Dark Me smiles and I recognize this smile because it's *my* smile and it's meaningless. It's a lie. It's me, pretending to care about the petty problems of whomever it is I'm talking to.

"Because, Josep, you are the most beautiful thing I've ever seen."

And because I'm a liar, I can't tell if this is some existential exercise in knowing oneself, or… I'm just hallucinating and the whole conversation is pointless.

"Can't you see it?" Dark Me asks. "Can't you see how God has touched you?"

I make a face. The word 'God' alone is enough to trigger this face, but the underlying sentiment is equally repulsive. "That's ridiculous," I tell myself. I mean, Dark Me. "God has never touched me."

"Were you not human once?"

"I'm not having this conversation with myself, Dark Me. So if you want me to participate, morph into someone else."

It wriggles on top of me, kind of... humping me. Its hands start caressing me, its legs moving alongside mine, its cock growing against my stomach. And even though I don't want to be turned on, my cock grows in response.

In response to what, Josep? Yourself? The madness of this whole thing suddenly hits me.

What if it's just always been me? What if the Darkness is nothing more than my own insanity?

"What if," Dark Me says, "you have always been *me*, dear Josep? What if that were true? What if *you* are the Darkness? Have *always been* the Darkness? And this entire life you've been living was just your own personal actualization?"

* * *

I sit up in the dirt. Mouth full of it. Heart beating so fast, I can't seem to catch my breath. I can still hear Paul above me. He's still talking to the scions who didn't join us in the dirt. "Now go. All of you. Hunt me some wolves!"

There is a small commotion above, then a dispersal.

Paul, in a lower voice, says, "Come with me, blood lover. I have big plans for you."

What is he doing? What is he plotting now? How will he fuck me over?

Whoever he is talking to, it's not Ryet because even through the dirt, I can smell his rotting corpse. Ryet's body has been decimated by the scions all around me.

No, whoever leaves with Paul is someone new.

But it doesn't matter who this new person is, whatever Paul is up to, it's got something to do with Ryet. He has an unnatural obsession with that man. Ryet is a tool. That is all he's ever been, and Paul knows this. But Paul, he's an ideas man. He has lots of them. He's always up to something. Something he shouldn't be up to, of course. But he likes it that way. It's part of the chase for him. The deception, the waiting, and the angst that comes from the waiting.

I don't understand him. Not even a little bit.

"Well, Josep," Little Baby Darkness coos into my head, "haven't you always been my tool too? And haven't I loved you the most, above all others?"

But the Little Baby Darkness is wrong. She is the hammer and I am the nail.

The blood bag, not the blood.

"*So?*" I say back.

"I gave you favors, I gave you magic, I gave you everything."

"So what?"

"So, this is how Paul feels about Ryet." Little Baby Darkness pushes some hair out of my face because she's next to me now. Here in the dirt. Which means this is, again, some kind of dream.

I can't seem to find reality. And it bothers me. Because Paul doesn't seem to be having the same trouble.

She leans over me, covered in dirt, pushing it off my face and caressing my cheeks. "That's because Paul isn't *you*." Little Baby Darkness boops me on the nose with a fingertip when she says this last word.

And why am I calling this thing a she? It's not a woman. It's not anything, really. It's a fucking freak of nature. Well, no. It's not even that. It's a freak of... the *unnatural*. Because it's not alive, it's not real, it's not—

Little Baby Darkness takes my face in her hands, forcing me to look at her. "You're not listening."

"You're telling lies."

She presses her lips together and shakes her head. "I'm not."

"You're not Little Baby. You're not her."

"Well, you're right." She smiles at me. "I'm not. I'm just a hallucination. But she's still here, Josep. Little Baby is waiting for you in your cave. And trust me, I am *her*. I am all over her. I am inside her. Everything about her is *me*."

I let out a breath and some dirt falls into my mouth, but I don't even bother spitting it out because it's all around me.

"You want her, Josep? Do you want the Little Baby? Your own creation to keep forever? As your partner? As your friend? As your lover? A blood lover just for you? This is what Ryet is to Paul. A pet. Do you want a pet, Josep? I will be your pet. In *her*. And *that* is real. All you have to do is get up out of the ground and come find me. Then we can be together forever."

I sigh, tired of this conversation with myself. Because that's what I think it is. Me and my own damaged mind.

"You know that's not true." Little Baby's voice is sweet now. And even though I'm under the ground with dirt all around me, I can see her plain as day. So it's not real. And I'm not listening.

"OK," she says. "Fine. I will tell you something true."

I'm not looking at her. My gaze is focused on a twisted tree root in the dirt above my head. It's white, and gnarled, and branches off in many directions that lead many places.

"I am the root, Josep."

I scoff. "That's your big revelation?" I scoff again. "Of course you're the root. I've used you thousands of times to move across time and space underground."

"But you see me as a highway. Something to be traversed."

I don't even bother scoffing. I just sigh, bored. Ready to die if none of this is going to work out in my favor.

"There is no death, Josep. This want of yours, this desire to evaporate into nothingness, it's so irrational."

I redirect my gaze to the girl on top of me and study her. Really see her. If she were Echo, it would be a reason to keep going. The two of us could hunt this Darkness together. We could subdue it, enslave it, drink its power, become a team, and rule the world as we built up the new American Vampires.

But I killed her. Not literally, she's beyond that now. Because I gave her the blood we mixed during Ryet's third birth and now she is part of *It*.

It is inside her. It has corrupted her. And I find that I'm truly sorry about that. I was too focused on Ryet and Paul. Too caught up in his plan.

"Yes," Little Baby Darkness says. "Exactly. None of this is you, Josep." She morphs back into Dark Me and I stare down at myself, suddenly able to see through his eyes.

"What do you know about me, Darkness?" I ask. But I'm watching myself say this as the words spill out of my mouth.

What a trip.

I lay my head on my own chest, then ask myself to hold me. "Hold me," I say. But it comes out of both of my mouths at once. Like an echo.

My arms wrap around Dark Me, but this is when I realize I'm not the man lying in the ground, nor am I the man on top of me. I am both of us.

"Exactly," Little Baby Darkness says, but only inside my head. "You are me, and I am you, and we are the same. This is why you're insane, Josep. You've been touched by God. You've been touched by me because I am God. And your mind was never able to process it until now."

"What's so special about now?" I ask. There's doubt in these words, but this insane dream is actually starting to make sense. In a small way, at least.

"Now, you can see yourself in me."

Dark Me lifts his head up off my chest and we stare at each other. He's pretty. That's the word for him. He's *so* fucking pretty. And the moment I think this, all the roots in the ground around me begin to glow the lightest of purples.

"I'm you," he says. But I'm saying these words as well, at the very same time. So no matter which body I'm inside of at the moment, I'm saying this to myself.

"I'm you. You're me. You are the Darkness. I am the Darkness. And if you want my power, you don't have to work with Paul to steal it. It's yours, blood lover. All you have to do is *merge*."

Here it is. I mean, I'm many thousands of years old. Temptation and I? We're old, old friends. The Darkness has been tempting me from my earliest days. Merge? I mean, come on. How fucking stupid do I look to this thing that it thinks I would fall for this simple trick?

"It's not a trick." But it is. Because these words come out of my mouth, and I'm looking down at myself as I say them. It's always been a trick.

"Let me help," Dark Me says as he sits up, displacing dirt all around his body so that it falls on me. He's straddling me now, smirking. "Let me help you understand. Watch closely."

And then his hand slips down to his cock and he fists it.

In this same moment, I *feel* this. I feel his grip on my own cock.

He begins to stroke himself and when I look down at myself I can see the indentation of his grip over my shaft. I feel him *squeeze* me.

"Because *you're not you*," Dark Me says. "You're me. And if you want my power, it's yours. I put it all inside Echo to keep it safe. Didn't you wonder why you had an urge to save her at the last minute? Didn't you wonder?"

"Because I wanted a partner."

Dark Me nods, squeezing his cock tighter and pumping harder. His breath is heavy and hitching now as he jerks himself off. "She's yours," he says, eyes closing. "And we put all our power inside her to keep it safe from Paul. So if you want your power back, all you have to do is come and take it."

I come. He didn't even touch me, nor did I touch myself, and I come, spilling the Dark Seed all over my stomach. A sense of utter relief washes over my body and I close my eyes, relishing it.

"It's proof." I expect these words to be in my head, or come from his mouth. But they don't. These words come out of *my* mouth. "I'm the Darkness."

I have always been the Darkness. Something foreign and alone that was born in the realm of infinity. Forever looking for a way to fit in and experience this world in a way that makes sense.

Because the realm of infinity is emptiness and all I want is to be *full*.

Dark Me is still straddling my hips, but now he lies down on my chest. Then… then he *melts* into me. Just… merges with me.

And that's that, I guess.

We are One.

* * *

Once again, I sit up in the earth, gasping for breath. And once again, I feel like this is reality, but I can't be sure.

I look around, expecting to see nothing but dirt, but that's not what I see.

I see light. Purple and gold light. Thin strands of it weaving all through the ground around me like a web. Like the Darkness is a spider that spun a web and I am caught in the middle of it.

When the ground lights up like this, the earth actually disappears.

Or… maybe it's the other way around? I'm not sure. But when I travel in the earth, I'm not walking through dirt. It's just mist.

But I've been here many times before and now, like any other time, I enter the Dark highway in the ground and I move towards the place I want to be and the next thing I know, I'm emerging from a wall inside my cave. The whole place is thick with purple and gold mist. Which is magic. Which is good. Because Little Baby Dark Echo is going to need that magic if she wants to rise again.

I walk over to the pool and slip into the water. It's warm and feels wonderful on my naked body.

Then I turn and take a good long look at my work.

Little Baby's skin is very pale, but she is whole again. Her hair is long and silver, her body lithe and slim, yet full in all the right places.

She is a vessel and inside her is me.

Though I still don't trust the Darkness, even if it is me, what it said makes sense.

If I put Dark power inside Echo to keep it safe from Paul, this would explain my sudden irrational desire to save her.

Of course, loneliness would explain this as well. But loneliness is sad and pathetic.

A grand plan to usurp Paul though? That's not sad and pathetic at all.

That's clever.

Which means this girl in the water with me truly *is* something special.

6 - Echo

I want him to eat me all night and day.

He is crooning in my ear when I wake. "I love you, Little Baby."

And Lucia is gone.

Was she ever here?

Was I dreaming?

Oh, please, God. I beg of you, let this all be a nightmare. Let me wake up in my parents' house in Spokane. Let me be in my childhood bedroom wearing layers upon layers of black eyeliner. Let me be wearing that tattered Offspring t-shirt, and my black velvet bell-bottoms, and my Docs, and let me be in my lumpy twin bed that I've been sleeping in since I was four. Let my parents be downstairs, fighting. Screaming at each other. Drunk and high. Let me be there. I would give anything to just go back.

"Welcome, my Little Baby. Welcome back to your new life."

I begin to sob, my whole body shaking.

His arms are around me, and I'm in the pool, and I want to pray for my own soul, which I am now very sure exists and has been sold with my full consent.

But before I can do that, his lips touch mine and a drop of blood slips into my mouth. And then… then the fight is over.

I am the definition of lost.

That's all it takes. Just one drop. Because in this drop lives everything I could ever want.

I close my eyes and go limp in his arms, letting the rhythm of his chest, moving up and down under my body, lull me into a half-waking slumber.

Be careful.

The words in my head aren't mine, they're Lucia's. It's a warning. That I should not let this monster overtake me.

You know what's happening here, Echo.

"I'm not Echo." To my surprise, my words come flowing right out of my mouth. Well, they don't exactly flow, they are more of a croak. But it startles me because for a moment there I think I forgot I existed.

It's the blood, darling. And again, it's Lucia's voice in my head. *It will always be your weakness and you will always want it. There's no getting around that, Little Echo.*

"Little Baby?" Josep says. His voice is so low and rumbly. So soothing and calm.

He's a complete psychopath, Lucia coos. *But do you know, even psychopaths have weaknesses? He left me alone for centuries. Do you want to know how I got him to do that?*

Josep is petting my head now, kissing my cheek. "Little Baby, can you hear me? Come back to me, Little Baby. It's all right now. You're all better. I made you all better."

"Tell me," I say.

"What should I tell you, Little Baby?"

But it's not Josep I'm talking to. It's Lucia. "Tell me."

Josep kisses my lips, nicking the upper one with his sharp teeth. He starts licking me, his tongue sliding in and out of my mouth. "You taste so good. Is that what you want to hear?" He kisses me, hard. Like we're lovers who have been separated for months. Who haven't seen each other. Lovers who only want one thing.

Not sex, though I see that coming.

But blood.

Blood lovers.

His weakness, Lucia continues, *is his vanity. Fall in love with him, Little Echo. Give yourself to him. Utterly and completely.*

"That doesn't sound like a very good solution," I mumble.

"What?" Josep pulls back, but not very much. An inch, maybe. I force myself to open my eyes and his are right there. Red. Blood red. He smiles at me. He's much too close for me to see that smile, but the outer corners of his eyes turn up, giving it away. "It's OK," he says. "I'm here, Little Baby. You're mine now."

Give yourself to him and he will love you, Little Echo. And Josep's love is that of the Darkness, which flows inside you, just like it does me. It is favor. It is privilege. It is... immunity. Tell him he's yours. Quick. Right now! Do it! Say it!

"No, my lord." I swallow hard and choke out the next few words, looking him in the eyes. He's frowning at my rejection. "You." I say this word with firm resolve because I can see rage in those eyes. I can see his fury and imagine his wrath if this were all there was to my statement. So quickly, I finish. "You, my lord, are *mine*."

He relaxes. Smiles. Holds me tighter.

See? Lucia is standing in a dark corner of the cave now, holding her own decapitated head in her hands, just staring at me with black pits for eyes. *His weakness is his vanity. If you just love him, Little Echo, he will give you anything you want. So love him. Let him do anything he wants with you.* She turns her body away from me when she says this part, like she doesn't want to think about this, but it's just a fleeting gesture. Nothing but a moment of recollection. She is thinking about the past. About what she let him do to her. Then her resolve is back. *You won't regret it, I promise.*

Which is a lie, I think. Because while I can no longer see her regret, I can feel it.

"That's right," Josep says, interrupting my thoughts. He lets out a long breath, holding me to his chest, rocking back and forth like I really am a baby. "I'm yours, and you are mine, and together, Little Baby, we will be the new Darkness together. I am the master now." He pulls back and with one clawed hand he rips open his throat. Blood comes gushing out.

Instantly, I have the urge to catch it all in my mouth. To lick up every drop. But I don't even have to move because Josep lowers his neck down to me, right over my mouth, and gives himself to me without hesitation.

"Drink," he says, eyes closed and moaning, like giving me his blood is better than sex. "Drink, Little Baby. Take every bit you can."

And I do. I let his blood gush into my mouth and slide down my throat. I take it all, and then he feeds on me, taking it all back. When he is done, I drink him again.

I know we've done this before. I can't remember where, or how many times, or what happened after, but I know we've shared the drink like this.

This time though, it's different. Because I'm awake. I'm aware. And the longer it goes on—and it goes on for a *long* time —the more I like it.

And the more I like it, the more I like him.

So when, finally, the drink is over and the two of us are spent and sprawled out on the wet cave floor, completely naked and tangled together in each other's arms and legs, I smile.

I am… maybe not happy. But I'm not sure happy is better than content.

And that's what I am.

Content.

                              * * *

When I wake up I'm in a bed. A very nice bed that is not inside the cave.

I sit up, looking around, trying to figure out where I am because I've seen every nook and cranny of the Montana compound and I've never seen this room.

This is when I hear the traffic outside.

I throw the covers off, get out of bed—completely naked—and walk over to the window, pulling the sheer curtains aside.

It's a city.

"You're awake." I turn and find Josep behind me. He's wearing loose pants and no shirt. And my God, is he a god? Because he's got the body of one. And the face—which is perfectly symmetrical, like it was meant to display those blue eyes of his like art. His hair is long and blond and a bit wavy. He looks like a… well, god really is the right word.

I blink. "I'm awake. Where are we?"

Josep smiles. "In my dream, of course. I don't like to leave the cave. And why should I? I can go anywhere I want without ever leaving home."

I look around, trying to see the blurry edges that might reveal the truth that this place is a lie, but I can't find them. "It looks so real. It feels so real."

"Reality," he says, "is dysfunctional, Little Baby. It comes and goes. It's all very here and there."

I frown, pretty sure that this is not _my_ definition of reality. "Shouldn't reality be… like… you know, _not_ very here and there but just one or the other?"

Josep laughs, crossing the room, coming right at me. I have

an urge to back up. To get away. Because he's a monster. I know this.

But he's smiling at me, and reaching for me, and there's really no time to get away, or anywhere to go, since I'm caught in some kind of trap. So there's a moment here where my anxiety is through the roof.

It's a very short moment, though. Because his hand comes up to my cheek and I feel his love. It relaxes me.

A trick. I try and make those words form in my head in Lucia's voice. Because if she says it, it's true, isn't it?

But Lucia is definitely not here. Not even in my head. And the words are just me, looking for a reason to doubt him.

My maker.

My god.

"My Little Baby," Josep says, looking down at me with adoration. His eyes flash purple. "What is going through that head of yours?"

Be his, my own inner voice says. *Be his and he will give you everything.*

I blink. Relax. Breathe. Smile. Then I bow my head, drop to my knees, and press my lips to the tops of his feet.

Which surprises me, because I don't even know where this comes from.

"Oh, that is cute, Little Baby. What god doesn't like adoration? We all do. It's flattering." But he's leaning down. Far enough to gently grab my arm and pull me to my feet. "But all that is over now. You're already mine. You made the promise when you drank me. And I made a promise back when I drank you."

I frown, still looking down. Because his promise feels a little bit like marriage. Did I marry this monster when I drank his blood?

I can't look at him. If I do, I might scream, and if I scream, he'll know. He'll figure out that this is a lie, that I'm using him, that I hate him. That I think he's a demon from Hell and that I have no desire to be his plaything.

But there's no reprieve for me because his finger is tipping my chin up. My eyes follow—reluctantly—until I am staring straight into his soul.

Or lack of one. A pit of evil might be a better way to describe what's beyond those eyes of his. They are absolutely purple now. No doubt about it. "Do you need more blood?"

I exhale loudly. "Need, my lord?"

He laughs, and, to my surprise, so do I. "Do you *want* more blood, Little Baby?" His hand comes up to my cheek, caressing it like I'm his most cherished possession.

I do. I want to suck on him for the rest of my life. But I have questions. "If this isn't real"—I pan my hand around the room— "am I really drinking?"

"Come," he says, taking my hand. "You've earned a little baby peek."

"A peek?" I don't understand. I feel like I've fallen down a rabbit hole and all around me is a sparkling, shining, glittering, blood-covered Wonderland.

But Josep is pulling me now. Across the room, through a door, and then... it's dark. There is nothing beyond this door but emptiness.

Josep stops in the middle of this emptiness then maneuvers me in front of him, his hands on my shoulders, his hips pressing up against my lower back, his hardness very evident.

"Concentrate," he says. "Look into the emptiness, Little Baby, and see what's there."

I lean forward a little, squinting, trying to do what he says. And I'm just about to say it's not working when the space shimmers and a kind of fog appears.

A gasp comes out of my mouth. And at the same time Josep's hands slide off my shoulders and down the front of me. His fingers fondle my breasts as the image in the fog resolves.

It's us. We are on the floor of the cave all tangled together.

Which makes sense, because I knew this. I remember this.

Our naked bodies are covered in blood. It is smeared all over us. I'm on top of him, leaning down into his neck, drinking. His hands are caressing me, rubbing up and down my legs and over my back. His eyes are closed, his head tipped up to give me easy access to his jugular, and he is moaning. Every time I draw his blood out of him, he moans. Like we're fucking.

Except we're not.

"Not yet," Josep says, still fondling my breasts on this side of things. "Sex is… well, a bonus. It's the drink I want, Little Baby. It's the drink I will take whether you agree or not. Sex is something else. Sex is something you must take from me."

I can't move. I can't speak. I don't have anywhere to go and I have no idea what to say back to that.

"I am not Paul," Josep says. "I will not use it the way he does. Even though you are my Ryet, I will not *force* you to be my Ryet. I will not chase you through time, practically begging for your love. I will not wait for it, either." His hands come back up to my shoulders and he gently turns me around until we're facing each other. "You will take it from me, Little Baby. Or it will never happen. And if it never happens, I'll get it somewhere else."

And this is when I figure it out.

This is when I understand.

"Lucia didn't take it, did she? She didn't fuck you."

Josep laughs. "She's inside your head, isn't she? Telling you all sorts of things." He doesn't give me time to deny it, so I don't bother. "No. She never did. But she was nothing compared to you, Little Baby. She is weak, and stupid, and nothing but a low-class trashy bitch." His hand comes up to my cheek again. "You are my princess, Little Baby. She was nothing but a slave. And I never wanted her in my bed, so I never gave her any encouragement. You, however…" He pauses here to smile. "Oh, if you deny me? If you want to play hard to get? I'll just tempt you, my Little Baby Darkness. I'll tempt you like this…"

He leans down, pressing his lips to mine. I expect him to bite his lip and give me blood, but he doesn't. He just… kisses me. Not hard and demanding, but softly and with tenderness. His arms wrap around me in an embrace, our bodies pressed together.

Everything is slow now. Like the chaos across that fog—the blood lust—isn't happening. Like this moment here is entirely ours.

When he pulls away, I suddenly miss him. Ache for him. So I look him in the eyes. "I will take your blood," he says. "Any time I want. But I will not take your body unless you give it."

Then he turns and steps into the fog.

"Wait!" I panic. "Where are you going? What am I supposed to do?"

His body is only marginally there, like he just became part of the fog. But he looks over his shoulder one last time. "Do whatever you want. Live here." He nods his head behind me. "Stay in the hotel. Go out into the city. Spend money. Buy pretty dresses. Meet people. Fall in love, Little Baby. You can live your whole life here and it will be a good one."

"A dream," I say. "This place is nothing but a dream."

"They're all dreams, Little Baby. They're *all* dreams." He grins. "But I am hoping that you, like me, want reality. And if that's the case, then come along." He turns away and takes a step, and then he's… well, he's just him on the other side of the fog. Josep, on the floor of his cave. Covered in blood. Me on top of him. Drinking. His hands caressing my naked, blood-covered body as he feeds.

He made this place for me. A place all my own where I can live forever inside a delusion. And that cave on the other side of the fog, that's what he made for himself. A world where I am his and he is mine and probably all we do is fuck and drink.

We can live—if that's even the correct word—we can live separately and still get what we want. But it won't be real. It's just a dream. So it will never be enough.

And no matter what I choose right now, I *am* his. There is no possible way back from this now.

"Choose him." Lucia is standing at my left shoulder. Close enough to me so that I feel her shrug. "I've already traveled that other road. You might as well just… be his. Wholly and completely. Because trust me when I say this"—she turns her head to look at me—"it's as good as it gets."

Then she's gone. Like she was never here.

I let out a breath, feeling completely crazy. I mean, being a halfbreed was insane enough. I only ended up here because Lucia was attracted to my boyfriend. I was a tagalong. He was killed years back now. I don't even remember his name, actually. He died, I stayed.

It's not that I was invisible. I had pink hair, after all. People saw me, but no one took any notice of me.

Not until Paul came up from the ground and made me his.

Not until Josep came up from the bunker and made me his.

In the foggy cave Josep suddenly opens his eyes. They are so bright and purple, they light up the darkness on this side of things. "*I see you,*" he says. Then he smiles, shoves me off his neck, and presses his mouth into my throat.

I feel the bite. On this side of things, I *feel* it.

And it feels good.

The pull. It's glorious. I want him to eat me all night and day. For eternity.

And I don't even have a choice in that. He's going to take it, he already told me.

So… why not take something for myself?

Why not take *him* back?

As soon as I think this, I'm out of the dream and back in my body in the cave. On top of him. Covered in blood. Lusting for it.

But not just the blood. I am lusting for this god of a monster beneath me.

I reach down, grab his hard cock, and put it inside me.

He pulls back from my neck, teeth dripping with blood, and laughs.

He did it.

He tricked me.

I gave in.

And it was my choice.

But I don't regret it.

I don't regret anything.

Carrots and sticks

The first page of the book is a mirror. And even though this is weird, it feels inevitable. A mirror. A mirror.

A *mirror.*

Looking into the mirror I see myself, but a moment later I see Ryet and Paul in a bed. Our bed. I mean, mine and Ryet's. And since this is a book, I know what to do with the mirror. I enter it, of course. That's what I've been doing with all the books since I came back to the Guild, so it's practically a habit now.

And then I'm her, the woman in bed with Paul and Ryet, and we're feeding and naked. All twisted together and writhing on the scarlet-stained sheets.

My eyes are closed and I enjoy the feeling of the pull coming out of both sides of my neck. It feels *so* good. It has to though, doesn't it? Because I'm not the kind of woman who has two men at once. It's not my thing.

It wasn't, at least.

But I find that I like being with Paul now. I desire him. Not in all the ways, but in this singular, specific way. I like being his food. I like being his... well, I'm not sure what I am to him or he to me. His part comes off as kind of custodial. A guardian. Which is ridiculous, because the word 'guardian' implies a level of protection and so far nothing about what has happened to me feels anything like protection.

Though I suppose it could always get worse.

"You think too much, Syrsee." It's not Paul who says this, it's

Ryet. Which is a clue. A clue that this isn't real. But of course, I knew that. I literally stepped into a book. A story. A fiction.

This whole thing, it's nothing but a fantasy. A good one, for sure. But *fake*. I know this.

"You don't know anything. You're a baby, dear Syrsee," Paul says. His face is right up against mine, smiling. And his teeth are dripping with my blood. "Nothing but a baby." Then he laughs and dives back down into his meal, which is me.

My grandma's words come back to me in this moment —*magnificent promises.*

It bothers me. Because while Paul did casually reference a few promises while we were making our way to this point in time, they have nothing to do with why I let him feed on me in these dreams. Nothing at all, actually.

I let him feed on me for the same reason I allow Ryet to do it too.

Because I like it.

It's as simple as that. I let him do it because it feels good.

A hand slips between my legs and when I turn my head, Ryet is smiling at me. His mouth is covered in my blood too. And not for the first time I wonder… how long will it last?

How long will they desire me? How long before I lose whatever it is that attracts them? How long before I am an old, empty bag of skin that tastes like a bitter pill?

It's going to end. Everything ends eventually.

"You don't have to worry about that, dear Syrsee."

I turn and look at Paul. At his bloody mouth and dancing eyes. "Why not? I mean, it's a logical worry if you ask me. I'm not a vampire. I'm a Black witch. And Black witches get old, so why wouldn't I? My blood will get stale. You'll make more Black witches and they will be young, and sweet, and gullible."

He places a hand on my cheek, still smiling. "So. You like it, do you?"

"It's impossible not to."

"Not impossible," he counters. "But it's very hard to fight the Darkness. Especially on your own. It knows, Syrsee. It knows exactly what you want. And it's powerful enough to give it to you—at least temporarily. And it has no conscience, so it doesn't care what you're feeling. It doesn't care if it chews you up and spits you out. And while all your desires are becoming manifest, you don't care either. It's the way of evil. It's always been the way of evil."

"This doesn't make me feel any better."

"No?" Paul laughs. "It wasn't supposed to. All of this"—he pans a hand to the bed, and the blood, and Ryet, who is still feeding on me while his fingers dance between my legs—"all of *this* is meant to make you feel better."

I blink. Because an understanding manifests. I blink again. "Where am I?"

Paul pets me like I'm a kitten. "You're right here, darling."

"No. *Where am I?*"

He chuckles, looking down at me with adoration. "You're. Right. *Here*. With me, Syrsee."

With him? But he's... and I'm..."But... the Guild?"

Paul shakes his head. "You're not there."

"But the books! I can read them!"

"You could always read them, Syrsee. It was always your choice not to look."

"But Myer! And... and our apartment!"

"Again, it's all real. I guess." He shrugs. "I did the best I could when I dreamed it all up based on what I know. Or, rather, what I could see inside your head. I even told you that you and your body would be separated. Remember? I told you that."

"You did, but—"

He shushes me with a fingertip to my lips. "Shhhhh. Quiet now, Syrsee. It's time to face the truth. I need you. You need me. Ryet needs us both."

I look down at Ryet, who is still blissfully sucking on my neck. It's like he's not here. But it's like I'm not here, either.

"Are you ready for the truth?"

I shake my head no without hesitation.

"Too bad. I've been careful with you, Syrsee. I really, really have. I've taken it slow. I've given you all the time you've needed. From the day you were born, to this moment right here, I have been careful with you. But that's all over now and I need you to commit."

"Commit to what?"

"To him, of course." Paul smiles as he looks down at Ryet feeding on me. Paul's hand slides up to my cheek and then he pushes a bit of hair out of the way as he gazes into my eyes. "You've done a good job. You've bonded with him, and fed him, and let him put the Dark baby inside you. Such a good girl you are."

I recoil back, repulsed. Not by his words, but because he's right. I did all of this. Everything he said. *Magnificent promises.* I am repulsed by the realization that I am an active participant in my own nightmare.

No, Syrsee. The voice in my head is my grandma. *You are the nightmare.*

The promise, I now realize, was the pull. The feeling of being fed on.

Which makes me feel cheap and stupid.

"It's OK," Paul soothes, as he pets me. "It's OK, Syrsee. You never had a chance. You're but a baby with no knowledge of anything and I am…" He chortles. "Well, I'm the fucking king. The fucking king, Syrsee. I *am* the American Vampire." He caresses my cheek now. "You never had a chance."

I wake up suffocating on darkness.

I try to sit up, but there's a heavy weight on my chest. I'm no longer in a bed with the man I think I love and his… *our*… master. The euphoric feeling of being fed on is gone.

I am in the dirt.

I know this because it falls into my mouth when I scream.

* * *

You're such a little rebel, aren't you? Hmmm?" Paul is smoothing the sweaty hair away from my face again. We're back in bed now. "Always looking for the blurry edges. It's a dangerous want, you know that, right? To seek the blur? It's asking for trouble."

"This isn't real."

"Of course not." And he laughs at me. "Everything that is good in your life, Syrsee? It's all fake. All put there by me to make things easier on you. That's how much I love you. I give you these things to give you time. To allow you to mature. So you can accept it. And you can't even get mad at me about this." His voice was soothing and low when he started, but it ends rather demanding and forceful. "You can't get mad about the fictions I've created. You enjoyed them."

"But…" I look up at him, searching those evil blue eyes. They are ringed red right now. Like the blue is just like everything else in my life—nothing but an illusion. "Was I ever at the Guild?"

"Of course. You had to grow up somewhere. I'm certainly not responsible enough to raise a baby. Even if I do love them." He smiles. "I'm a terrible father. That's why I gave you Ryet. He loves all that father shit. It's gonna be fun, you'll see. The two of you and…" His hand slips down to my belly. "*Him.*"

I close my eyes and wonder how hard it would be to kill myself and why I didn't go through with it back in Paul's Montana lodge. I was *so close* to freedom. True freedom.

And I backed out.

I *chose* this. I chose evil.

"Oh, come on, Syrsee. You're being dramatic."

"Dramatic?" My eyes fly open and I stare at him. Ryet is still feeding on me, but the sensation of the pull is gone. Like he's nothing but an illusion, which I'm sure he is. He's not at the Guild any more than I am. He's in the ground, choking on dirt. "I'm a bag of blood. I'm a womb. A factory. That's it. I don't want to do this."

"Well, of course not. Who would? But that's because I haven't explained your reward yet."

"*Reward?*" I scoff.

"Carrots and sticks, dear Syrsee. You respond much better to carrots. And once you have this baby, my bouncing baby Darkness, I will stuff you full of carrots. So many carrots that you won't mind that I stole a life from you." He smiles here. A big warm lie, this smile. "If it all goes well, I will steal many lives from you. One after the other after the other. And you will not care. It's a very good trade, dear Syrsee."

"What are you talking about?"

"A fiction, you see. I've planned it all out. A special little place for you and Ryet and"—he gestures to my stomach again —"a never-ending supply of babies. You see, I have a plan, Syrsee. And it's quite complicated. Some of it happens here—" He pans a hand to indicate the illusion we're currently part of. "Some of it *there*." He flicks his fingers into the air, like wherever 'there' is, it's ethereal. "Here and there," he continues. "That's the best of both worlds. But I'm getting ahead of myself. The babies are necessary for things that will happen 'here'. And that is where you come in."

This is when everything that happened at the cabin comes back to me. *There is a cycle, Syrsee.* I am not a feeder. I'm a *breeder*. I look at Paul. "My reward is living inside an illusion?"

"Just think of it as a book." His smile is delightful, like he is the most cunning and clever thing in the world. And he is, so I guess he's earned that smile. "You made such a big deal about reading the books. And now you get to live in one. How fun is that?"

"I don't want to live in a fiction."

His words come out angry and frustrated. "Everything is a fiction, Syrsee. There's no reality. It's fake. It's an illusion. The Darkness rules this world." He lets out a breath, takes one in, and composes himself. "And it needs to stop. That's why I'm doing all this. We've got to put an end to it! And the babies guarantee that. Ryet as well, of course. But I would never leave him to die. I would never do that. Not after all the trouble I've gone to. Not after all my careful work. He'll be safe in the end." But right after he says these words, his eyes shift. And I know it's a lie.

I scoff again. "You're trying to save the *world*? Do you really expect me to believe that?"

He waves a hand in the air. "Who cares what you believe.

You're a vessel. Filled with blood and babies." He smirks down at me, one eyebrow cocked. "This is as good as it gets."

I wake up again, choking on dirt, trying to claw my way up. But then Paul's voice is in my head. "*Do not* leave him in the ground, Syrsee. *Do not.*"

"I'm not gonna leave him! I'm trying to leave *you!*"

"You can't just claw your way back up to the real world, Syrsee. You have to *feed* him."

I make myself pause here. To try and come to terms with what the actual fuck is happening to me. But I don't know. I can't think my way through this. "What has happened? Tell me what is going on, or I swear to God, I *will* leave him and all your careful work will be for nothing."

It's a lie. I won't leave Ryet. He's all I have left and I'm gonna fight for this man until my last dying breath. And while Paul should know this, he hedges. Then, he answers. "He's buried next to you, just a few feet away."

"Why didn't you just bury us together? Could've saved me some time clawing through the dirt."

"Because we weren't sure who would wake up first. You or Ryet."

"Why does that matter?"

"Well…" Paul's chuckle reverberates in my head. "Because he's a *monster*, Syrsee. And while you're no angel, you're no match for him."

"What are you saying? That if he had woken up first, he'd have torn me apart?"

"See? You're not so stupid."

I close my eyes, willing this all to be a nightmare.

"This is as real as it gets because this is as good as it gets."

Paul repeats this phrase with his trademark smarmy charm that I'm sure, if I could see him, would come with a matching smarmy smile. "This, finally, is your reality, Syrsee. You make blood and babies. And for now, you feed me and Ryet. I rather like how this has turned out. You're pretty, and your blood is sweet, and those babies of ours will be gorgeous. They will ensure an everlasting rule here in this realm we call reality. Which is still a dream so you might as well just give in and enjoy it with me. Ryet sure will."

"You don't know that."

"Oh, but I do, Syrsee. At first, he will be all instinct, just like he was when you first made him, feeding on you when he's hungry and throwing you away when he's full. But he'll come around again. I promise, he will. The promise of babies is his lure, not yours. He liked being a father. It worked for him."

"What?"

"You haven't thought much about motherhood, so yeah. It's an adjustment for you. But trust me now, Syrsee. You'll see. It's all going to turn out perfect. It will be you and Ryet and the babies in your belly forever, and ever, and ever..."

"Forever? No. It's not forever, Paul. Because I'm not a vampire. You told me twelve. Twelve babies. So I get twelve years of a fake life as a demon's broodmare and then... then what? I die and go to Hell?"

"You were *always* going to Hell, Syrsee. You're made of Darkness. So that's got nothing to do with me. I'm trying to make it all better. And I've said this several times now. I'm tired of repeating myself. *Just do your job.*"

These last few angry words of his echo in my head, but once that subsides, the silence left behind is deafening.

I am alone, in the dirt, with an evil, dark thing inside me.

And this is where I will stay until I get myself out of it.

* * *

I doze for a while, my head filled with nightmares. And slowly, I begin to hurt. I can't really move in the dirt. I mean, I understand that it's possible—with clawing and struggle—to get out of the ground, but it takes an effort and a will that I don't really have at the moment.

But I do manage to displace enough dirt to move my arms around, and my new evil superpower seems to be night vision, so I can see what is causing my pain. Because it's everywhere, all over my body, all at once.

It's bite marks. That's what I find. Bite marks all over me. Glowing a sick, fluorescent purple. There are so many, it's like every vampire in the world used me as food.

Which doesn't really make sense because aren't Paul and Josep the only ones? Well, and Ryet. But isn't a vampire a rare thing? How could two vampires have made such a mess of my body?

I don't know. Nothing makes any sense and I feel like I'm already in Hell, so... I doze, trying my best to find the purple dreamwalk so I can make reality go away.

But it's not easy. Not like it was. It's like the purple knows I'm different now and wants nothing to do with me.

That's when I remember the gold. I have two mists at my disposal. And while the purple was part of Paul, the gold is part of me, the Black witch.

The *nightmare*.

My nightmare.

I think about this for a while, letting the gold mist surround me in this new place in my head. Letting it heal me. I think. I hope. And I settle into the idea that Paul doesn't know everything. He doesn't know about the nightmare. About that little girl and her… beast. What was her name again? Coyrah. And the monster was called the aquis equī—which was like a cross between a seahorse and an octopus.

If Lucia was telling the truth—and there's really no reason to believe she was because pretty much everyone in my life is lying right now—but if she was, then that little girl who tamed the monster is my ancestor.

The start of the Black bloodline.

I feel like Paul has very little respect for this blood of mine. Not the actual blood, which he feeds on, but the genetics. And his dismissal of it—*of me*—feels wrong. Deceptive. Because if I was weak, he wouldn't need me. He wouldn't have gone to so much trouble to curate me, and raise me, and keep me close.

Which means I'm strong. I just don't know it yet.

And this strength comes from Coyrah. That's what Lucia was telling me.

I am a Black witch and a Black witch is nothing to fuck with.

* * *

Eventually I have to concede that I can't stay here in the dirt. My body still hurts from all the bites and it's not getting any better. I don't think it will get better until I drink from Ryet. And whatever is happening to him, that won't get any better until he drinks from me.

For better or worse, I love him. He's my partner. And even if he is a monster now, with little or no resemblance to the man I met in White River, he's all I've got.

I'm not gonna give him up. I can't. If there's a way to keep him, I will find it.

It feels like a hollow promise. Something lackluster. I mean, it's not romantic at all. It's practical. And I really hate that.

But I cut myself some slack and let out a breath. Because none of this is my fault. Yes, I have made some seriously bad decisions over the past couple of months, but it was mostly reaction to circumstance. It's not like I planned on becoming something evil. It's not like I had a choice, either. This is what was handed to me. I'm just doing the best I can to save myself. Which, again, feels a little gross. But self-preservation isn't a sin. It's an instinct.

This word makes me cringe because animals have instincts and I'm already feeling less and less human as the moments tick off. But my way out was a choice I gave up back in that bedroom in Paul's lodge. When I saved Ryet, I agreed to walk this path and now that I'm here, I had better start thinking of *me*.

No one else is.

Whatever Ryet is to me, whatever he will become, remains to be seen. We are in a relationship. It's symbiotic through the blood lust, so it's not a romantic relationship. But it is a relationship. A new one at that. In fact, even though Ryet and I have been through some serious shit over a short period of time, we don't actually know each other yet.

We're still in the honeymoon stage. Granted, he's a monster and I'm a witch and our attraction is mostly about the blood lust, but it doesn't *have* to be that way.

He could love me. If he's capable of it. If he's not, well… then what I do next is even more important. If I don't want to end up like my grandma, then I need to make calculated decisions from this point on.

I need to make sure Ryet and I have a chance to get to know each other again. I need that dream life Paul cooked up for us at the Guild. We were getting along. We were a team.

And if I choose my steps carefully, we can be a team again. I can save that dynamic between us even if I can't save myself.

Misery loves company.

I don't like the way that sounds but I refuse to walk into my future without an ally when he's literally in the dirt next to me and is most likely more than willing to come along. Even if it is only so he can feed on my blood.

So that's what I have to do. I have to feed him. Hopefully, once I'm done, and if he's sane, he will feed me back.

That's the only choice I have at the moment. That's the only way to keep him.

* * *

Making my way through the dirt is a slow process because I'm deep in the earth and the dirt has to go somewhere and the only place is the cavity I leave behind me. One handful at a time, I make enough room to turn. Then, one handful at a time, I start inching sideways.

I'm not sure how long I've been doing this when I smell his blood—maybe an hour? Maybe a day? Maybe a lifetime?

But the scent of him wipes away all the exhaustion I am feeling and I claw faster until, finally, my hand finds his shoulder.

I stop here, inhaling deeply, and close my eyes. Because his blood is so close. But this pause is barely a moment because my drive to feed on him is so strong, I couldn't stop what I'm about to do next if I wanted to. And I don't.

Both hands are now furiously scooping dirt away from his body and pushing it behind me. "Ryet?" I whisper. "Can you hear me?"

He stirs, but doesn't wake.

I can see his neck now. I've uncovered most of his face and the top of his chest. And I just stare at his jugular—which is throbbing and pulsating with such a fervor, I almost lean down and bite it.

If I had fangs, I would. There would be no stopping me.

But I don't have fangs. It would be a very gross chew to open that vein.

I'm looking right at him when I think this and his eyes fly open.

I laugh in surprise. "Ryet? Can you hear me? Are you awake?"

He doesn't look at me. I'm not even sure he hears me, but he starts clawing at the dirt on top of him, scooping handfuls and pushing it underneath him in a way that feels very practiced. Like he's been digging his way out of the dirt his entire life.

The word 'instinct' come to mind again.

Like he's a mole.

While I'm thinking this, he begins to move upward. Then everything starts happening so fast—his hands, the dirt, the empty space above him—and before I know it, he's leaving me behind!

I grab on to his shoulders at the very last moment, hooking my arms tightly around his neck. And it's a good thing I have instincts too because if I had waited another second, he would've left me buried behind him.

Moments later we're breaking through the surface of the earth, the dark, inky night sky a refreshing and rejuvenating sight.

I did it!

We did it!

We're out.

As Ryet steps out of the ground, I unwrap my arms from around his shoulders and land on my feet. Then I start laughing. It was so much easier than I thought it would be.

Ryet turns and…

My smile drops and my laugh dies.

He and I lock eyes. I don't know what mine look like, but his are red and there is no trace of the man I love in there.

The next thing I know, I'm falling backwards to the ground and his teeth are ripping through my throat.

Too much is the only answer.

I go outside and start making my way to the lab, my mind still caught up in the dreamwalk this morning. The three of us. I've never been interested in Paul that way and if you had asked me a couple of weeks ago whether or not I'd be up for sharing my girlfriend with a demon, it would've been a firm no.

Which bothers me.

Not really the 'no' part. Well, that too. Paul. I dunno. I can't go there right now.

It's mostly just the fact that I can't count on anything anymore. Reality is so… unstable and unreliable. And it makes sense, I guess. I did turn into a vampire and I am living in some sort of second body.

That's another thing, too. Second body? Paul did explain it. Kind of. He was all, "you could split yourselves" and "be in two places at once" and "walk away from your soul." Which, looking back, really should've been the flashing red warning sign where I focused all my attention.

Walk away from your soul? What the fuck? Soulless? And we agreed to this.

It was the blood lust, I'm sure of it. Blood. It makes you do weird shit.

This last thought is still swirling through my head when I realize there's no one around. Like… no one. I stop on the walking path and look all around. Empty. Every trail, every path —just empty. I'm kind of in the woods now, so I lean to the side, trying to get a glimpse of the clearing up ahead where some shops are, but again, no people.

I throw up my hands. See? This is what I mean. Un. Reliable. I need some stability here. *"Where is everyone!"* I yell this into the forest and it echoes back in a weird way, like my own voice mocking me.

"Funny you should ask."

I whirl around and find Paul sitting on a bench about twenty feet behind me. "What the hell are you doing here? And… nice coat."

"Isn't it though?" He grins as he straightens the lapel on his fur coat. An actual fucking grin. Which is so out of character for him—his usual expression is more of an evil smirk—that it knocks me back a step. Because… it looks good on him, that grin. "It's wolf. It's not real, of course. It's made of magic purple dreamwalk." He looks down at his left shoulder and brushes a leaf off the coat. "But I'm having one made just like it back at the compound."

I blink my eyes and shake my head a little to snap myself out of whatever trance I'm falling into, then point at him. "How are you here?"

"How do I get anywhere, Ryet? I dreamwalk it."

"I understand that. But it's not answering my question."

"Because you haven't asked that question yet, Ryet." He pauses here to smile at me. Not a grin or a smirk. Just a smile. Kind of a sad one. "You're afraid to ask that question."

I blow out a breath. I know what he's gonna say and I don't want to hear it. I really, really don't. So instead, I say, "I can't live like this."

"Good news." He beams. "You're not."

I shake my head. "I can't do it, Paul. I really can't. I've lost all sense of reality. I have no idea where I am, or what I am, or who I am."

Paul stands up and walks towards me. Our eyes are locked together as he approaches. We stand, facing each other, mere inches apart. He speaks first, pushing a piece of hair away from my face like I'm his fucking lover and he's trying to be tender. "It's temporary. I told you that. Remember? It's all temporary."

I think back to a conversation we had not that long ago. *"If we had a herd,"* he said, *"it would be easier. Right now, all we have is Syrsee. So we must share. It's temporary. Black witches are hard to farm."*

I turn my back to him and stare off into the forest. "We're not here, are we?"

"No."

I turn back, furious. "Why? Why are you doing this? Are you trying to make me insane?"

Paul laughs. "Insane? Dear Ryet, I'm saving that mind of yours this very moment. You're doing remarkably well—thanks to me." Now he glares at me. "But I'm glad you brought it up."

"I didn't bring it up, *you* did."

He waves a hand in the air. "Regardless. If you don't pull back and rein it in right now, you're going to decapitate our one and only Black witch. And while I see the draw of this act—all that Black blood all at once would certainly be the feast of a lifetime—we don't have a backup food source. So." He throws up his hands. "That's why I'm here. Pull back, Ryet. *Right now.*"

And then he's gone.

And then I'm gone too. All of it is gone. The woods are gone, and the Guild is gone, and the lab is gone. It's all gone because it was never real to begin with. *Split in half. Be in two places at once.* It's crazy. Even crazier that I fell for it.

I blame the blood.

But I can think about that another time because while I am not longer in the woods of New Hampshire, I am in some other woods. Covered in dirt. Nothing about me feels normal and everything hurts. My whole body screams with pain. The only good thing about this moment is the blood gushing into my mouth like water coming out of a firehose. If water was sweet, and Black, and magical, that is.

I open my eyes and it takes a moment to make sense of what I'm seeing. All the while, Black blood is rushing into my mouth. A moment later I realize I'm looking at… hair.

With a shock, reality comes back and I unlatch my mouth from Syrsee's neck. She falls back, out of my arms, limp and lifeless on the freshly disturbed earth.

There's a hole in her neck where I was feeding. A *hole.*

"Syrsee?" My voice is deep and almost unrecognizable. "Syrsee?" Then the panic sets in. I shake her. "*Syrsee!*" I stand up and the moment I do, my wings spread out with a great whooshing sound. I look down at myself and recognize the blue-black skin of a demon, but there are marks all over my body. Fang marks. Like a hundred vampires were feeding on me at once.

I look around, frantic. I'm at the compound. I can see the lodge off in the distance. We're behind it, in the woods just north, and I can see the blue glow of the lit-up pool in the back.

Syrsee has the same marks on her body as well.

I fill up with rage and the anger flows out of my eyes as a maroon glow, illuminating Syrsee's body with a sick red light that turns into a mist before my eyes.

Feeders. He turned us into *feeders.*

For who? Just him and Josep?

No. There are way too many bites.

I want to figure this out, it feels very relevant, but Syrsee—she looks bad. I pick up her in my arms, shaking her a little. But this just makes it worse because some of the muscles in her neck have been damaged by my feeding, so her head just lolls back and forth like the broken neck of a dead bird.

But the really gross thing is that I can see her jugular throbbing, blood spilling out of it as I watch. Which means she's not dead.

Not yet.

She needs blood. A lot of it and right now. I bring my wrist up to my mouth, tear it open with my teeth, and let the blood drop into her open mouth. "Feed, Syrsee! Feed on me!"

The blood coats her tongue and spills over the side, pooling. But she doesn't swallow. "Come on," I say, shaking her again. "Come on!"

She chokes, spilling my own blood back into my face. But it's better than nothing.

"That's it, Syrsee. Take it. Swallow, *please.*" And I silently say that word again, *Please, Syrsee. Please. Do not make me the one who kills you.*

Which is a selfish plea, but it's an honest one too.

Do not make me the one who kills you.

She coughs again, sputtering. But she's not swallowing. She's not taking it in.

Think, Ryet! You're a vampire now. A real fucking vampire. Which means you have all sorts of powers at your disposal. Use them!

But I don't know what they are. Paul never explained anything. I have no idea what I am, let alone what I can do.

Which… isn't entirely true. I do know how to do one thing. Dreamwalk.

I sit down in the dirt, Syrsee cradled in my arms, and close my eyes. Concentrating. Beckoning the purple mist.

Immediately, I'm inside it, still holding Syrsee's limp body in my arms, but there are no bite marks and her neck isn't practically torn in half. She looks like she's sleeping.

I take a breath, hold it, and slowly let it out. "Wake up now, Syrsee. It's time to feed." I say this in my Ryet voice, not the demon one I was using back in reality.

Her eyes flutter, but don't open. That's OK, though. I don't need her awake. She doesn't even need to bite me because I'm dripping blood into her mouth on the other side of the purple. I just need her to swallow.

Which she does. Once, twice. But that's it.

I pull out of the dreamwalk and look down at the woman in my arms again. She's gurgling now, but I can see that the wound in her neck is beginning to heal. Just along the ragged edges, but the blood is clotting.

She'll be OK.

I stand up, holding her close to my chest, and carry her like I would a baby towards the lodge.

She'll be OK.

I'm heading towards the pool because it's the most inviting place I can see at the moment. A place fit for a woman healing from the attack of a vampire.

Everything is lit up around here, but I don't see any of the halfbreeds. Not a single one, which is weird. Because there are lots of them and they keep strange hours. I keep searching as I walk up to the pool, but the place is truly empty and the silence gives me chills.

What the fuck happened here?

I want to know, but it'll have to wait. I need to heal Syrsee first. I walk straight into the pool. It's heated, so it's warm, but as I enter, the water gets exponentially hotter and I recall a memory of Paul in his demon form making the pool water boil when he swam. Well, mostly he floated on his back, staring up at the sky with his arms spread open wide, like he was daring God to fuck with him.

But I don't float. I take a seat on the steps that face the house, half in and half out of the water. And then I open up my wrist again and start the process of fixing what I did to her.

How many times will I need to do this in the future?

How many times will I hurt her so badly, I will need to summon Dark magic to heal her?

How much more of her will I take?

Too much. That's the only answer. Too much.

A noise from the direction of the lodge startles me and I look up to find a shadow backlit by the lights inside the house. A man.

He says nothing and neither do I. We just stare at each other for what feels like a pretty long time, but is probably only about thirty seconds.

Then he clears his throat. "Ryet? Are you… Ryet?"

It's not a voice I recognize. And he smells weird. Even from here, I can smell him and it's… wrong. "Who the fuck are you?" Back out here, in reality, my voice is not something I recognize. This guy, whoever he is, doesn't recognize it either. Not as Ryet's, because he doesn't know me. He doesn't recognize it as… human.

"I… well… I'm…" And then another guy appears. Backlit as well. Then another. They flank the guy in the center. One by one, more men appear until there is a semicircular line at the end of the pool in front of the lodge, all staring at me.

This is when I understand who and what I'm looking at.

Paul's scions.

This is where the magic lives

Kael is an exceptionally fast driver, which I appreciate because we make the drive down into White River in record time.

"This is it," I say, pointing to a sign announcing White River as we flash by.

Kael slows down the truck, kind of squinting his eyes as he looks around. "Here?"

"That's right. White River is one of my towns."

"What the hell do you do out *here*?" He sneers these words out. But the sneer seems to be his default setting, so it has little impact.

"You're about to find out. See that church up ahead? Pull in the back. By the food pantry door."

"Church?" He's still sneering, but this time it comes with a chuckle laced with a healthy dose of ridicule. He looks at me, amused with himself. "What is it? Satanic or something?"

I offer him a patient smile. "Something like that."

He pulls the truck into the parking lot of the First Methodist Church and slides up next to the pantry door, slamming on the brakes so we both jerk forward.

I take a deep breath and do a very good job of controlling myself while I side-eye him. "Wait right here."

He snickers now—"Yes, sir"—and pops off a mock salute.

I get out of the truck, close the door, and enter the pantry, welcomed by the jingling of bells above the door. I look up at them just as a familiar voice says, "My lord! You're here? You didn't even call!"

My smile is immediate because Joshua Reed comes out from behind a curtain-covered doorway and he is a complete delight. He's submissive, accommodating, and clever too. It's a rare combination that I value. Especially his cleverness. And when you add in his deceptive clean-cut good looks, it makes him downright dangerous. Beauty and danger are both things I value. "I didn't have time," I say. "Things are moving quickly now, Joshua. We're nearly done."

"Already?" He makes a face of surprise, which looks very good on him. Though he looks good all the time by my standards. Blond hair, blue eyes, that square jaw that is mostly clean-shaven. He was a very pretty child and his beauty did not abandon him as he grew.

"Yes. Already. It's gone better than I'd hoped, with one tiny exception."

Joshua smiles at me. "You're having second thoughts, aren't you?"

"Second thoughts?" I ponder the idea. Briefly. "No. Not quite anyway."

"It's Ryet. You love him."

Which I cannot deny, so I don't. "I do." And these words come out as a sigh, forcing Joshua and me to take a moment to appreciate my unlikely regrets. "But"—I rally, of course—"it needs to be done. And anyway, I have a plan and that plan is sitting in the truck outside."

Joshua snickers. Which is an entirely different kind of snicker than the one Kael snorted at me mere seconds ago. Then he walks over to the window behind the front desk that acts like a checkout stand—though there is no checking out happening here, all the food is free—and pulls a light blue curtain aside. After a moment, he turns back to me. "He looks…"

"Dangerous?"

Joshua points to me. "That."

"He is. That's why I came to the pantry instead of the coven."

"Oh!" Joshua gets it. "Emily's not here, but let me give her a call. She'll know what to do." Then he turns back the way he came and disappears behind the door curtain.

"I'm sure she will," I absently say, tracing my finger along the side of a large wooden crate holding watermelons. Which are way out of season, especially for Idaho, but, of course, they were grown in the greenhouse, so they are not out of place.

Then I wander down a narrow hallway until I reach a long set of shelves filled with jars of herbs. I study Emily's stock for a moment. I've never been curious about kitchen magic since I have the Darkness inside me, but now, I find myself reading labels.

All of the jars contain a specific dried herb. These jars hold ingredients, not potions. Which is a quaint word that I quite like, but Emily calls what she cooks up with them 'teas.' It's a human-friendly word, so she says.

Joshua comes back. "OK. She gave me a list of options. Not these," he says, pointing to the jars. "Back here." Then he leads me deeper into the innards of the church and we stop in front of a locked room. He keys in a code, opens the door, and invites me to go inside.

Which I do.

Now here… *here* is where Emily keeps all her incredible and innate talent tightly sealed up in little vials. The White River coven is the only one I have, but there are many other kitchen-witch covens in this part of the world and we do trades with them. The church pantry isn't actually a food bank, it's the storefront for my very lucrative apothecary.

Joshua follows me in, closes the door, and starts reading off the list he made, adding a question mark after each statement. "Dizzy? Sleepy? Exposed? Living Dead?"

"Hmmm." I ponder these options. "What is 'exposed'?"

Joshua's eyes flick up to the ceiling like he's thinking. Then he looks back at me. "It makes you kind of… impressionable? But with a healthy dose of 'don't give a fuck.'"

"What do you suggest?"

"Well." He takes a moment to think again. "Are we going to kill him?"

"Definitely."

"Milk him?"

"Yes."

"Sex?"

"Orgy."

Joshua smirks. "Well, that's fun."

"I certainly hope so. He's kind of a dick."

"And what are we harvesting? Liver? Heart? Gonads?"

"All three, I think. But we'll let Emily decide once we get up to the coven."

Joshua nods, collecting the jars off the shelf. "OK. Well, if Emily's tweaking, let's just take all four."

"Perfect," I say. "Do you want to ride with me? Or meet us up there?"

Joshua glances in the direction of the pantry, then looks at me. "I'll meet you there. He's…"

"Scary?"

He points at me. "That."

"Well, you won't have to worry about him, Joshua." Then I

reach over and place a loving hand on his cheek. "He'll never touch you. He'll never even get the chance."

* * *

The entire town of White River is mine. All of it, including the people. They are all part of the coven of witches I've been breeding for the last hundred and twenty years, give or take. But they are nothing like the line of witches that Syrsee comes from. There is no Black blood running through my women. In fact, it's the men who have most of the power in my line.

The women, like Emily and all the cooks who came before her, are good at manipulating the inherent properties of plants and mixing them all together in certain proportions using recipes passed down through generations of mothers and daughters. But the potions can only do so much. They help things along.

All the real magic is in the secretions. And manipulating secretions is the magic of men.

Which is why I keep an ample supply of scions. It wasn't a hedge against Ryet. Well, maybe a tiny hedge. But I knew he was going to work.

No. I keep the scions, like Kael here, for his blood. Blood that is half mine. Which makes it all mine. And then, should I ever need some help to move things along, I come up here with a scion, have a little ritual, kill him, milk him, harvest him, and give that all to Emily—or whoever was in charge of the kitchen at the time, which hasn't always been Emily, but nonetheless, it is now— and this little kitchen witch will cook me up a custom potion and put it in a vial, or cook me up a pudding and put it in a jar.

Most of the time I take the potion or eat the pudding myself and then I offer Ryet a drink. This is how I slowly, *slowly* changed him over the last several decades.

It wasn't the Darkness.

It was *me* using the Darkness and the men of the White River Coven to create a special kind of magic that I call the Dusk.

I smile at the wordplay, amused at my own cleverness.

If the Dusk was a beer, it would be called Darkness Lite. It takes a little more to get the same buzz, but I'm not looking for the Darkness kind of buzz. I'm going to kill this man. I only need him cooperative and willing until the ritual is over.

I go back outside and get in the truck.

Kael looks at me expectantly, waiting for some kind of explanation. When all I do is stare back at him, he becomes agitated. "*Well?*"

I smile, picturing him naked. "You have a nice body, you know that, Kael?"

He snorts a little. "Yeah. So?"

"I'm going to enjoy it."

Now he smirks, confident in his own sex appeal. "Is that what this is about? Sex?"

"It's always about sex, Kael."

"Well, for me it's about blood. So… when do I get some?"

I chuckle and grin. "You're gonna get some all right." Then I point at Joshua's beat-up silver Chevy pick-up as he comes around the side of the church. Joshua smiles at me from the other side of the windshield, then nods his head towards the road.

"I'm going to take you somewhere now, Kael. Somewhere Ryet has never been."

Kael side-eyes me. "What kind of place?"

"A place where magic is made."

"Do I get blood at this place?"

"You do." I picture how this will go down and grin. "You're gonna get more blood today than I've given you before."

"And sex too, huh?"

"Oh, yes. There will be lots of that as well. It's going to be a pile of sweaty, bloody bodies, Kael. All fucking, and sucking, and getting off. Me, and you, and him." I jut my chin at the waiting Joshua. "Plus many others."

"Any women involved in this?"

"If you want one, sure. There are plenty of women."

He nods a little, probably picturing all this in his head. "All right. So what's the catch?"

Kael is smart. There's always a catch. But he's nearly twenty in scion years if I recall correctly, so he understands how I work. I do not lie. I always tell him what's going to happen. So he knows there's a tradeoff coming.

"We're going to use you, Kael. Your blood. I need to make some magic. So we're going to feed and fuck and then I'm going to take your blood and your seed and mix it up with all of ours to make this magic. Does that sound acceptable?"

He stares at me for a few moments, eyes narrowing. "That's it? Feed and fuck and make some magic?"

"That's literally it."

"And Ryet has never been here? Or done anything like this?"

This is Kael's fatal flaw. Jealousy. He hates Ryet. He's always hated Ryet. He wants to be my blood lover. My one and only. Not because he loves me—Kael here is a psychopath, he's not capable of love. He wants to be my one and only because he has grand dreams of usurping me.

Which is ludicrous. I have more Darkness in a single strand of hair than he does in his whole body. But you don't know what you don't know, so I can't fault him for dreaming big. And anyway, these big dreams of his are the whole reason he's going to say yes to this offer.

"Is this guy a vampire?" Kael nods to Joshua.

"No. He's a witch."

Kael snorts. "A witch, huh? Aren't witches women?"

"They can be. But mine are men. They're more… agreeable when it comes to the blood loving. Easier to convince, if you will. More inclined towards the debauchery that comes with it."

He huffs. "Debauchery. What a word."

I smile patiently. "So. Are you in?"

He side-eyes me. "Fuck yeah, I'm in."

I pan a hand at him and grin. "See? So easy to convince."

We follow Joshua out of White River and turn onto a little gravel road that leads up the mountain. Everything is wet and muddy with snowmelt, so it takes a while to weave our way through the forest, but eventually we arrive at the top where there is a collection of charming A-frame houses and buildings reminiscent of Old Europe and all made of wood hewn from this very forest, as if Zecharyet Wagner handcrafted this village himself.

I love it mostly for this reason. It reminds me of Ryet.

Of course, he's never been up here. He will never come up here. Even if my plans had worked out and he and Syrsee had stayed in White River for their transformation, he would never have seen this place.

Because he was meant to die in a grand scheme of world domination and not some simplistic sex ritual to make a potion or a pudding. And that's the only reason a scion of mine would ever come up here.

To die.

There are lots of people around when we get out of the truck. All the women and girls are wearing long, linen dresses with a traditional feel to them. Mostly light blue—they love that color for some reason—but there are several dozen wearing undyed off-white or mustard-yellow dresses as well. A small handful of them are wearing peach, which only started showing up a few years ago when Emily took over, so it must be a special dye she cooked up.

All the men are wearing brown trousers and blue or undyed work shirts with suspenders and boots.

Only Joshua, and Kael, and myself are wearing outsider clothes. All of us in jeans, boots, and flannel shirts.

It's very charming, but it has to be, doesn't it? I mean, this is a place of dark death and I want my scions to feel comfortable when I kill them to cook up the kitchen magic.

Kael comes around the truck to stand next to me. When I give him a sideways glance, I find him leering at the women. "You like them?" I ask.

"What?" He's not even paying attention to me.

"The women? You'd prefer one of them?"

He looks at me now, suspicion on his face. "What's that supposed to mean?"

"I'm asking you a question about your preferences, Kael. Clearly, you like women."

"Of course. But if you're asking if I want to trade one of those stupid whores for your blood, the answer is no."

That wasn't what I was asking, obviously. But I don't bother explaining. Kael here might be cunning, but he's also very primitive and I'm kind of in a hurry, so not in the mood to humor him. "Take your pick," is what I say as a reply. "Which one do you like?" I point to a young woman who was much younger the last time I was here. Rachel, I think her name is. "I've had my eye on that one there for years now. How about her?"

Kael looks at the woman with a critical eye. She's in her early twenties and wearing one of the peach dresses and it's got a yellow apron, so she's festive. Her face is round and welcoming once she realizes we're looking at her. She's got dark hair, so she comes from the oldest line of breeding, but while she's nice to look at, she's not much of a cook. Which is fine. Emily's our chef so this one's only job, literally, is to tantalize. And she does it well, cocking a hip and her head as she lifts her chin up, daring someone to approach.

All of this is directed at Kael, not me. And Kael responds. "All right," he says, a little bit breathless. Like the few moments he took to study the woman were spent in fantasy. "Yeah, she'll do." Then he turns to me. "And you. You're not gettin' out of this, Paul. I want the blood."

I place a hand on his cheek, much like the one I placed on Joshua's, but without the care or concern. "It's yours, blood lover." I point to Rachel. "Would you like to join us?"

She smiles, knowingly, then does a little curtsey and bows her head. "Of course, my lord."

When she meets my gaze again, I point to Kael. "Make him happy for me."

She curtsies again and then comes over and hooks her arm into his. Kael smiles, despite his misgivings. He knows something's going on here, but the promise of blood and sex with me and a pretty woman seems to have alleviated his initial suspicions.

"Let's go." Then I nod my head in the direction of a large A-frame building that is used as a gathering house.

This building is where all the rituals are done. Inside it's dark because there are no windows, but it's not inhospitable. In fact, it's quite the opposite of inhospitable. It's inviting.

On the far end is where all the business is done. There is a depression in the center of this space with four stone steps leading down to the grand altar made of Nero Marquina marble quarried in Spain that has been so meticulously polished, it gleams like obsidian.

The altar is on the same spatial plane as the floor so as to offer up the perfect view of what takes place on top of it for those watching from a distance, and at seven feet long and three feet wide, it's impressive.

On either side of the altar are dozens of candelabras. Three women are lighting them now, but there are so many candles, it will probably take another ten minutes before they're all ablaze.

Behind the altar—where one might find a crucifix if this were *that* kind of holy place—there is a font of the baptismal variety. Though it's genuine, it's not used for baptism. Which makes it more of a crucible, I suppose.

On this end, where Kael and I are standing, is the wall of cutlery where every kind of knife you can dream up has been arranged on the wall for easy access so anyone who wants to can use the altar for an impromptu ritual or whatever. Though they don't carve up scions, obviously. Mostly likely rabbits or... I dunno, perhaps a goat?

The middle of the room is where all the fun happens. A

massive patchwork of feather beds covers the floor from edge to edge. The duvets are light blue, or off-white, or mustard yellow, or peach linen, just like the dresses of the women outside. The pillows that line the edges of the feather beds are the same color, and this whole scene gives off a vibe of whimsy.

It's lovely. Absolutely lovely. Much, *much* nicer than the clearing in the woods where we used to do these ceremonies in the early days.

Kael is studying the beds as I watch him. Then he turns to me with eyebrows raised. "How many people are you expecting?"

As if on cue, the double doors behind us open and every grown man under the age of thirty enters, already unbuttoning shirts or loosening trousers. They don't say anything as we watch them undress.

Once they are naked, they go to the center of the room and start touching each other. Caressing each other. Kissing. And there's a little bit of grinding as they work themselves up.

This time when Kael looks at me, he's grinning. "You're sick."

I shrug. "It's why you like me, Kael. It's why you agreed to be my blood bitch in the first place."

He actually laughs. "Let's go then." He turns to the woman, eyes narrowed, giving her the first glimpse of his deranged madness. "Undress me, whore. And lick me while you do it."

This woman, she's gonna get a big reward from me later. Because she doesn't even blink. Just curtseys, like he's her lord now, and eases his jacket off his shoulders, then pulls his shirt up over his head. She pauses for a moment, maybe admiring the lust in his eyes, then drops to her knees as her fingers begin unbuttoning his jeans. She looks up at him as she wriggles them down his hips and dutifully licks his stomach while staring him in the eyes.

I let out a breath, very, *very* satisfied with what I have built up here with the coven and the kitchen witches who populate it. This is gonna be fun. And I have to be honest, it's been all work and no play for months now and I'm looking forward to the respite.

But in Kael, I find myself slightly disappointed. Not about bringing him here, he is the perfect choice for what comes next. But about his reaction.

Usually, when I bring a scion up to meet the coven and take them inside this building they begin to panic. Not a lot, not usually. But they at least glance questioningly at the cutlery displayed artfully on the wall behind us, and they often pay more attention to the altar than Kael has. They notice things about it. Like how it's just big enough to spread out a man. They notice the leather straps in the perfect position to tie down said man. And they notice how there are little grooves along the edges of the polished, black marble to catch his blood.

Situational awareness. Kael has none of it. And I'm disappointed. I feel like maybe, somewhere along the way, I failed him. So I let out a sigh.

"What's wrong with you?" Kael snaps. He's fisting the woman's hair now, grinding his cock into her mouth.

I simply smile in response. But it's kind of a sad smile. Then I notice that Emily has entered the building. I watch as Joshua greets her, leaning in to her ear to whisper something, spurring a chuckle out of his wife. Her eyes dart over to me and she nods, letting me know she's ready.

In that same moment Joshua turns in my direction and starts walking towards me, pulling off his shirt as he closes the space between us. I keep my eyes on him and only him because in him, and all these people who live in the White River coven, I got it right.

I love them. And while I say I love them all, I don't. Not like this. Ryet is the only one I ever put before these witches. The only one I ever put before myself. But the most remarkable thing about the people of White River is that they love me back. *Truly* love me in a way no one else ever has, and since this is my moment of illumination in regards to my buried emotional attachments, this is also the moment when I realize that this little village is… my *home*.

The Montana lodge is lovely and I like it, but mostly because Ryet built it for me. When I'm at the lodge everything around me is a memory of him and, as my first true offspring, it's natural to be irrationally drawn to him because of what he means to me and my future.

But Ryet doesn't love me back. Not really. He needs me, he likes me—*maybe*. I grew on him, I suppose. Became a fixture in his life. Something that was always there so he cannot imagine existing without me.

So it's different.

I had intended to have my fun with Kael today. He's attractive and he likes to do lots of nasty things with me that Ryet never would. But when Joshua reaches me, it's him I want to spend this day with. It's him I want to hold on to in my memories, not something disposable like Kael. So that, in a thousand years, when I think back on this day and how it all started, it will be Joshua I see. It will be Emily, and Rachel, and all the other lovely little snakes in my den of vipers.

Joshua stands before me, unafraid to meet my gaze. And why should he be afraid of me? I've never been anything but good to him. Yes, we sacrifice scions here to make Black magic, but he knows, with one hundred percent certainty, that he is not, and never will be, something I sacrifice.

So I place my hands on his cheeks, lean in, and kiss his mouth. I watch as his eyes close and his body gives in to me. Then I start walking backwards, still kissing him, until we're next to the other men in the village who are already lying down, jerking on each other's cocks.

The kiss ends and Joshua opens his eyes. They are a little glassy, like he might want to cry. "Don't," I tell him. "Don't be sad."

His smile is immediate. "Oh, I'm not sad, my lord. I'm full of happiness. So full, I'm overflowing. This is all I ever wanted. To be *yours*." And then he gazes up at me with complete adoration as he drops to his knees and pops the button on my jeans.

The true ritual begins the moment Joshua's lips wrap around my cock and I rip off my shirt. My pants come off next in a hurried rush, as do Joshua's. And then that's all there is. Twenty or thirty men in the middle of a large room, teasing the seed of Darkness out each other in every erotic way possible.

It's beautiful, and intoxicating, and, obviously, magical.

Until *Kael* interrupts the moment. "Where the fuck is the blood, vampire? Give me the blood!"

He's taking Rachel doggie-style a few feet away from me, his hips slapping against her ass with each hard thrust.

I smile. Not the same smile I gave Joshua just a few minutes ago, but a deliciously wicked smile. Because while I don't normally relish killing my potential offspring for the greater good, I'm going to get a lot of pleasure out of Kael when he meets his true maker.

But first, my Joshua.

I'm lying back on the floor now, the feather bed underneath me hugging my body in soft comfort. "Lie down, Joshua." He does this, placing his long, lean, naked body next to mine. I turn my head as he turns his and we smile at each other. He knows what's coming. And while witches don't crave the blood the way scions do, he likes it.

It will be Joshua that I feed first. And even though this isn't how we normally do it, I want him on my neck. So I reach up and slash my jugular open with a clawed fingernail and blood begins to flow in great pulsating bursts.

A moment later, Kael is nearly on top of me, trying to get his drink. But I simply fling him off, sending him careening across the room and slamming into the wall, my gaze still locked with Joshua's. "Climb on," I tell him.

Joshua straddles my body without hesitation, his blue eyes bright with excitement, his large hands splayed out and pressing into the featherbed on either side of my shoulders, his cock hard against my stomach as his hips grind against mine. Then I turn my neck, baring myself to him, and a moment later, he's feeding on me.

Automatically, my eyes close. It doesn't feel the same as when Ryet, or Josep, or Syrsee feed—it's *better*.

Kael must be passed out and concussed, because he doesn't interrupt us again. Joshua drinks, and drinks, and drinks until he literally passes out and falls off of me.

Then Emily is there, milking her husband as his cock spits out magic. When he's depleted, she and the rest of the women pull Joshua away from me, and, already understanding my plan, start directing the other men to climb on and have their drink too. The closest one does, grinding against me to get himself off.

He is milked for magic as well. And then the next man

climbs on. I slash my own throat dozens of times as each of the men takes their drink and spills their seed into a chalice that Emily holds. She chants things as she collects. It's Latin, and though I am fluent, of course, I don't pay attention to what she's saying because I don't have to.

When all the men are spent and satisfied, I get up, covered in my own blood in various stages of coagulation, and walk over to Kael's body, still slumped against the wall.

I actually chuckle as I look down at him. He didn't even finish his fuck.

Which doesn't matter. We'll make sure he's satisfied before we kill him. That's the whole reason he's here. I look at Emily as I nod at Kael. "Let's get him on the altar and tie him down before he wakes up."

Immediately, every woman in the room is grabbing at his body, lifting it up and carrying it to the other end of the room. They place it on the altar and tie him down.

They are just buckling the last restraint into place when Kael begins to moan, his head jerking back and forth as his hips rise up from the marble slab in protest. It takes a few more minutes before he is capable of opening his eyes. He must've hit his head hard when I threw him aside, but it's not concerning.

"Kael," I say as I lean down into his face. "Can you hear me?"

He groans and spits out croaky words. "What the fuck?"

My smile is genuine and big. "You tried to cut in line, little friend. Which is against the rules. You are not in charge and you've always had a problem with that."

"What the fuck is going on?" He's mostly back now, his voice stronger, his struggle more forceful. "*Where's my blood!*"

"It's *my* blood, Kael. Not yours. But don't worry. I need you euphoric when we take your seed, so even though you don't deserve it, you'll get the blood." I look at Emily. "Are we ready?"

She's holding the four vials we brought with us from the apothecary and she lifts them up. "Let's use them all."

"You're the boss." Then I take a step back and the women come forward and start caressing the loud and objectionable Kael. He lifts his head up, looking down the length of his body at all the women. He's breathing heavy with fear, but it immediately turns to lust.

God, he's so predictable.

They are touching him. Dozens of hands caressing his body. They slide up his legs and down his arms. They pump his cock and play with his hair. One fingers his mouth and he begins to suck. This finger is laced with the first potion. And I watch as this woman teases his mouth with her finger and he comes for the first time. There is a chalice waiting to catch what he spills. And then it repeats. Fingers in his mouth, fists on his cock, tits in his face, and Kael sucks down all the potions and becomes more pliable and happier.

So happy, he stops struggling and just lies there as the women take his seed over and over again. His eyes have been closed for several minutes now, but they lazily open, trying to focus on me. "Blood," he whispers.

I nod my head and smile. "It's time, blood lover. It's time." Then I slash open my wrist with a claw and let the blood flow into his mouth. There's no way this animal will feed on my neck the way my witches did. He doesn't deserve it. He is nothing but a little factory to me.

As soon as the blood hits his mouth, his soft cock becomes erect again.

This is the seed we need. What we already took was just the milking. The emptying of the tainted, worthless semen.

This now? This is where the magic lives.

The women pump him one final time and when he spills again, his seed is purple.

In that same moment, Emily's scalpel slices him open from throat to groin. His blood spills out, drips down his body, and flows into the channels cut into the marble, forming a river that empties into the baptismal font that has been moved into position.

Kael is so happy, and satiated, and, let's face it, drugged, he doesn't even flinch when she begins to remove his organs.

I take Joshua's hand and lead him back over to the bloody featherbed to join the rest of the men, who are now waking up from their drink, and we insert ourselves into the pile of sweaty bodies and begin touching each other for pleasure this time. We writhe together in lust and sin, until, hours later, the magic has been made.

Then I get up, shower with Emily and Joshua, let the women dress me in clean clothes, and leave the White River coven with the magic I need to change the course of everything.

My name is King.

"Never."

That's the word I whisper into her ear as Little Baby and I lie on the floor of my cave, having finally found reality. Because never is the number of times I've felt connected to anything outside of myself.

None.

That's how many people have loved me in my lifetime. Because none is the number of loves I thought I deserved.

And now… one.

Which is perfect and whole, in and of itself. Which is all I ever wanted. Which is what I have now with my sweet lollipop, Little Baby. Someone to accompany me into the dark infinity of the eternal nowhere. Someone to be nothing with me.

The blood has dried and caked all over us, leaving my skin feeling deliciously itchy. It's a feeling I haven't had in a long time, but I've missed it and it's good. Because when I'm covered in blood like this—all crusty and flaky—it's a sign that there is someone next to me.

Someone not just being fed on, but feeding back.

Little Baby is sleeping now, satiated with blood in her stomach and my seed in her womb. Her head is on my chest, one leg thrown over me in a gesture of possession, her soft breath both satisfying and comforting. Because she is alive and because she is mine.

I hold her tighter as these thoughts weave their way around

in my head the way the roots weave through the dirt. Winding, but purposeful.

If Paul can turn Syrsee into a blood mother, why couldn't I do the same with Little Baby? I am, after all, the Darkness itself. It is me who controls the magic of the unliving. The possibilities are endless now. I can populate the whole Earth with vampires if I so choose.

I have the power. I have always had all the power and it's a simple thing, really, to make new monsters. I think these words in my head like they are nothing, but they are not nothing. They are very much a something.

Because I've been hunting for power for so long. And now I feel a bit silly. Because it was mine for the taking from the very beginning. There's a part of me that wants to rage at the Darkness for not telling me sooner. But that's stupid.

I *am* the Darkness.

It was only me deceiving myself.

How ironic.

Carefully, so as not to wake her, I ease out from underneath Little Baby. Then I kneel at her side, watching as her breasts rise and fall with each of her soft breaths.

She's truly here.

She's truly mine.

I take a moment to really internalize what I have accomplished. And the most ironic thing is, I didn't even do it on purpose.

When this thought manifests, I'm looking at my Little Baby's body, and in this same moment it illuminates. Soft purple lights flows out of the once hidden, but now visible, markings that I used to make an offering to the Darkness back when she was my sacrifice, when a family and home of my own was just a dream. Something I felt was unattainable.

Little by little, each of the symbols that I carved on her begin to glow brighter until I can see them all. My name, Paul's name, and the little pictures I drew of the family I thought I wanted. Me, and Paul, and Syrsee, and Ryet. We were all there inside the crude depiction of a house.

I wave my hand over her body and all those markings disappear.

Then I smile and start carving out a brand-new future.

I take my time because Little Baby doesn't care. Wherever her mind is right now, it's happy and content. She can't feel the pain of my claw. She is living the dream.

I should probably wake her up and get her opinion on things.

But do I *really* care about what she wants?

Yes, in a sense. But only as it pertains to me. That's all that matters. And there's no way she can't want me. There's no possible way for her to deny me. Because she *is* me. Just like I am the Darkness. She is me.

We are two sides to the same coin. Yin and yang. Fire and water. Order and chaos.

I want a new little baby. A real baby. *Offspring.* And if I want it, then I shall have it.

I am, after all, the king.

I chuckle when that thought manifests inside my head. The king! This was always Paul's goal. A vampire's offspring is his kingdom and Paul has always fancied himself a king.

An offspring gives meaning to the blood lust. It forces it to make sense. For if you have a woman who needs this blood, and if you can put a seed inside her the way a human might, then it's… natural. Good, and wholesome, and organic.

This baby is not a blood baby like Ryet.

It's a seed baby like… well, like Little Baby herself. Was she not human once? She was. And now, with her help, I will have a true, and good, and wholesome, and organic lineage of my own.

Forget about being king, I will become *God*.

And once that happens, I won't *need* Paul.

This makes me laugh. Not that I won't need Paul, but that I ever thought I did. Because I'm inside Paul. I'm all over him. I'm inside Ryet, too, though to a much lesser extent.

If I wanted to *be* them, I could be them. I could open my eyes and see through their eyes the same way I saw through the eyes of Darkness.

But I don't have time for that. I'm sure it's a process. Equally as sure that there'd be a fight—especially from Paul. And I don't want to tip the balance of things right now.

It's all going too well.

It's all going my way.

I lie down next to Little Baby, propping myself up on my elbow so I can look at all the new markings I just made on her body. Right in the middle of her stomach is a big circle and inside the circle is what will keep us together forever.

I name him Dark Baby after the both of us.

And then I smile, and lie back, and slip my arm underneath Little Baby so I can pull her close to me. When the figurative and literal long-held breath comes out of me, it brings a sense of wellbeing and peace. It brings relief.

Because finally, I know why I'm still here.

Not only that—I'm smiling wide as I gaze up at the dancing glow of purple light that flickers along the roots in the cave ceiling—I know where I'm going, and I know how to get there, as well as what will be waiting for me.

A family and place of my own.

✳ ✳ ✳

Little Baby stirs underneath me, wriggling, like she wants to get free from the tight embrace I have her in. Reluctantly, I loosen my arms and lift my chest off her back so she can reposition.

She tries to get up, but I pull her back down, my words coming out in a low and soothing tone. "We're not in a hurry, Little Baby. We have all the time in the world."

She lets out a breath, only to quickly take in another one and hold it. She's confused, and she has a right to be. Who knows what she remembers?

"Where am I?"

Oh, just the sound and timbre of her voice is enough to fill me with happiness. "You're in love, Little Baby."

It's me who's in love, so I'm projecting, but I'm the king of kings and master of everything. I am God, and so what I feel is what everyone feels. Her love for me is absolute. There is no other way for her to exist.

She holds her breath again. I can tell because when it comes out, it's a puff on my arm, which delights me—to have someone I love so close I can feel the life inside them when it comes out.

"I mean," Little Baby attempts to clarify, "where, in... location, am I?"

"Oh!" I chuckle. While I was daydreaming, I seem to have moved us out of the cave and into a hotel room. "We're in a bed, Little Baby."

This time her breath is quick and rushed, but I still like the feeling. "I can see that we're in a bed, but where in the world is this bed located?" All these words come out through gritted teeth, which delights me.

"You're feeling better, I take it? Since you're being rude?"

"What?"

"I'll let you be rude to me. It's fine because it's a sign that you're… your own person. And that's very important to me."

She struggles out of my grip and even though I don't want to release her, I do. Because she's confused and needs more blood and sex.

Besides, she's naked and as she slips out of bed, I take a good long look at her full breasts, and round ass, and pussy covered in fuzz so blonde, it's nearly white.

"You're perfect," I tell her. "I made you so perfect."

She walks over to the window and pulls the sheer curtain aside, ignoring my words. Then she scans the city, shaking her head. "This… this isn't real." She turns to face me, making those glorious tits jiggle. "This isn't a real place! There are…" She pulls the curtain aside again and takes a second look. "There are horses and buggies down there. People all dressed up like… God-lovers, or something."

I actually laugh. "God-lovers. That's so adorable. You, Little Baby, are *so* adorable."

"That doesn't explain this fucking city!" She points to the window. "*Where is this?*"

"*When*, my dear. *When* is this. And it's…" I shrug up a shoulder. "I dunno. 1900 maybe? It's not historically accurate because I was underground at that time. But who cares, right? I like the sound of horses. I like all the clothes people wore at this time. All those undergarments to get through before you can fuck your women. I mean, you can always just bend them over and hike the skirts up, taking them from behind. But that's just cheating in my book. I like a naked woman."

Then I leer at her. Good and long too. I open my mouth, bare my fangs, and lick one with my tongue. "Come here." I pat the bed beside me. "Come, Little Baby. You're irritable because you need blood and sex."

She looks at the bed, then looks at me, baring her own fangs, hissing like a feral cat.

Oh, I like that. I like that very much. But she's getting precariously close to crossing a line with me and I feel it is my duty, since she is newborn, to give her fair warning.

Instantly, I'm across the room and I've got my hand around her throat. Equally as quick, I push her into a wall, pinning her against it.

Then I open my mouth, bare my fangs, and growl back. "Because you are my first, and confused, and deserving of respect in your own right since you are mine... I will let you be a brat for today and today only, Little Baby."

Her eyes are wide with fear and she's gasping for breath under my tight grip on her throat. Her hands clamp over mine, her fingertips trying to pry it off.

It's of no use. I am the Darkness, after all. And she is just my Little Baby.

I wait until her face turns bright red, and her eyes start to flutter, and her muscles go limp before I ease up and let her breathe again. She slides down the wall like a rag doll, her legs all spread open in front of her as she sucks up air. I wait, motionless, until she regains herself.

And this patience of mine pays off when she looks up at me.

She's so helpless. So weak. So... *fragile*. It turns me on.

Naturally, my cock begins to grow. And since it's not very far from her face, she notices this. Is drawn to it, actually.

She licks her lips.

I bend down, open my legs as well, and then I take her face in my hands. "You need blood and sex, Little Baby. And you'll feel all better."

There are tears streaming down her cheeks and she doesn't answer me.

I'm just about to become annoyed with her reaction when I remember that I have forgotten to tell her the good news. No wonder she's crying. She doesn't realize who and what she is yet.

I stand back up and offer her my hand, then bow my head in shame. "Forgive me, Little Baby. I'm very sorry. I haven't given you the good news yet." I look at her now, with downcast chin and upcast eyes.

After some hesitation, she places her hand in mine and allows me to pull her up off the floor.

Then I look her straight on and smile. "I forgot to tell you." I slide behind her, my hands slipping over her hips to caress her stomach, her heavy, round breasts resting on my arms. "We're expecting."

There is a pause here, and I allow it. I want her to work through it on her own time. And she's smart, so it's only a few seconds. "Expecting… what?"

I caress her stomach as I lean down and place my mouth right up to her ear. "We're expecting a Dark Baby, Little Baby. One made of you and me. It's a boy, of course. You are his seed mother and I'm his seed father, and together we will raise him and we will be a family."

Little Baby sucks in a great breath and when it comes back out, it is a *scream*.

* * *

How much time passes before my Little Baby wakes again? I don't care about time, so I don't know. And anyway, I was busy. While she was tripping through eternal Darkness and endless Eternity, I was planning my next move. Which means it's perfect this time.

I made a mistake. I realize this now. She was not properly prepared.

Of course, I'm new at this so I don't beat myself up over it. I just course-correct.

Her screams followed her into the abyss I sent her to, but lucky me, I have a mute button, so I wasn't bothered by it.

But I want to hear everything as she comes out of the untold infinity because it's exciting. It's life. Her fear and anguish are proof that she's real and not just a sliver of myself.

So I enjoy it. I relish the idea that she is wailing and screaming with insanity.

But mistakes need to be corrected with haste or the results thereof will linger. And while I would still love my Little Baby if she spent all of eternity with me being belligerent and insane, that is not the happily ever after I'm envisioning.

It might, this attitude of hers, rub off on Dark Baby. And that I cannot tolerate.

So when Little Baby next wakes we're not in some default hotel room bed, we're in the earth. Which doesn't seem like much at face value because we've been in the earth in my cave this whole time. But we're not in that kind of earth. We're in the Dark Earth.

The glowing root system. The magic.

I'm going to teach her how to travel.

She already knows about the blood and how good it is, but that's not even the best part about being part of the Darkness. There are so many perks that come with being my seed vessel and traveling through the earth is but one of them.

But this gift of travel is one of the best.

You can be anywhere in an instant.

Anywhere.

And I am going to show her everything.

And then she will not only love me, she will fall in love with my dream.

One Dark Baby is but the beginning of what I have planned.

Soon the whole of humanity will know my name.

Which is King.

I am the king of kings.

If this is as good as it gets, I'll take it.

When I open my eyes all I see is purple. All around me is nothing but purple. It's blurry, and misty, and magical. But as the seconds tick off, my eyes begin to focus and the fuzzy haze condenses into something recognizable.

Lines. Squiggly lines of *glowing* purple. Like a neon sign might glow.

"They're roots, Little Baby." Josep speaks these words directly into my ear. "The Tree of Life." He laughs softly and this laugh sends a chill through my body that makes the little hairs on the back of my neck stand straight up.

Not in a bad way, either. It's… a shiver. But the good kind.

This realization almost sends me into a panic because—

"Little Baby?" He interrupts my thoughts.

"What?"

"Don't overthink it. Just… enjoy. Enjoy everything. I'm sorry for waking you up earlier without the proper preparations. I made a mistake. But I've since course-corrected. Forget about everything that came before this moment right now because none of that matters."

I can't say I agree with him. I can't say I disagree with him either, of course, because he's…

"Insane?"

He knows what I'm thinking? He can read my mind? This is like the abusive relationship from hell.

Josep chuckles. "I'm not reading your thoughts, Little Baby. I'm part of them. I'm part of you. I'm inside you. Both as the

Darkness and as the Seed." His hand, I realize, is caressing my stomach.

This is when I remember what happened earlier and what he said. *We're expecting a Dark Baby, Little Baby.*

Immediately, my heart begins to thump inside my chest and I start sucking in air in short frenzied gasps.

"Shhhh," he says, petting my head as he continues to caress my stomach. "Don't panic. I'm going to show you what this all means and how beautiful it is. And then we're going to drink, and fuck, and sleep, and grow old together." He laughs again. "Well, we won't grow old. Ever. We will be the same pretty demons we are right now in a thousand years. Because you are the Dark Mother, Echo."

When he says my real name, something inside me changes. Some little part of me—the part that was dying—starts to come alive again.

"*Echo.*" He repeats my name right into my ear, causing another inexplicable shiver of delight. "You're my Dark Queen, Echo. You're my Dark Mother. But first and foremost, you're my Little Baby. My one and only. Forever and ever. For all infinite eternity."

Despite the fact that I know better—that I understand what this thing is and what it has done to me—I relax and begin to feel… safe. I guess.

I must be drugged. Because the one thing I am not is safe. Not with him.

"I understand your misgivings, Little Baby. I am quite a spectacular creature, after all. But look around. Look at what we're a part of."

I let out a sigh and refocus on the roots all around me as they glow the gentlest of purples.

"Are you looking?"

"Yes."

"And what do you think?"

"It's… pretty?"

"It is. I really like being in the earth. It's so soothing, isn't it?"

I want to deny this, but I can't. He's right. The glowing roots *are* soothing. It's something out of a fantasy. Like a fairy realm in a movie.

"Do you know what they do?"

"The roots?" I ask.

"Yes. The roots."

"Well… they… feed the tree? I'm really not a science geek, OK? I dropped out in eleventh grade. I failed biology, so—"

Josep's laugh is loud and it startles me into silence. "No. Forget about the trees. These roots aren't part of the trees. Well, they are, in a sense. But these are the roots of time, Little Baby. And for us, they are a highway to go places."

"What? What are you talking about?" I'm so confused.

"The Tree of Life, Little Baby, isn't a tree. It's a timeline. We can use the roots to go anywhere we want. Just like we use the purple to conjure up new realities."

"Purple?" What he just said did not enlighten me in any way. "I have no idea what you're talking about."

"Of course not. You were born a human. This is what I'm trying to explain. Humans are… boring, and powerless, and limited. You can't see the purple mist that surrounds your pathetic and contained reality, so you can't use it to conjure up a new one. But you, my dear Dark Mother, are no longer human. When you took my blood, you took my magic. And this is what you're looking at. The magic is purple and showing you how to use it properly is my birthday gift to you. Come."

The moment he says 'come', we're somewhere else. A dark and empty place with no light at all. No roots, no earth, no purple. It's—awful and even though I can't sense any movement at all, I feel this dark emptiness pushing in on me. Encroaching. And then suddenly, I remember that I was in a place like this before I woke up.

"Yes," Josep says. "I put you in the Dark Place so you could understand. We are part of that Darkness, Little Baby. It is us and we are it. And in this Dark Place there is no time. And if there is no time, there is nothing but…" I wave my hand at the emptiness all around us, but of course she can't see this because we are the Darkness now. "There is nothing. It is insanity for a sentient being. Which we are, obviously. Because we are still communicating.

"In order to bring sanity back, and with it a clarity of vision," Josep continues, "we must have time. Because the Darkness is the eternal infinity. Or infinite eternal, if you prefer. Darkness, Little Baby, is… well, nothingness. And it's quite boring. In fact, if we stay here too long we'll get lost in the insanity. Because if there is no time in the eternal infinity, then there is no existence. Do you see?"

I'm shaking my head through all of that. "No. I can't see shit."

He laughs. And to my surprise, so do I. "Of course not. I didn't mean literally. Do you understand that if there is no time there is no… *living?* There are no experiences here, Little Baby. You are nothing but a bit of purple mist. Reach down and touch yourself."

"What?"

"Anywhere. Your arm, your stomach where my Dark Baby lives. Anywhere."

"This is a real thing? You want me to touch myself."

"I do."

I let out a breath and reach down to my stomach. I don't want to because the thought of that baby being inside me is…

There's nothing there. There's just air. I wave my hand in the air, trying to find myself, but I am not here! "What the hell is going on? I'm invisible!"

"No," Josep says, in that calm, deep voice of his. "You're not invisible, you simply don't exist."

"But that's impossible! I'm thinking thoughts, so obviously I have a brain!"

"Not a brain, Little Baby. A consciousness. Weren't you listening? You are nothing but a consciousness. That's what it means to live in the Darkness. You are nothing but ideas. And while it can be fun for a short period of time, it will drive you insane. You see, when we are nothing but Darkness, we don't exist. We can't feel anything. We can't express ourselves. And we certainly can't drink blood and fuck, which… I mean, that's pretty much the best part of having a body, don't you agree?"

"Well… I guess."

"You guess?"

"Sure." I sigh. "Yeah. Blood-drinking is pretty fun. And so is fucking. So. All right. I'll give you this point."

"We don't want to live here in the Darkness, do we?"

"*No.* I completely agree. I do not want to stay here one moment longer than I have to. In fact, I want to leave right now."

"Of course you do. We crave existence. Everything does, really."

"So how do I get out?"

"In the beginning, before I thought it through, I was planning on leaving you here. Forcing you to find your power and all that growth bullshit humans like to brag about. But that's not a gift. That would be making you work for it and a gift is something you give freely. So I'm going to teach you, Little Baby. And I want you to know that I have never told a single other soul how to do these things."

"Not even Paul?"

He laughs. "Paul doesn't wait for explanations. Paul is a force. He plows forward like a bull, crashing his horns into anything and everything that gets in his way. He never needed my help. But no, even if he did, I wouldn't have obliged. Power isn't something you teach, it's something you learn."

"Well, you just said you're going to teach me, so…"

"I'm going to teach you the 'what,' not the 'how.' But you don't need the 'how' because you're with me. I'm your 'how,' Little Baby."

I blow out a breath that only happens in my mind. But I understand what he's not saying just as well as I do what he is. He wants me to know him through his power. This is a very typical thing in a controlling relationship. And I've been in quite a few of those, so I'm on guard here. He wants me to need him. So no, he's not going to teach me how to get out of the Darkness. He's going to *take me*. So I am in debt to him.

But, of course, I don't say any of that out loud. He can read my thoughts, anyway. "So… are you trying to tell me that I'm special?"

"Yes." And even though he hasn't got a face and I don't have to see it, I hear him smiling. "I understand—at least, I'm trying to understand—that what happened to you… what I did to you… it was…"

"Unconscionable? Abusive? *Evil?*"

"No. It was careless. And I care for you, Little Baby. So I'm going to make up for my misguided actions when you took my Darkness into yourself."

If I had eyebrows, they'd be hiked up on my forehead right now. "Misguided actions? And did you just blame me for what you did?"

"Did I?"

"*Yes*! That was a rhetorical question. Look." I sigh. "I get it. You're in control. You're the big, powerful Darkness. You're the insane vampire. And I'm a high school dropout with pink hair who gave up my eternal soul because Lucia wanted to fuck my boyfriend and make him drink her and I was so insecure, and my self-image so damaged, that I would rather get in on that and follow him to a vampire's lair into the pit of Hell, Montana, and become a halfbreed than be *alone*. But I"—I point to myself. Well, I would, if I had hands and a body—"I am not responsible for what you put me through. And if you think I don't remember? And I'll just forgive and forget because I'm carrying your stupid Dark Baby? Well." I huff out some air. "You're mistaken, mister. I might be a coward, and a dropout, and a pathetic example of an empowered woman—but you know what else I *am*? A grudge holder. And you're not getting out of this that easy. I'm damaged! *Damaged*! And I... hate you."

There. I said it.

What he does with this outburst is his business. He might torture me. Or leave me here. Or... something worse. Because it can always get worse. But I don't care. I said what I said and I mean it.

So I say it again. "I hate you." And then I just let it all spill out. "I will never love you. I will never love this baby. I'm going to trick you into... I dunno. I'm gonna kill you, I think. And this baby. And then myself. Because... you're... you're... *inhuman*!

And I'm going to blame you for everything that has ever gone wrong in my life and I'm gonna feel pretty fucking good about that. I'm gonna absolve myself of all responsibility and—"

He's laughing.

And I'm fuming. "What's so fuckin' funny? There's nothing funny happening here! I am literally pregnant with a demon's offspring, I live on blood and sex, and I'm standing in the dark pit of Hell itself. *There is nothing funny happening here!*"

But instead of answering me, he hugs me. His arms wrap around me, and he pulls me close, and I can feel him, so we're real now. I can feel his body against mine and it's… nice.

It's really nice. This hug, it's a genius move on his part. Like 5D chess move, or whatever. Because it works. I like it. And I never want him to let me go. Because no one has ever loved me. Ever. And even though he's a demon, and he's evil, and he's not even human, even though he's given me demon blood and put a demon baby inside me… I don't care right now.

I *want* this hug. I need this hug. And if I could make it last forever, I would.

"Open your eyes, Little Baby."

"Why? There's nothing to see but Darkness."

"Open them."

So I do. And I'm wrong, of course. Because I'm never right about anything. We're still in the Darkness, but there's a purple mist now. Not a thick one, but it's enough to give meaning to the endless eternal infinity of emptiness.

"Where would you like to go, Little Baby? On Earth, I mean."

"A real place?"

"A real place."

"Like… Machu Picchu?"

"Machu Picchu?" He chuckles and this makes his chest vibrate.

And since he's hugging me, this vibration resonates. Like it actually enters me, and calms me, and so I sigh. "I've always wanted to go there and see those ruins. It's dumb, but you asked."

"Well, if that's where you want to go, let's go. Take me there. Let's explore it together."

"Take you there, how?"

"In the purple. The Tree of Time, remember? Imagine it, and then take a step forward. Keep hold of my hand and I'll come with you. Let go of it, and you'll leave me behind."

Is he giving me a choice? To bring him along or go alone? "Why bother leaving you behind? You'll just follow me."

"No. I won't. You have to come back to me. You need blood and sex, remember? So why should I chase you if you want to be alone? I'm not insecure. Do you want to see Machu Picchu alone?"

"Why would anyone go anywhere alone? It's only fun to do exciting things if you can share it with someone."

"And that's why I want to be with you. So we can share. Because I'm alone too, Echo."

Again, he uses my real name. And this is his way of letting me know that he sees me. I am his Little Baby, his pet. And he's serious about that. But he's not delusional. He *knows* I'm something else too.

"I do not have to force you to do anything. You will come to me whether you want to or not because you need blood and sex. But don't you want more than blood or sex? Because I do."

I close my eyes and let out a deep breath. Then I press my

face into his chest, listening to his heart beat. Which is stupid. Because we're not even here. We're not even real.

"It keeps time," Josep says. "That's how it works."

I look up at him now. At his beautiful face. "How what works?"

"Everything. The heart, it keeps time. And all you need to make a place real is time, Little Baby Echo. Something to tick it off. So listen to my heart and make something real. Let's go to Machu Picchu and look at all the ruins. Take me there."

But I don't want to go there. Not now. I'm too tired. I'm exhausted. And I'm… sad. I just want to go to bed. But I don't want to go to bed alone and I don't want to leave this hug, so instead of imaging the mountains of Peru, I picture a bedroom. Not the hotel room we were at, but something all brand new.

My own bedroom. A dream bedroom.

And the moment I think this, we're in a bed. And his arms are still around me, and he's kissing me, and holding me, and I realize he's a very good abusive partner because… I *like* this. And it's crazy. Because he took me to the pit of Hell, and carved up my body with his claws, and put evil symbols all over me, and then turned me with a long drink, and then used me to poison the halfbreeds.

They tore me to shreds. I remember it. I remember every moment of it.

And still, his attention is enough.

This little bit of kindness—which isn't kindness at all, I understand this—it's enough. I won't forget, but I will forgive.

Because I'm not about to give this up.

I will never love him, and I might throw up just thinking about what's growing inside me, but if he will hold me, and feed me, and fuck me like this? Whether his love is real or not, it's more than I ever had as a human.

It's more than I ever thought I deserved.

I roll over in the bed, looking straight into his purple eyes as I climb on top of him and straddle his hips. I place my hands flat on his chest and lower myself down until we're so close, we could kiss. Then I reach down, grab his hard cock, and gently slip it inside me as I lift my hips.

He almost closes his eyes, which I interpret as pleasure. And then we smile, and kiss, and fuck. And after the fucking... we feed.

* * *

Much later, though I am not paying attention to the ticking of time so I have no idea how much later, Lucia shows up in my head.

Josep and I are cuddled up together under the luxurious comforter, his arms around me and his leg hiked over my hip in a possessive embrace.

"I want to say this is brilliant," she says. "But I'm concerned, Echo, that you might be buying into his lie."

I mentally swat her away. Not because she's wrong. She's not wrong.

I *am* buying into this lie.

But if I'm buying into it, is it a lie?

"You need to find the Black blood, Echo. He's got a vial of it hidden in that cave. That's how you kill him. You feed him that and—"

But I'm not listening. In fact, I banish her from my thoughts.

And then I turn, press my face into Josep's muscled chest, and let him hug me harder.

It's not a lie.

I like this.

And if this is as good as it gets, I'll take it.

This is the Kingdom of Darkness

I never knew that scions had a stench to them.

They reek like… *rot*. Like something two days dead that's been left out in the hot sun. The scent of one was bad enough, but there are at least a dozen staring at me from the opposite end of the pool, looking like backlit shadows.

The silence lingers because the scion who appeared first, the one who was talking to me, didn't finish his introduction when his buddies came up behind him.

"Get out of my house." My voice is nearly unrecognizable. It's the demon voice. Which matches my new demon body.

The leader, if that's what he is, bows, falling to his knees and prostrating himself. "My lord—"

"I'm not your lord."

He looks up at me, but doesn't lift his head, only his eyes. "OK. Ryet. That's who you are, right?" I don't nod or agree, so he just assumes his guess is correct and keeps going. "There are scions underground. They got to feed off you and they're transforming as we speak."

"Get to the point."

"The point is," he says, getting to his feet and staring me in the eyes. It comes off as a challenge and even though I'm not his lord, I feel slighted at his overt gesture of disrespect. "The point is that we haven't fed, *Ryet*."

"Am I supposed to care?"

The man sighs and there is some murmuring from the

others standing behind him. "I don't know," he admits. "I just know I'm starving."

I think back on my own experience as a scion, trying to remember a time when I was starving, but can't. I mean, the lust was always there. If Paul bled, I wanted it. But I don't recall a single time when I ever had to go begging for it. Especially from someone I didn't even know. "Where is Paul?" I ask him.

"He left. He took Kael and left."

"To go where?" I notice that my voice is starting to normalize. It's no longer demonic-sounding, but not quite back to my regular voice, either. My skin is changing too. Instead of the bruised blue and purple color, it's going pale. And the bite marks that were all over me just minutes ago are starting to heal and disappear.

"No one knows," the scion says.

"What is your name?"

"Jeff."

"*Jeff?*" I snicker. "Jeff the vampire? I don't see it."

Jeff sighs like he's tired and then his eyes flicker a weird shade of gold. "Me either." And these might be the truest words I've ever heard from anyone.

"All right, Jeff. I need things. If you help me, I'll help you."

"What do you need, my lord?"

"And don't call me that. I'm not your fucking lord. I'm no one to you and you're no one to me. Don't get attached to me or my blood, because I'm not Paul. I'm nothing like Paul. Do you understand me?"

Jeff nods. "Yes. Now how can I help?"

I stand up and get out of the pool, cradling Syrsee in my arms as I walk towards the group of scions. "Where is Josep?"

"No one knows," Jeff admits. "He was in the ground, but

there's a lot of disturbed dirt over there. Even before you came back to life. I know Paul left, we all saw that. But there's a lot of turned-over dirt now. Like…" He pauses to take a breath. "Like some of the scions came up too."

I blow out a breath, silently cursing Paul for causing this mess. "How many? In all, I mean? How many of you are there?"

"Fifty-four in total, but there's only twenty-two of us left who didn't get to drink and go into the earth."

"Twenty-one," another man says. "Kael left with Paul, remember?"

Jeff nods. "Twenty-one then."

Fifty-two fucking scions. Fifty-two bets hedged against me.

Well, I guess I know where Paul really stands. "OK," I say. And while my voice is totally back to normal now, my body is doing weird things that I would like to cover up with clothing sooner rather than later. "I'll feed you." There's a great murmuring conveying relief. "But"—I hold up a hand, gesturing for them to shut up—"I need to take care of Syrsee first."

"That's your Black witch, right?" Jeff says this innocuously enough, but he licks his lips. Like he'd like to taste her.

"Jeff? You're never going to drink her. And if, by some chance, you find yourself presented with an opportunity to drink her, you're still not going to drink her. Because if you take her blood without my permission, what you're really doing is taking mine without permission." My wings suddenly unfurl with a great whoosh of air. And even though all these scions must surely have seen Paul doing this very same thing at some point, they all gasp and take a step back. *Do you understand me?* These words come out in an entirely new voice that is deep, and resonant, and echoing with a very serious don't-fuck-with-me sentiment backing it up.

They all drop to their knees and bow their heads. Some of them say, "Yes, my lord," out of habit for Paul, probably. But Jeff says, "Yes, Ryet," like a good little minion.

"All right then. Stand up and… go do something productive."

"Should I keep working on the coat?" some random scion in back asks.

"What coat?"

Jeff answers me. "Paul wanted us to hunt wolves to make him a coat."

These words make so little sense to me, I don't even bother trying to understand them. "I don't know. I'm taking Syrsee up to my apartment. When she's better, we'll talk again."

Then I fold up my wings and simply walk past them, entering the lodge. They're not entirely satisfied with this outcome, so they grumble behind me, but I don't care.

What can they do?

They are just scions. Helpless, in-between creatures that smell like rot.

And it is quickly becoming very, *very* clear that I am something else entirely.

* * *

I don't think about Syrsee's limp body in my arms as I make my way over to the north side of the lodge where I have an apartment. I get stuck at the door because I don't actually remember the code and have to kick it in. And then I pause for another handful of seconds to take in how easily this solid wood door broke under my will. Well, my foot. But it might as well have been my will, that's how little effort it took to crack it.

The problem with breaking the door is that it won't close

behind me. But this is a secluded section of the lodge, that's why I put my personal space here. So I don't care. I just carry Syrsee over to the bed and lay her down. Then I push some sweaty and dirty hair out of her eyes, open my wrist with a clawed fingernail, and let my blood drip into her mouth.

I wait.

It takes nearly ten minutes before she actually swallows. Relieved at this good sign, I get into bed with her. We're filthy, absolutely covered in smeared blood and dirt, not to mention the scent of the rotting scions that were obviously feeding on us. But I don't even know if she's gonna live, so who cares what we look like.

There's a part of me that thinks my doubt is absurd. I mean, she's a Black witch and she's filled with the blood of two old and powerful vampires. Not to mention whatever magic was done to her with those jars and vials we consumed back at my cabin.

But there's a limit. There has to be a limit to this protection, if that's what is. This ability to live long past your scheduled demise, and then come back, even better than ever.

Which is a relative term.

This is when I start thinking about *me*.

I'm… a vampire.

Which should not be a shock, considering all the decades it took to bring me across this finish line. But it is.

I am a vampire.

Not some creature in a book. Not some actor in a movie.

This is my *life*.

And I have wings.

I'm lying in bed next to Syrsee, who hasn't moved at all from the position I put her in, but I'm sitting up, resting against pillows, so I can see my body. And it's not the blue-black bruising body, either. I'm pale to the point of almost being silver. And there isn't a bite mark on me, thanks to Syrsee's blood. "What does it all mean?"

"It means you're complete."

I look over at the open door and find Paul staring back at me. He looks the same. Beautiful. Dangerous. Predatory.

"Oh, come on, Ryet. Let it go." He comes in my room without asking and walks over to the bed, bending down to pet Syrsee's head as he looks at her with adoration. "You're magnificent. Admit it." Then he looks back up at me.

We just stare at each other for a while. I don't know what he sees in me, but in him I see the truth. That he is evil. That I am evil. And Syrsee is, too. "We do not belong in this world."

Paul scoffs. "It is *them* who don't belong here, Ryet. This realm belongs to *us*." He stands up, walks over to a massive wingback leather chair, and sinks down into it, crossing his legs and leaning on one of the wide arms as he props his head up with a hand. He looks tired, but exuberant at the same time. "You know what I don't understand about you, Ryet?"

"Tell me." My reply doesn't come out snide or condescending like it used to and I'm surprised to realize that I actually want to hear what he doesn't understand about me.

"All that church-boy shit you did growing up and you never found it. I mean, it's all spelled out in there, Ryet."

"Spelled out in… where? I have no idea what you're talking about."

"See?" He points at me. "This is what I mean. Your… innocence? It's adorable." Then he laughs, because I'm getting irritated and I think it's leaking out of me as red light from my eyes, because Paul will not stop staring at me. "The truth, Ryet. It's right there." He pans a hand across the space in front of the chair as if the truth is something tangible that can be with us in this room.

"Why do you have to be so cryptic, Paul? Why can't you just say what's on your fucking mind with as few words as possible?"

"Like you?" He chuckles.

"Yeah. Like me. It would save a lot of time."

"I'm a poet, Ryet."

This makes me guffaw. "Is that right?"

"Yes. I like symbols, and nuances, and allegories, and, of course, the playfulness of a good double entendre."

"Well, I like candid, forthright, plainspoken truth."

"'If you can fill the unforgiving minute with sixty seconds' worth of distance run, yours is the Earth and everything that's in it, and—which is more—you'll be a Man, my son.'" He smiles at me.

I just sigh.

"I'm Kipling, Ryet."

I roll my eyes. "OK."

"You're a textbook. Both are good in their own way. I make beautiful things, such as yourself. But you? You just want to peel back all the layers of that beauty and see the bloody inner workings. Which is fine with me. As a poet, I can appreciate the abstract elegance in scientific illustrations."

"*Anyway.*" Why do I even bother trying to talk to him? "You were saying? About me missing something in the church?"

He sighs now. It's a long one. "One day you'll understand. One day you'll see all the symbols and nuances that I planted along the way." Then he gives me a sad smile and a long moment of silence. I'm just about to demand he tell me about the truth about what I'm missing when he speaks again. "This is a place of evil, Ryet. You *know* this, but I'm telling you again. This is the Kingdom of Darkness. It says as much in the Book. There is no goodness here. It's not meant to be good because this place is not meant for us."

"But… *us*? You were talking about humans. We're not human, so we're not a part of that 'us.'"

"No. We're not."

"Then what does it matter?"

"It matters. Trust me, it does. Now." He lifts his body up a little so he can reach into his pocket, and then he pulls out a vial, holding it up so that a stray beam of morning sunlight can illuminate the contents within. "This is why I'm here. It's for Syrsee. I made it special just for her. And by that, Ryet, I mean… just for *you*. You understand that, right?"

I don't say anything at first. Just let these words of his roll around in my head so I can filter out the nonsense poetry from the actual facts. *Just for me.* He wants me to know he loves me. And all of this comes from that.

Any logical person would see the deception here. I mean, just look at what he's done to me. Look at what he's done to Syrsee. It's… gross. And wrong in every way possible. No amount of love can change that.

But in his mind, this all makes sense.

"Do you want me to feed that to her?" I ask.

"No. You drink it, then feed her. That's the best way because your body will metabolize it better and she will have fewer reactions."

"What will it do?"

Paul smiles. "Save her, of course. It's going to save her and—" And then he stutters or… hesitates. Like he almost said too much. And I know—*I know*—this is the important part. That I should make him say it. That I should refuse to drink whatever's in that vial until he does. That I should seek the truth.

But I'm tired and even though the thing that loves me most in this world is a mere ten feet away and he's offering me his version of salvation, I feel forsaken.

So I see the logic in the poetry. It makes all kinds of sense because it's a way to pretty up the evil.

Paul stands up, walks over to me, and offers me the vial.

I take it and then he turns away, heading towards the door. "Hey, wait," I say. "Where are you going?"

He doesn't turn and look at me, just throws a side-eye over his shoulder. "I've got things to do, Ryet. We're on schedule now so don't procrastinate with that blood. Drink it, feed her, and then we'll talk."

He walks out.

He wins

I am on a long, great sheet of ice and the wind is blowing so hard, tiny pinpricks of snow hit my face like pebbles, stinging it and making me cower.

There is a tribe of people in front of me, all formed up in a circle. They are wearing furs, and have dark hair, and they look ancient. They are all holding torches, looking down into a black hole in the ice.

Then, without any preliminaries, the monster emerges from the water screaming like something from Hell.

In the dreamwalk Lucia took me on, this was some kind of octopus horse thing. But in this one, it's a snake. A giant viper with its mouth open and fangs dripping with poison.

"It doesn't matter what shape it takes."

I turn and find Lucia standing next to me. "What?"

Lucia shrugs. She's not really here. She's dead, I know this, but even if I didn't know this, I would understand that she is not here because she's… transparent. "It doesn't matter if it's a snake or an aquis equī, Syrsee. It's all the same thing. Look. *Look closely.*"

I turn back to the snake and watch as the little girl all dressed up in fur approaches and starts to mount its head. But as I stare at it, it changes. Turns to black sand, and then, once the girl is sitting on top of it, it… crumbles.

That's the best word I have for what I'm seeing. It turns to black sand and falls apart, taking the girl with it. She simply disappears, like she was never here.

There is a great roar from the people dressed in fur as they lift their torches up into the air. Then they are dancing, and lighting fires, and there is cooking going on. Tents are pitched, right there on the ice. Right in front of the black hole.

They begin fishing, and I watch as the low-hanging sun goes down below the horizon, and the moon chases it, and that whole day-and-night dance happens in time-lapse. The ice shifts, melts, and freezes again as this small camp inches its way back to land. Then cabins appear where there were tents. Hordes of people live here now. The buildings get bigger. They are made of ice and summer never comes. These people make massive boats and bring in great nets full of fish and seals.

And then this little village is a city.

Then a bigger city.

Bigger.

Until, finally, it is a castle made of ice.

This is when the purple mist appears.

"Why now? Why did the purple wait so long?"

Lucia looks at me. "Why do you think?"

"They… didn't know how to summon it."

"Everyone starts somewhere."

"What did they do? How did they get the Darkness to cooperate?"

"They gave it a girl, of course. A Coyrah, which in the ancient language is just a word, not a name. A word that means 'trade.' You see, there are many girls like you and it's been going on for thousands of years. If you want something magnificent from the Darkness, you must trade it something back in return. She is Coyrah. Just as the last girl was Coyrah. Just as you are Coyrah."

I let out a long, tired sigh.

"You all get your own personal monster, Syrsee. And yours is called Ryet."

I turn and look her in straight in the eyes. "I thought you said this was something magnificent?"

"Well, it is. It's amazing. This is your bloodline, Syrsee. This is where your Black blood comes from. But it's more than that, it's your destiny as well. It's where you go when you die." She pans her hand at the ice castle. "These people weren't stupid. They made a good deal."

I almost snort in disagreement.

Lucia shrugs. "They got the magic, didn't they?"

"They turned themselves into... I dunno. Some kind of cult. And the magic is dark. The magic is... gross."

"Power is power."

"I don't agree."

"No, I don't suppose you would. You are, after all, the sacrifice. But when you die, you'll feel different when you don't find yourself rotting in Hell. Because you'll be here." Again, she pans her hand to the ice castle. "Ready to be recycled."

It takes a moment for that last bit to internalize. "What?"

"I told you. She is Coyrah. You are Coyrah. You are all Coyrah. Or maybe a better way to explain it is... Coyrah is *you*. Every Black witch that has ever lived is... *you*."

"That's not possible." These words come out loud and strong. "That's just not possible. It's not even logical. It doesn't add up. My grandma was a Black witch. I mean, I know they are few and far between, but—"

"They are you."

"But it can't be! I am *me*. And no one else."

Lucia gives me a sad smile. "Didn't Paul explain the severing of souls?"

"What? No!"

"That's a lie. Don't lie to me, Syrsee. It's counterproductive. I'm only here to help. Are you, or are you not, carrying the Seed of Darkness inside you right at this very moment?"

I just stare at her with my mouth open and my eyes wide.

"Well? Are you?"

"I… might be."

"You are. And Paul, in order to preserve you to keep Ryet compliant and happy, split you in half and put you in two places. Do you think two is the limit?"

I shake my head. "This doesn't make any sense."

"Doesn't it? Well, we'll have to agree to disagree here. Because it makes perfect sense to me. You are *the trade*. Your soul is trapped in the Darkness. It claimed you, right out there on that ice, thousands of years ago. The reason there are so few Black witches is because the Obscurati can only split you so many times before the Darkness is too dilute to matter. Paul stole a little bit of you when he, and Josep, and I left the Old World. A tiny drop of blood. Josep took that blood and grew it the way a scientist might grow a mold in a Petri dish. He stole you. Clever, clever Paul. I wish we were friends, because I would really like that story. How he got that little drop of you out of the Old World is something akin to divine intervention."

"You're telling me that I am my own grandmother?"

"Your own mother, as well." She pauses here to smile. It's a sad one. "You're the nightmare. Do you see it now? The horse *and* the rider. Eating its own tail."

A perfect image of the logo for the Guild Lounge pops into my mind.

"The ouroboros," Lucia says. "And the creature in the symbol is a snake eating its own tail. But in your case, it's a mother eating her child."

I start shaking my head. "No. *No.*"

"You're not really eating your own child, Syrsee. Keep up. It's you, devouring yourself. Recycling at its best."

This is when I realize that no one ever told me that it was called the Horse and Rider. I made that up because that's what it looked like when I first saw it.

But it's not a horse or a rider. It's me and the evil I carry inside me.

Not the baby, but *the Darkness.*

"Come on now. Let's put all the pieces together, shall we?" Lucia's voice is soft now, and she tucks a piece of stray hair behind my ear, trying to soothe me. "Did you think that the Black mother killing the Black daughter at birth was a joke? It's power, Syrsee. Your power. You're killing a daughter, you're snuffing out a future piece of yourself to build up your current incarnation."

Suddenly, I'm in that cabin again. It's New Year's Eve and my grandmother smells like death because she is dying.

Magnificent promises.

"He is going to promise you something you want very badly, Syrsee."

"What, though? I don't need anything, Grandma."

"No. You don't. But someone you love will. So be very sure about the man you give your heart to, my love. Because he will be your downfall. He will steal your soul."

* * *

"You were told this. This should not be news to you," Lucia says. "At the very least, you should recognize the truth in it. Did you ever know your mother?"

I'm still halfway in the past with my dying grandma when Lucia asks me this, so it takes a moment for me to completely come back to her. "What?"

"You never met your mother."

"So?" I'm irritated now. Why am I always the last to know everything?

"Have you ever seen a coven of Black witches?"

"No. Have you?"

"Of course not." Lucia laughs, making her eyes sparkle. "They don't exist, darling. Only *you* exist. Coyrah. The trade."

Finally, I've had enough. "Look, either you tell me what the fuck is going on and what I'm supposed to do, or *go away*! I don't have room in my head for this shit right now! And I want it spelled out for me, OK? Short, simple sentences. Give me the fucking bullet points!"

Lucia looks a little stunned at my outburst, but she composes herself quickly. "Fine. You want the bullet points? Here they are. One. You're an eternal sacrifice. Your soul is trapped in a constant recycling of a single human girl. Two. Your purpose is to carry the Black blood into the future. Three. The future is now."

I stare at her for a moment, waiting for point number four, but she remains silent. "Don't stop, Lucia. I'm fucking serious here. Four. Keep going."

Lucia sighs, side-eyeing me. "Four." Her voice is low now. "You have two choices. End it all or don't."

"End... all... of what?"

"You. Ryet. Paul. Josep. This whole bloodline." She gives me a weak smile. "And me."

"You're already dead, Lucia."

"My soul is trapped, just like yours. But in a different way."

For a moment I think she's sad that she's a part of this. Of the bloodline, as she calls it. But then I remember back to when Paul cut off her head in the Montana lodge and all the things she told me that night.

Well, fragments of it, anyway.

She wanted to die, that I remember for sure. But she mentioned second-level powers that would come with it. "What do you get out of this?" I ask.

"I get to move on, Syrsee."

"To that ice castle place?"

"That's right."

"But that's not a place for you." This is a guess on my part, but if what she just told me is true, then I'm right. I'm the only Black witch there is. She doesn't belong there, *I do*. "That's a place for *me*."

But that's a lie too. And I realize this when Lucia frowns.

It's not a place for me any more than it is for her. I'm stuck in an eternal process of recycling.

"If you could go there, Syrsee," Lucia says, "would you?"

I want to say no, but that's just a reaction. So instead, I take a moment to really think about it. If I am stuck, and living out this Black witch Coyrah thing is all I have to look forward to for all eternity, then… I sigh. "I suppose."

Her reaction is a single raised eyebrow.

"Fine," I huff. "I would, I guess. To get out of this cycle. Yeah. I'd rather spend eternity in some fantasy ice castle with people who traded me for the power to leave this world for good than keep going as the horse and rider."

"The ouroboros, you mean."

I wave a hand in the air. "Whatever."

"Let's return to our bullet points." She smiles. "Five. In order to break your cycle you must kill them all, Syrsee. Ryet, Josep, and Paul. Then, and only then, will you be free."

But it's a lie. I can *feel* this lie. Because she left something out. Something I can't really articulate, and I know almost nothing about, but she hasn't even *mentioned* the Obscurati. Who must have a part of me as well. So it's a lie.

Lucia is shaking her head. "That's not what's happening here, Syrsee. Paul *made* you. You are a brand-*new* Coyrah brought to life by the Darkness itself and living inside that baby you're carrying right now."

"So who is the Black witch across the ocean?"

"Not a who, but a what. It is a bloodline that is too dilute to continue. Something that was merely dying, but will soon be dead."

"Six," I say, continuing the bullet points. "How do I kill them?"

Lucia smiles, and my God, it is evil. "You feed them the dead Black blood. There's a vial in Josep's cave. He brought it with him from the Old World. Paul used that blood to coerce him into joining up on this quest. Find it. Drink it. And let them feed. One and done."

* * *

"Ah, *there you are*. I've been looking everywhere for you, Syrsee."

Lucia is gone now and in her place is Paul. I'm no longer standing on the ice, but lying in a bed next to him.

It's a nice room, at least.

We're both staring at the ceiling, quiet for a few moments.

I don't know what he's thinking about, but everything Lucia just told me is swirling through my head like a cyclone.

Finally, he breaks the silence. "I take it you know now?"

I'm surprised at these words. "You and Lucia planned this?"

"Of course not." He snickers these words out. "Lucia is a tool, not a confidante. But she is part of the plan. Her betrayal of me, at least."

"So you know she wants me to kill you?"

"She's wanted me dead for hundreds of years."

"She wants me to drink Black blood and feed you all. This is your plan?"

"No." And he chuckles. "My plan is to save Ryet."

"What about me?"

"Well, if he's alive, dear Syrsee, then you are too. He cannot exist without you."

"What about you?"

"Oh, I don't matter much." He turns his head to look at me now. "Don't worry about me, Syrsee. I can take care of myself."

"How many?" I ask. "How many of me are there right now in the world?"

Paul sucks in a breath, like he's silently counting. "Well, I have three."

"*Three*? Assuming this baby inside me counts as one, where's the third me?"

"She's a baby still. Only two. She's living up in White River with my clan."

I look back up at the ceiling, trying to internalize this news.

"But there are many more than three, Syrsee. There are a few clans of Black witches up near Seattle who are still breeding the line I gave them about a hundred years ago. But that line is very dilute and I don't expect any of those girls to make it to my bed. Then, back in the Old World, the Obscurati has its own line." He pauses to think, sighing as he does this. "I don't know for sure. But I would guess at least fifty or sixty. They feed the entire population back there, and there are a lot more vampires across the ocean than there are here."

"How could I be this many people? I mean, I only have one soul!"

"Oh, that soul is very tattered, my girl. It's fraying, and not just along the edges. And fragile and fraying things are very easy to split. But it's nearing the end of your cycle. Especially across the ocean. They can't make magic with it anymore. They need every bit of your Black blood to keep themselves alive. But they will die soon, all on their own. I don't have to do anything to make them die, they did it to themselves. And once they're gone, if my plan works, Ryet will be the only one left." He side-eyes me. "And you, of course. You're the key to everything."

I'm afraid to ask, but there's no going back now. "What does all that *mean*, Paul?"

"Well." This word comes out... *sad*. A little. And this throws me. Because he's Paul. Paul the Vampire. Paul the cocky one. The charming asshole. He doesn't do *sad*. "Well," he tries again. "It means we have to... say goodbye. For a little while, at least. That's why I'm in such a rush to complete Ryet. I need him strong when you go."

"Go *where*?" There's a little bit of panic in my voice now.

"The Long Death. All your pieces must die so you can collect them again. In the Old World they call it the Mors Longa and it is not due to happen for another seventy or eighty years." Now he smiles, but he's not looking at me, he's looking up at the ceiling. "I would say that we're off schedule, but"—he does look at me now—"we're not." Another smile. This time very wide.

"You planned this."

"Of course I did. I'm trying to *end them*, Syrsee. We all have a job to do. We don't like the job we're doing, but we do it, nonetheless."

I think about all his words for a moment, trying to force them to make sense with what I know, but I can't. "I don't understand. I thought you were trying to *make* an army? The American Vampires?"

"Every journey begins with the first step."

"What does that mean, Paul?"

"What does that *mean*?" He's still looking at me, and this time his smile is small. But as small as it is, it's also genuine. The smarminess he's known for is nowhere to be seen. "Ryet is my hedge." He sighs. "I don't want to give him up. I know it's wrong, I know I'll pay for this, but I don't care." And now he frowns. I'm not sure I've ever seen Paul frown. "I can't explain it. I just… love him."

"So he's not part of your job?"

Paul scoffs. "No. I am decidedly off task when it comes to Ryet. But you see, Syrsee"—he turns in bed now, facing me like we're best friends ready to gossip—"you see… it's one thing to know one's job. It's quite another to live it for two thousand years, and get used to who you are, and gather minions that you love and care for, and immerse yourself into the lifestyle and… well. It wouldn't be the first time that a spy has gone rogue, now would it?"

I'm… *shocked*. "What. The fuck. Are you talking about?"

"I am human, after all. I mean, I was. Once. And there's… you know, desires in there." He points to his chest. "We're not perfect."

I just shake my head at him. "Who the hell do you work for?"

He simply laughs. "It doesn't matter. Because I'm… I'm going to see this through. I'm going to make sure that Ryet lives. And don't worry. I'll save you too. Even if he didn't need to feed on you, I would still save you, Syrsee. I have to now. Because he wants you. And I will do anything to make Ryet happy. Even give up my eternal soul. I mean, who needs it at this point, right? Mine was taken by the Darkness long ago and… well, I've seen Hell, Syrsee. I've looked that Devil straight in the eyes. It doesn't like me because it's never trusted me. For good reason. But I answer to someone far more dangerous than some silly Devil. Still, I think I'll be OK."

I blink. Because… is he saying what I think he's saying? "Paul, you need—"

But he's gone. And while I am still in a bed, it's not the same one. It's a real bed and Ryet is looking down at me with a worried face.

"Syrsee?" His voice is low, nearly a whisper. "Syrsee? Can you hear me?"

I nod my head, but I can't answer him with words because everything I thought I knew about myself, and Paul, and Ryet, and the Darkness, and the Black witches—well, none of it is true.

"How do you feel?"

How do I feel? I suck in a long breath and slowly let it out. "Tired. I'm tired of this."

Ryet presses his lips together and nods. "Yeah. Me too." He lies down next to me, pulling me into his arms. "Do you hurt?"

I mean... I almost laugh at this absurd question. "No, Ryet. I don't hurt." Which is a lie, but what's one more in the grand scheme of things? Still, I don't like lying to Ryet, so I add in a little truth. "At least not on the outside."

"I'm so sorry for attacking you like I did. I wasn't myself."

I scoff, then actually let that laugh out. "Yeah. I'm not really myself either."

Ryet hugs me a little tighter. "It's gonna be OK."

And I just nod and agree.

Because whatever happens, I'm not in control.

Paul is.

And if there's one thing I know about Paul, it's this: He wins.

So I decide to believe Ryet and just let him hold me as I drift back asleep.

I hope he's worth it

The leftovers are waiting for me in the main floor grand lobby when I make my way down there. They are all lined up, like they've planned a little ceremony.

Twenty-one. Twenty-one lost men. My army.

I pause on the last landing to sigh. It's not Legion, by any means. But it will have to do.

One of the scions steps forward. "My lord!" And when he says this, they all kneel in unison, bowing their heads and staring at the floor.

The one in front lifts his eyes up. They are a nice shade of gold, which I like because he reminds me of Ryet, and this is the only reason I know his name. Everything I do these days goes back to Ryet. Since the moment he was born, it has always been about Ryet.

Why, though? Why am I obsessed with that man? There's no rhyme or reason to it. He's attractive and I am drawn to him for that reason, I'll admit that. But this one here, Jeff, I like him naked as well. And though this one does balk a bit at times, he never positioned himself as an adversary the way Ryet did. He's much easier to enjoy, that's for sure.

So why Ryet?

When I don't say anything, Jeff gets anxious and stands back up, which compels the others to do the same. "We haven't completed the coat yet, but we have secured some pelts from a local fur trader about twenty miles south, so we're..." Jeff looks over at another guy. "Well... tell him."

"Yeah." The other guy looks very nervous. "I did check the YouTube and I did find a pattern for Jon Snow's coat. But—"

"Stop." I put up a hand. "I don't have time for this. What the actual fuck are you talking about?"

This guy's eyebrows shoot up in confusion. "My lord?"

"What are you going on about? We're in the middle of a battle of Biblical proportions. Why are you talking to me about a *coat*?"

This one and Jeff exchange a look. Jeff clears his throat. "Well, my lord, you asked us to make you a Jon Snow coat out of wolf pelts."

Without thinking I guffaw. Then do it again. And it feels good to let my strung-out emotions free like this, so when I'm done laughing, I suck in a deep breath and slowly let it out. "I'm sorry. This is the dumbest thing I've ever heard. Jon Snow is a pussy. Do I look like a Jon Snow? I'm not cosplaying Jon Snow. And this isn't a fantasy!" I kinda roar this. "This is reality! And you're my Army of Darkness!" Here I pause. "Wait. No, wrong movie. Never mind that. We're *not* the Army of Darkness! *They* are!"

Every scion head nods in agreement. But it's one of those cautious, 'he's insane' kind of agreements. And now I do kind of remember something about Jon Snow, and I might've asked them to make me a coat.

So I feel dumb.

Also… crazy. Have I lost my mind? Has the whole ordeal finally caught up with me? Is this how Paul the Vampire goes out? A deranged lunatic who can't discern dream from reality?

Only if I let it be.

"I'm sorry," I say, sighing, but also rallying. "I'm not myself right now. We're in the middle of things. It's confusing for everyone." They emphatically agree with me now. "And I never really explained your role in the endgame, so it's all my fault. But"—I smile at them—"you are…" I need the right word here. Something that conveys all the meanings and bolsters their faith in me. "You are… the Chosen." Oh, yeah, that's perfect. "That's right. The Chosen. I chose you—"

But before I can finish, the front doors of the lodge slam open and a ray of sunshine bursts through them. And behind that ray of sunshine is—well, whoever it is, they are backlit. So it takes me a few more seconds to recognize Tristin after he steps forward.

"My lord!" He's bellowing at me. "What the *fuck* are you still doing here?"

This is when I realize I don't know. I felt so sure of myself when I took Kael up to White River. I had a plan, the plan was for Ryet and Syrsee, and it was executed. This internal wordplay nearly causes me to snort at my double entendre.

But now I'm confused.

Which isn't something I typically allow myself to be.

I close my eyes, breathe, and try to calm myself. Because I'm acting strange. Even if there weren't twenty-one scions and Tristin looking at me like I'm insane, I can feel my approaching madness.

Something has gone wrong. *Again.*

Tristin walks towards me with a concerned look on his face. "Paul?"

"What?"

"Are you OK?"

"I'm fine."

"All right." But he doesn't believe me. And when I check the faces of the scions, neither do they. "So why are you all still here? And where did the scions go?"

"They're right here, Tristin." I pan my hand to my Army of Not-Darkness.

"Not *them*," Tristin snaps. "The ones we *poisoned*!"

A flash of sanity hits me and suddenly the plan is back in my head. "What? They're gone?"

"Yeah, they're gone."

"They can't be *gone*, Tristin. We put them in the ground."

"We did," he says, trying to be patient with me. "But there's nothing but displaced dirt where they used to be. They dug themselves up. They're not there. Trust me, I looked."

"Then where the hell are they?"

Tristin growls at me. "That's what I'm asking *you*. You know, since you're the king of the American Vampires and in charge of this entire fucking scheme!"

"OK, perhaps it's time for a meeting—"

"Meeting?" Tristin cuts me off, scoffing. "There's no time for a fuckin' meeting! We're on a schedule here!" Then he turns to look at the scions. "And why haven't they changed? What the fuck is happening?"

I'm doing my best to sort out his words before I speak so I don't sound crazy, but there's no hope. My mind is… not well. Because I say, "Is there a costume change that I missed?" And even though these words just came out of my mouth, I hear the absurdity.

"*Costume change?*" Tristin is aghast. "Holy shit. You've lost your mind. We're not actors in a fucking movie, Paul! We're about to annihilate the Darkness, remember?"

I laugh. Because that's right. I do remember that. "Yes. The Darkness. But—"

"You haven't fed them yet!" Tristin pans his hand in the direction of my leftovers. "How the hell are we supposed to fight the Army of Darkness if you haven't given them the proper weapons?"

I point at Jeff. "See, I knew the Army of Darkness was relevant here."

Jeff nods, but he side-eyes Tristin at the same time.

"We need to find Josep."

"No." Tristin laughs this word out. "No, Paul, we *don't*." He's red-faced with frustration now, so he takes a moment to breathe through it and collect himself. "OK. I... don't know what happened to you, but you're... confused. So I'm taking over."

"Yes." I point at him. "Agreed."

He turns to Jeff. "We need to get the fuck out of this lodge. Josep could come up at any moment and this asshole is not going to save us. Where can we go so everyone can drink?"

There is a bit of excitement here among the scions. They are hungry and I'm starving them. Not on purpose, though. I was just... preoccupied with something else.

I just can't remember what that something else was at the moment.

Have I actually gone insane?

"The purple rec room?" Jeff says. "It's all the way across the compound, but I'm pretty sure Josep doesn't even know it exists."

"Don't count on that." Tristin laughs. "That thing is not stupid. And we're..." He pauses here to look at me. "We're at a serious disadvantage."

"It's still the best place," Jeff says. "It's small, and out of the way, and near the woods."

"All right," Tristin agrees. "Get over there and get ready. Paul and I will be right behind you."

Tristin waits until all the scions have left before turning to me. He's concerned. "Paul, what is going on with you? Where have you been? I've been waiting at the rendezvous since last night for you to arrive. I only came here to look for you because it was the last place I expected you to be." He looks around for a moment, then lowers his voice to a whisper. "Where is Josep? Is he in the bunker?"

"I… I'm not sure."

He and I just stare at each other for a moment. I can tell that he wants to get angry with me, but he's doing his best to control it. "Do you know what we're even doing?"

"We're… killing the Darkness, of course."

"Of course. Yes. But… you *do* remember who the Darkness really is, right?"

It hits me then. And things start coming back to me. "Of course. And I was busy all day yesterday *preparing*."

"Preparing? How? Because you didn't feed the scions, Paul. That was literally your only job!"

"I was killing Kael up at the White River camp. For Ryet and Syrsee."

Tristin blows out a breath. "So you're really going to jeopardize everything for him?"

And with these words of his, clarity manifests for me. I remember everything again. Who I am, what I'm doing, and why I'm doing it. "Yes," I tell Tristin. And as soon as this word comes out, I'm back. Calm, calculated, smarmy. "Yes, Tristin, I'm going to risk everything. And anyway, it's done. I sacrificed Kael, got the blood I needed, and have already given it to Ryet. He's probably feeding Syrsee right now."

Tristin gives up. "All right. You're the king. But this decision of yours? It might ruin everything. By trying to save Ryet, you might kill *everyone*. So I hope he's worth it."

Then Tristin turns away and follows the scions out the door.

I hesitate, playing his words back in my head. Yes, I might actually kill everyone. Or at least sentence them all to an eternity of Darkness.

But I need to get *something* out of the last two thousand years.

And Ryet is my something.

* * *

Tristin watches with an almost lustful fascination as, one by one, I feed my scions. It is during the feeding that my mind begins to return to me. I hadn't anticipated the insanity that came with the Blood Mother ritual. And, in fact, I haven't even fully comprehended the consequences of it yet either.

This is the only expected thing that's happened all day—my confusion. Because how would I know? I've never made a Blood Mother before, let alone an Army of Not-Darkness. There's a learning curve. I can't be expected to know everything, all of the time. I have fallible moments every now and then.

But I feel confident that my memory is on track to catch up with the times. And, as proof, I realize that as the feedings go on, other things start to make more sense too.

Things like... *me*.

Where I started and how I got here.

Bits and pieces come back to me. Of course, I never actually forgot what I was doing or why. It just... stopped being important somewhere along the way. Two thousand years was more than enough time to talk myself into the idea that it never happened that way to begin with.

That it was a dream?

A nightmare?

A trick?

It could still be all three.

But it's not. I know it's not. From the moment I saw Syrsee in that dreamwalk on New Year's Eve, I remembered. I just didn't spend much time pondering the significance of that memory.

And now, as I pass my blood magic onto these men, it's all I can think about.

Syrsee. And how she showed up in the bath that night I was made. And how she washed my back, wings poking through, and gave me hope.

Because I have to be honest here, I wasn't feeling hopeful that night I was born. The only thing I was feeling was forsaken.

Why? Why *me*?

What had I done to deserve this… curse?

A book was written, back in the day, that answered these questions. But that account was written before third-born Paul killed the Fifth Roman Emperor, so it was never completely accurate. To the victor go the spoils. The 'good guys' always get to write the history books.

But I do remember the true story of how and why I was made. And even if my path from that moment to this one here is quite crooked, here I am nonetheless.

The scion who is feeding has finally had enough and he falls to the side of the bed, unconscious. Tristin, this being his one job, jumps into action and grabs the man under his shoulders so he can pull him off the bed and drag him across the floor where the rest of my fully satiated scions are all lined up.

I sigh, looking over to the men still in line. There are five of them, all staring at me with hungry eyes as they bare their teeth and lick their lips.

But they don't rush me. They wait like good little almost-vampires.

They will never be vampires.

I mean, I suppose it's possible that one survives the change, but it's highly unlikely. Josep and I have made hundreds and hundreds of scions over the years and Ryet is the only one who took. These men never had a personal feeder who was bred for the sole purpose of helping them through the transition.

But they will not take as long as Ryet to emerge, either. I glance up at the clock on the wall and see that it is nearly dawn now. They will sleep off the blood intoxication and be awake by this evening.

It might be too late. And when I think these words I inadvertently glance over at Tristin. Because he's been reminding me on repeat that feeding these scions was my only job and if, by some chance, Josep doesn't come hunting us before they wake, it will only be by luck.

"Are you *trying* to ruin this operation?" That was another thing he said.

And, if one looks at it objectively, there could be an argument for this last one.

I don't feel particularly concerned about things. There is no sense of urgency now that the final feeding has commenced.

This is how it used to be. This… *indifference*. In the first days, in the beginning days. When that insufferable child of an emperor would torture me and the only escape I had was my mind. And the mission.

I hadn't forgotten about the mission. Hadn't given up on it, either. It just stopped being relevant. When you're in survival mode you do what needs to be done. Good or evil no longer matters. The only thing that matters is to keep going.

But, as I sit here feeding my scions their death drink, I am once again thinking about that night when Syrsee showed up in my bath, back in the times of the Roman Emperor, Nero. It was the night of my third-birth and Syrsee appeared as a blur of golden light. Something not quite there, but also very real. I couldn't see her correctly. Like some magic had been done on me so I couldn't make out her face.

But I always knew. And I am considering the idea… entertaining the notion that I… might have… gotten some of this… *wrong*.

Oh, I have thought about that final conversation I will have with my Maker about all he has put me through. I've thought about that a lot. What I would say, the way I would seethe, and spit, and accuse. And I still plan on doing that. But I haven't put any intellectual effort at all into what comes *after* that.

I'm a hell of a vampire. I mean—I actually chuckle out loud here—*legendary* really is the right word for the Vampire Paul. I embraced it. I embraced all of it. The blood, the sex, the magic, the Darkness. It was all mine for the taking.

Even the Darkness was mine. I'm sure it would disagree on this point, because it tried very hard to deny me the magic. But still, the magic came to me. Somehow, some way, it came to me like I was the true owner of that evil. And it did my bidding like I was the true demon it was made of.

This is how I got here. From that Roman bath to this little

building in the Rocky Mountains. Every step of the way was paved in debauchery.

A word that perfectly describes my third-born life.

I have become what I once despised.

And that's depressing.

Also not true. It's easy to put myself in the category of those who were Fallen and named in the Book because I have committed many a sin and I have accepted the Darkness inside me and done its bidding. But there is a plan at work here. And I'm playing the starring role.

Good or evil, it is me.

Here I pause to chuckle and this chuckle disturbs the scion currently feeding on my wrist. He pauses his drink, eyes heavy with blood lust, but also suspicious. If a vampire is laughing at you as you feed, might this be a concern?

I pet his head and smile. "It's OK. Drink. Drink all you want."

The scion lets out a relieved breath, then dips his mouth back down to my wrist and continues his suckling.

He is not the cause for my chuckle. I am the joke here.

Me.

It's always been me.

But I haven't gotten this far without merit.

And it wasn't the Hand of God that did *that*.

In the beginning it was Syrsee. That one visit gave me hope.

The Obscurati knew I was something special. I did, after all, kill the Emperor. Then, in the following year, I killed three more. They were all vile. Nero turned Rome into a complete shit show. Everything was up for grabs back then. I was a bit out of control so the Obscurati made it a priority to reign me in.

It was during this period that Josep and I first met. He didn't mean anything to me back then. He was just a wretched creature in a prison. Something to be forgotten and it would take another eighteen hundred years before I saw him again and started figuring things out. By this time, we were both insane.

He wanted the Long Drink. To end it and start over again, I guess. The Darkness hadn't understood the depth of human greed and depravity when it first manifested inside the body of beautiful Josep.

But it learned.

Still, Josep was done. I tempted him with the dead Black blood, promising him that little vial in exchange for his help in getting away. Starting over in the New World.

And by the time we got here, he was ready to try again.

But all of that was but a step.

The leaps didn't come until I created my little coven of witches. It took a while to hunt down the distant descendants of the Coyrah in the New World, but I knew they were here.

Over the many thousands of years that the Coyrah was recycling, many had escaped. Nero wasn't the only monster who ruled Rome, after all. As vile as he was, he had nothing on Caligula. It was Caligula who diluted the Black blood so badly, it was nearly worthless. He made so many little Black witches. Hundreds in the span of just a few years. So many, they lost track of them. Black blood babies were being born everywhere.

That's how the Darkness spread around the world. Of course, looking at it objectively a couple thousand years on, even I have to admit that it feels more like a plan than a mistake.

And now these distant descendants of the old Coyrah line make Dark magic for me through the blood of my sacrificial scions.

Because that's all a scion is.

Nothing but a sacrifice.

And Ryet is no different. Because by now, he will have consumed that blood and fed it to our dear Syrsee.

Who lives.

Who must live.

Who *will* live.

I know this because Syrsee came to me.

And that time in the bath was but the first.

She is my plan.

She was always the plan.

Without her, we lose.

What's one more day?

Little Baby is life. She is my new purpose.

We are lying together on the floor of my cave, panting and sweating from the sex, and this, I think, is my first experience of bliss that is not about blood.

She's on top of me, her soft breath fluttering against my chest like butterfly wings, and she is sleeping.

I love.

I am able to love.

It's a surprise because loving her was not my intention. I had imagined a slave. Sex, blood, whatever I desired her to do—to me, for me—I saw her doing it.

But a slave isn't real. And ever since the Darkness tricked me into thinking it was Little Baby while I was underground, I can't seem to get it out of my mind.

What is real?

I admit, I haven't thought about it much. And it helps that the Darkness explained that it and I are the same, I just forgot we were the same.

But it's *the Darkness*.

And the Darkness doesn't have regrets, or attachments, or ponder the meaning of life. It's unable to do any of those things because it exists outside of time. Without time, there is no progression. Without progression, there is just... well. Darkness.

But the Darkness does have one thing: Goals.

Or, more accurately, *a* goal.

It wants to be in this realm with *us*. Just because this realm belongs to it doesn't mean it can partake.

It wants to partake. To be vampires and humans. Plant and animal. It wants blood and sex. And it needs both good and evil —black and white—to fully exist. It needs this or else it is just insanity.

I wouldn't care if it was tricking me if Little Baby wasn't here. I wouldn't care because before her I truly was the Darkness. I realize that now. The Josep who came before Little Baby is someone other than the Josep who came after.

My arms are wrapped around my new precious demon as she sleeps and my thumb is absently stroking her shoulder.

She must be real.

I must not accept anything less than real.

So she is the reason that I gently roll her off me and cover her up with a fur. Then I stand over her, looking down at her face, glowing and pink with life.

She can't be another illusion, she just can't. If this little demon was the Darkness, she would be talking to me. Trying to make sure I was doing my job. Trying to influence me and keep me on track.

But she's not.

It's enough to convince me for now. And I have things to do.

Not because the Darkness wants me to, but because I need to keep her safe. I need to provide her a future. And at this point, there is only one way to do that.

Kill Paul.

Has he always been trying to kill me? Dark Me, specifically. Not Josep Me.

I don't think so.

I understand that he was sent on a mission and that

mission did involve annihilating the Darkness, so at first glance my logic appears to fail. But becoming a vampire is a disorienting process. The past few days alone are proof of that.

You get lost. It's hard to find reality. You forget things. Things like… you and the Darkness are actually one and the same. Or things like… you're on a mission from God.

So while I'm sure it was there, inside him, this hatred for me —I'm not convinced that he understood it.

Which is why I went along with many of his ideas.

The Vampire Paul is an infection and he's contagious. It was easy to get caught up in his plans.

Especially the American Vampires.

There can only be one king.

Just one, no more.

And I'm not talking about one American king, either.

One World King. One king to rule over everything in this realm.

This is how it was written in the Book.

There is but one, he rules us all.

And that One is me.

For I am the Darkness.

And this world was my promise.

* * *

I leave my bunker and go upstairs. The floor of the grand foyer is stained with the blood of halfbreeds where I poisoned them using the girl called Echo.

My head tips up and I smell the air. Paul was here and so was Ryet. Recently. Looking around, I realize Ryet is on the other side of the lodge. Close. So close my sensitive ears can hear him talking to his little Black witch.

But I am not interested in Ryet. He will be dead long before this is over. Whatever Paul did to try and save him, it won't be enough.

I always knew Paul would betray me for Ryet. How could he not? Ryet is his firstborn. A true vampire. He's a magnificent achievement, even I will admit that.

My feelings for Little Baby and Dark Baby are the same. There are powerful threads of loyalty attaching me to them.

I knew this was coming and I prepared.

Ryet, as far as I'm concerned, is not worth my time. He's going to die and Syrsee will be the one to kill him.

Smiling, I turn towards the door and walk out into the sunshine.

The air is cool and crisp and the breeze passing across my naked body feels magnificent. The path to the cave is nothing but a deer trail, but it's a well-traveled one, so it's not hard to follow. But even if it were, I would know the way—not because I've used this path before, but because there are fresh footprints in the dirt.

My scions.

Mine.

Not Paul's.

Mine.

They belong to *me*, the Darkness. Yes, they fed on Ryet and Syrsee and both of these creatures are technically Paul's. But Paul has no access to the Darkness except through me.

Did he really think I would hand over all that power without a down payment?

Without assurances?

Without precautions?

I chuckle as the cave entrance comes into view, thinking about how I carved up Little Baby's body with all those symbols. How I put my plan into blood. Then I laugh out loud about how, in the end, I have only ever been praying to myself. Only ever been begging myself for more power.

It was me, checking me.

It was me, empowering me.

I am a genius.

I am the Darkness.

And this is my world.

The scions are sitting on the floor of the cave entrance when I enter, but as soon as they see me, they jump to their feet.

I take them in as they stand, silent and with bowed heads.

A few of them are naked, but some still have tatters of clothes on. All of them are dirty since they all came up from the ground.

They are pale, and gaunt, and actually look like walking death because they are starving.

They need blood and none of these former men have their own personal little Black witch.

Which means they need me.

"It is time to feed," I say, panning my arms wide like the Messiah I am.

Some of them start to weep. A few fall to their knees. None of them rush me because all of them know better.

"But before we do that," I continue, "I need to explain your objective here. Look at me. All of you, look at me."

They do this. Their eyes are all blood red, a sign of severe starvation. They are trembling with anticipation and hunger pangs.

"Your objective," I say, looking into each set of eyes as my gaze sweeps across the group, "is to drink Paul until he is dry. You will each take a long drink, but you will not give it back."

There is complete and utter silence after these words come out of my mouth and for several long moments, they just stare at me.

Finally, one says, "My lord, how?" He squints his eyes. "How do you propose we do this?"

"And why?" another one adds. "Why would we drink Paul dry?"

"He's our maker!" a third chimes in.

The rage inside me surges with this last comment. *"He is no one's maker."* My voice comes out so strong and so loud, it shakes the cave, causing them all to fall to their knees. *"I am your maker! I am the maker of every vampire on this Earth. It was me who made you. Do you understand?"*

One scion presses his forehead to the rocky cave floor, sobbing. Then the rest follow. Not all cry, but they all submit. They have no choice, they are starving.

I suck in a deep breath, calm myself, and then slowly exhale, my words softer now. "Do not doubt me, scions. Blood of my blood. I will feed you now. You will drink my magic. You will drink my power. And then you will use this power to take Paul's."

Again, they are silent.

But again, it's only temporary. "My lord," one says, the sobbing one. "My lord, why would we want to do this?"

"Why?" I sigh. The obvious answer is because I fucking said

so. But that won't make them more efficient and answering this question honestly will. "Because he betrayed you, scions." They look up now, even the crybabies. All their blood-red eyes find mine. "He poisoned you." They start mumbling. "On purpose. You were never meant to ascend. Never. Paul only cares about Ryet. You were a way to experiment with blood while he used all his knowledge of Dark genetics to build up Ryet. Ryet, Ryet, Ryet—it always goes back to Ryet. Everything Paul does is about Ryet."

Of course, I was part of this plan as well, but they don't need to know that.

They look at each other now, confused.

But, as expected, this confusion turns to anger pretty quickly. They are *starving*. This is a bad thing for vampires and an even worse thing for scions. It's not a good look nor does it foster patience.

So they start bitching. I let them do this for several seconds, then put up a hand. "Silence." Which makes them stop, because obviously, I pushed their mute button. I needed to tell them about draining Paul to get them on board, but we're not going to discuss it further. Time is ticking and Paul's death awaits us. I didn't have to tell them anything, I could just direct them to do what I want, but Paul is part maker. I hate that, of course. But it's true. So I need them committed to this task. I need them to resist him. One of them alone could not harm Paul in the least. But all of them, plus me?

We've got this. As long as they stay focused.

So I focus them.

"Line up right here." I point to the cave floor in front of me. "It's time to feed."

There are about two seconds here where they check

themselves, making sure they heard me right. Then they clamber into line, pushing and fighting a bit as they jostle for position.

I beckon the first in line forward and he covers the few steps between us licking his fangs, hunger in his eyes.

My smile is wide as I place my hands on his cheeks. "Pledge yourself to me, son. Pledge yourself to me and me *only*, and you may drink my blood until you've had your fill."

He blinks, stunned. "My… *fill?*"

"You can take as much as you like. Take it all, if you can. I'll make more blood." He leans in, but I stop him with a flat hand on his chest. "First, you pledge."

"I pledge, my lord! I fuckin' pledge!"

I take a claw, swipe it across his neck, open it up, let the blood spill until he collapses, and then I bend down, open my wrist, and let my blood pour into his mouth.

I look up at the stunned scions waiting in line, slack-jawed and wide-eyed. "Don't worry," I say, my voice soothing and calm now. "This won't kill him. I am merely replacing his inferior blood with mine. And you all will get the same." I narrow my eyes. "If you pledge."

They nod, but not enthusiastically. Most of them are staring at the man on the ground at my feet. He's not moving. The blood I'm feeding him is pooling into his mouth, un-swallowed. So they are not convinced.

Fools.

It takes several long and painfully stress-filled minutes for the blood to drain out of this scion completely. But drain out it does. By this time, he is a shriveled-up husk and nearly unrecognizable.

The watching scions start murmuring, but then, just as they

are losing all hope, this one coughs and sputters. Blood comes flying out of his mouth.

His eyes open, focus on mine, then he comes at me like a fiend, grabbing for my neck.

Of course, he will not be feeding on my neck. I press my wrist into his mouth and he grabs at my hand instead, sucking on me, drawing out my blood in long drinks the likes of which he's never experienced before.

It feels good. So I smile and sway on my feet a little.

I don't know how long it takes before he is full. Twenty or thirty minutes, maybe? Then he stumbles away, presses his back up against the cave wall, and slides down it, slumping into himself like a heroin addict.

I look back at my waiting scions. There are dozens of them, so it's gonna take a while. But after waiting thousands of years, what's one more day?

I beckon the next in line with a crooked finger and he attacks me while I laugh and cut open his neck to drain him dry and fill him back up.

His name is Paul

Ryet is talking to me, and I say something back, but I'm drawn to another place and his voice fades along with my awareness of him.

I find myself inside the Darkness.

Here lies infinity. The forever. The eternal. The unknown.

Ever since my grandma died I've been looking for the truth. It feels like a mission now. I wanted to read the books because I felt like that was where my truth was hidden. Somewhere deep in the pages of antiquated thoughts, and magic recipes, and philosophical waxing.

But my whole trip to the Guild with Ryet was nothing but a dream. Nothing but a lie.

No wonder I was reading nothing but meaningless things. The Guild library doesn't hold my truth, I do.

I am the Coyrah and the reason I can't find my truth is because I have been shattered into so many pieces, there's not much left of me.

Which begs the question: If this piece of me I'm living in now is but one of hundreds, or thousands, or, who knows, maybe even millions—then what would I be if I was whole?

How much power over the purple and gold would I have if all of that knowledge was contained within a single consciousness?

And what could I do with that power?

Change Ryet back?

No. What's done is done. He's a vampire now, whether I like it or not. Whether *he* likes it or not.

Just like him, I am made of Darkness, but that's the past. It's done and there's nothing I can do to change it. But maybe I could use all that magic to bring forth a better future.

Not for the world—I don't speak for the world—but just Ryet and me. Couldn't I use my power to find a way to give us… *hope?*

It's a goal, at least. One that might be futile, but what else am I gonna do? If I am eternal, what better way to spend eternity than hunting down all my missing pieces so I can put them to good use?

This new confidence and understanding forces a change and slowly, the black emptiness fades and then I'm conscious again. Another minute or so passes before I try and open my eyes. And when I do, I wake up immersed in a mist of swirling gold and purple.

It moves around me like a slow-moving tornado, glittering, and sparkling, and catching the light. For some reason, this makes me feel safe. Kind of reminds me of a fairy realm I saw in a movie once.

Which allows me to relax, exhale, and look around.

After a few more seconds I realize it's not the pretty colors that comfort me, but some internal instinct that this is… home. Somewhere I belong.

My body starts to tingle and a sense of purpose and wellbeing comes over me. A surety, maybe, that I have… arrived.

The only question is, arrived… *where?*

It's impossible to know because there's no one to ask.

But I've been dreamwalking since I was a child. I might not know everything about it—certainly not the gold parts, since they are new—but I know enough to get places. To use it as means to an end.

To use it as a *road*.

My stomach flutters and my hand automatically drifts down to my stomach as I suddenly realize that there is something growing inside me.

A demon? A god? A vampire?

I don't know. The only thing I do know is that it's not mine. It's not Ryet's, either. It belongs to the Darkness. We belong to the Darkness as well, I think. But this baby is different. It's something very, very *wrong* and it cannot be born. I feel this all the way down to my bones.

It cannot be born.

I don't know what Paul thinks it is, or what Josep thinks it is, but I don't care what they think. They made it for all the wrong reasons. I think it's evil. And not in the same way that I am. Not even in the same way as Paul or Ryet.

It's more than that. It's like... Biblical. An Antichrist or something. At the very least, it's a terrible idea to bring it into the human world and an even worse idea for me to *raise* it.

I'm shaking my head as I think these last words. No. I'm not gonna do it.

And then I remember something. My own thoughts from months ago. From that night in the lodge bedroom when Lucia died.

Maybe the Darkness wins. Maybe the Darkness takes over the world. Maybe some woman really does pop out a bunch of evil demon babies. Maybe that's really how all this ends.

But I swear to that good-for-nothing God above, it's not gonna happen that way because of me.

I was so convinced. In fact, I was here, in this same frame of mind as I am right now. I had a choice back in the lodge bedroom when Lucia came to me and told me to kill Ryet and then myself and I didn't do it. I put myself on this path. I am this demon's mother.

It's my fault we're here. But this guilt, or self-blame, or whatever emotion it is that I'm feeling, isn't the important part.

The important part is that while it's inside of me, I'm in control of it.

"The ouroboros," I say, repeating the words Lucia spoke to me. The baby is power. And if Paul was telling the truth and my only purpose in this life is to make babies, then it's a *constant* source of power. Not for him, but for *me*.

He was going to take it, of course. Just like the piece of me that was my grandma took it from the piece of me that was my mother.

But couldn't I take it instead? Couldn't I just eat my own tail and keep all that power for myself? And, if I were to find all my shattered pieces, couldn't I scoop them all up and just... put them all back where they belong?

How dark am I? How close to being the actual evil of Darkness am I? Because these thoughts of mine make me feel more like a daughter than a distant cousin.

This final thought is the scary one. Not that any of the previous ideas were in any way calming. But the next thought is... if I did pull myself together and take all my power back, would I still be Syrsee? Would I still love Ryet?

Would I be able to control it?

Most likely not.

It's probably a really stupid idea to claim my birthright power.

It's probably gonna come back to bite me, just like that snake eating its tail.

But the only other option is to let everyone else dictate my future.

Paul, or Josep, or Ryet, or the Darkness.

If this is truly my life, isn't it better to try and change my future rather than letting others do it for me?

Yes.

I know this is the way because I spent my whole life up to this point being ignorant, and afraid, and on the run.

I don't want to run anymore.

I don't want this baby.

I don't want to die, either.

I want to live. I want my power. And I want Ryet to be my future.

From where I'm at presently, none of this seems possible. The deck, as they say, is decidedly stacked against me.

But it doesn't have to be that way. I could, for once, stop running and take a stand. Which sounds good in books and movies. Stories. They speed everything up and make a montage of growth or... something. Time passes, skills are acquired, coping mechanisms are learned. Because this is how growth works. You have to struggle. You have to live through things. This is how you grow. You don't simply wake up one day and say 'I'm a hero.' Because if one was able to simply become courageous, everyone would do it. It's just not that easy. You have to earn it.

I like personal growth as much as the next person, I just

don't have time for it. The Darkness is coming and I'm not ready. All of this is out of my control.

And… now I sound like a quitter. Is this my fate? To be food? To be a demon-making machine? To *lose*?

Even if it is, shouldn't I at least *try* to buck the system? Conjure up the essence of heroines in books and take control of my destiny? Be a girl boss? A strong female character who wins despite all odds?

I should. But it doesn't seem very realistic. And if you know you're just gonna lose, it's hard to commit.

Maybe… I should just… redefine winning? I mean, sure, living through this intact, not having a demon baby, and getting to spend thirty or forty years with a man I love—even though he's a vampire—is the actual prize I'm aiming for. But couldn't I… maybe… come up with a more magnanimous goal?

Like… saving the rest of the world from an eternity of Darkness instead of living my dream?

Because if this was my goal, then I could lose all three of those things above and still win.

As if I've hit on something important, the mist begins to change all around me. Instead of swirling, it starts to coalesce into tall shapes. I watch, slightly hypnotized, as the glittering gold particles separate themselves from the purple and become tall rectangles.

No. Not rectangles. *Doors*! Many, many of them. Hundreds, maybe, as I look around. I begin walking forward, trying to see into the ones closest to me.

In the one on my right, I see Ryet. I almost rush forward and walk through it, but I catch a glimpse of motion in another door, and in that one, I see Paul.

Choices. That's what these doors are.

Ryet is the Vampire. We're on a bed together and he's shaking my shoulder, leaning down. Probably because I'm not waking up and he's worried that I'm dying. I think this room is in the lodge, but that's just a guess, as well as a detail that doesn't really matter. Because I recognize this door for what it is. The present.

The other door, the one with Paul, is not the present. It's him running through the woods, but not the him of today. It's the him of that dreamwalk I took to the Roman baths. Which is the past.

Choices.

I would like to walk through the door with Ryet, wake up on that bed, and find a way forward with him at my side. It's so much better than doing this alone.

But if I choose Ryet, I stay the same. Nothing changes. No personal growth.

The present doesn't offer many opportunities to change your future. You are what you are. But the past... the past is where choices were made that got you here in the first place. So even though this isn't my past, it's Paul's, I walk through that door.

I choose Paul.

As soon as I say his name in my head, I'm there. In the forest, running alongside him. He's naked and dirty, breathing heavy and concentrating so hard on running, that he doesn't even notice me.

That's when I hear noises up ahead and realize Paul isn't running, he's hunting. And whatever it is he's after, it's just up ahead.

We come through a break in the trees and I see a naked man.

He looks over his shoulder, trying to see how close Paul is, and his expression says everything his mouth doesn't.

He's dead.

The man stumbles, falls, and then begins to weep as Paul catches up and attacks him like a dog, ripping his throat with his long, sharp teeth. He spits the chunk of meat out and dives down, sucking up the man's blood.

In the distance, there is a baying of hounds. And they are not that far away.

I squint down at Paul, watching him feed as questions rush into my head. "When is this?" I say it out loud.

Paul hears me, because he stops and looks up at me. His face is covered in blood, his eyes as red as the blood he's sucking, and his face is so gaunt and white, he looks even more demonic in this starved human form than when he's wearing the blue-black skin and wings.

His grin is lopsided. And if this were the future, I would recognize this grin as his practiced smarmy smile. But here, in the past, it's haunting and not the least bit playful.

He growls at me. "Now? You decide to come back *now*?" He doesn't let go of the dead man and he doesn't straighten up or stand. He remains there, crouched on the ground, with the dead food clutched in his claws.

"When is this?" I ask again. Because clearly time is not passing in the same way for us. In my weird, unreliable dreamwalk time, perhaps minutes have passed. Maybe a couple of hours.

But from the look of him, and his blood-red eyes, it's been… months?

The hounds are getting closer and this makes Paul cock his head in their direction. Then he looks back at me. "Do you have any idea how long it's been since we last saw each other?" These words come out past the blood in his mouth.

Paul is looking me straight in the eyes and, for some reason, he scares me. So much so that my stomach flips. I shake my head no.

"Seven. Years. Now ask me how long, before right now"—he shakes the dead man in his claws—"has it been since *he* fed me?"

It's a rhetorical question, so I don't answer. Just ask one of my own. "Who, Paul? Who is doing this to you? The Obscurati?" Because clearly, he really is starving.

He scoffs. "The Obscurati? The Obscurati works for Nero. That pathetic little boy who calls himself a ruler. Seven years. Since the night I was born. That's the last time he fed me."

Everything I thought I knew about Paul the vampire gets flipped upside down in this moment. He's scared. And starving. And dangerous. Very, very dangerous.

I blow out a breath. The hounds are so close now, we might have thirty seconds before they're upon us and nothing has been settled. I don't want to leave him like this because it won't change anything. So I push my wrist into his space. "Drink me."

"I don't need you." He's scoffing again.

"Drink me. I'm a true Black witch, Paul." I point to the body on the ground. "I don't know who this is, but a Black witch he is not. Drink me, kill Nero—everyone hates him anyway—and I'll be back to feed you again. Only next time, you will tell me everything I want to know. Do we have a deal?"

He looks in the direction of the hounds. They are so close now, and the baying is so loud, I almost miss what he asks next. "How long?" He looks back at me, his eyes dripping blood as if he's crying. "How long do I have to wait?"

"I don't know," I admit. "It's all very new to me and I don't have much control, but I will find you, I promise, I will. Now drink!"

Almost before those words are out of my mouth, he's biting my wrist. He's not careful, he just rips it open. And once again I'm reminded that he is not the practiced, calculating, master vampire that I know in the future.

He is a frightened newborn.

The hounds are suddenly upon us, and they attack. I slip away as mist, but not before I see what happens next. Paul turns, mouth still blood red, just as it was when I came here. But his eyes are now blue.

He is no longer starving.

My blood did that.

And whatever he does next, my blood does that as well. But I don't see it, because I'm gone.

It is in this moment that I realize what I have actually started here.

I am supposed to be killing him with dead Black blood, but all I have done is make him *stronger*.

And not only that, I promised to feed him again.

I'll find you.

I tell myself it's for answers.

But I think I have the answers I need.

I think I'm doing this for me, not him.

I think there's much more going on here than anyone has told me. And while everyone has kept me as ignorant as possible through the careful dissemination of truths and lies, I'm finally starting to see the big picture.

This isn't about vampires.

This isn't about Black witches.

This isn't about my eternal soul, this isn't about ice castles, or the Obscurati, or the magical purple mist, or even Ryet.

This is a battle as old as time.

The battle of *all* time.

And I have chosen my side.

His name is Paul.

Fuck losing. I'm not redefining anything. I am going to feed this monster, and make him strong, and no matter the cost, we are going to *win*.

* * *

Coming out of this dreamwalk with Paul isn't like *leaving* a place. It's more like an *exchange* of a place. One moment I'm in that forest, and the next I'm in the swirling purple and gold mist.

I'll need another word for what this is, because 'dreamwalk' doesn't feel right. Dreamwalking is what I've been doing all my life. This is something completely different.

But there's no time to make up new words. I need to get back to Paul. Seven years went by for him and it was mere moments for me. At least it felt like moments.

So as soon as I manifest, I go looking for the pathways. It's just… no matter how long I stare, I can't seem to find the doors again. The mist just continues to slowly swirl around me. I look around and down at myself, watching the mist. And this is when I realize that the baby bump is gone.

I just stare at my stomach for a moment, trying to find a way for this to make sense.

I mean, none of it makes sense. And the easy answer, of course, is that it's just an illusion. I'm not pregnant with a demon baby, was never pregnant.

It's a nice thought, I'm just not convinced it's true. I think I really am pregnant. I think there really is something very, very sick and bad growing inside me.

But it's such a relief to not see the proof that I can easily push that problem aside to concentrate on the other one.

Which is Paul. I need to find him. He knows what's going on and he doesn't seem as committed to keeping his secrets as the Paul I know in my own time.

I need those secrets. Desperately need those secrets.

So I stare at the mist. I squint my eyes, I cross them, I let them go lazy… but nothing works.

"Come on!" I say this out loud as I rub my hands down my face. "Where is Lucia when I need her?"

I look around, hoping that my wish becomes manifest and Lucia appears, but she doesn't.

But a shape does begin to form. I stand still as the mist bonds and more and more rectangles appear. But when I approach, there's something wrong with them.

They aren't doors, they're… I lean forward, squinting, trying to make sense of what I'm seeing. Some of them are easy. They show bedrooms, or hallways, or the interior of cars. But some of them show sky and the boughs of trees. Some of them are a blur, like everything is moving. And some of them are the ceiling of a bathroom.

Mirrors. The doors have become mirrors that show the human world. They are all places, obviously, but none of them are *Paul*.

An idea hits me—maybe that's how I got to the Roman bath? There was water in there. And the Coyrah was out on the ice.

It's the water!

The dreamwalk belongs to the vampires. Purple is the earth. The dirt. A highway across the present or a vision of the past.

But gold is the mist. Water. Doorways through time. And it belongs to *me*.

I turn my head and finally see something familiar. A pink-haired girl on the other side of a rippling pool of water.

And she is standing in a cave.

17 - Echo

How much do you know about mirrors?

I duck my head under the pillow and wrap it around my ears, but it's no use. I can still hear them. I sit up, pissed off and hungover, and scream at the top of my lungs. "Will you two shut the fuck up! Get a divorce already!"

If they even hear me, which is doubtful, they don't respond. They just keep fighting.

"Parents," I mumble.

I'm still kinda fucked up from last night and need at least a whole day of sleep before I can function properly, so I lean over my bed, fish underneath it with a grabby hand, and search for the bottle of pills.

It's not oxy—I kicked that shit, I really did. It's something else. Something this woman was selling at the club a couple weeks ago. They don't get you high, not the way I'm used to anyway. They take you places in your sleep.

It's like acid, but you're not awake. She called it the dreamwalk. Says it's spiritual and shit.

It's an OK trip, I guess, but not something I'd do more than once or twice a year. No one wants to sleep while they're partying.

But I'm not partying right now and sleep is the only thing I want.

So I shake two out into my palm, grab a stale can of soda, and down them.

Downstairs, my mother is crying now, which means the fight is almost over. They fight like this so much, there's a pattern to it. They don't even realize that fighting is a part of them now.

I side-eye my bedroom door. I will never be like them. I will do anything—whatever it takes—to stay free. Because if they weren't *married, they wouldn't stay together. And they're not here for me. That's a joke. They stopped paying attention to me when I was thirteen. My mother made me get a job cleaning houses with her so I could buy my own school clothes and food.*

It's not me that keeps them stuck in this rut.

It's the pattern. *And the familiarity of it.*

I'm not gonna get stuck. I won't fall into this trap.

I will never...

* * *

My eyes open and all I see is the ceiling of a cave. It's not one of those moments where one has to try and remember where they are. I fully understand where I am. It's just one of those moments where one needs to pause and reflect on how they got here.

It was my parents.

I'm the one who took Lucia's dreamwalk pills, that's a fact. But I wouldn't have done that if someone had cared about me. If someone was looking out for me, I wouldn't be in this situation to begin with.

I know Josep is gone, I feel his absence. And smell it too, which is weird. I hadn't realized that deficiency had a smell.

My internal monologue makes me chuckle out loud. Deficiency? Internal monologue? Did the blood make me smart? Because I've never used those words in a sentence in my life.

I think about this for a moment. Intelligence, and the lack thereof.

Before Lucia, I was not a smart girl. Which, now that I think about it, was why she chose me. I mean, really she chose my boyfriend, Boyd. But he was dumb too.

I was malleable. She could shape me.

And look—I chuckle again—she did.

I'm here. The concubine of evil. The Darkness itself has taken me as its partner.

"Oh, come on, Echo. You don't really believe that, do you? Please tell me you're not that stupid."

I sit up, then get to my feet and face Lucia. "This is *my* cave now."

She shakes her head as she studies her fingernails. "No, sweetie, it's not." She looks up at me with that penetrating glare she has. "He's using you."

"He's using me for what? I don't have anything to offer."

Her head lolls to the side, like she cannot believe I just said that. "You really are stupid. In my next go-around as an evil, conniving witch I will do an IQ test first."

"You know what? I don't have to take your shit anymore. I'm not your bitch."

"No, you're *his* bitch now."

I nod. "Yeah. I am." This is when I realize I'm naked, so I fold my arms across my chest. "And I like it, OK? He's… good to me."

Lucia bellows out a laugh that echoes off the ceiling. It's such a hearty laugh, it takes several seconds for the air to still after she's done. "Good to you? He carved evil into your skin, served you up as food to the halfbreeds, used you to kill them, let them destroy your body until it was nothing but tatters, and then"—she flips a hand in my direction—"brought you back to life so you can be his sex slave. This, my dear, is not what salvation looks like." Her gaze is trained and focused on me again as she stares into my eyes. "This is damnation, girl. You just don't have the good sense to understand that yet."

"Well…" I'm not sure how to respond to that, so this is all I have. But Lucia waits, allowing me to gather my wits. "If this is damnation, you're the one who put me here."

It cuts, but only a little. Lucia, from my perspective anyway, isn't the kind of woman who lets herself dwell on past mistakes.

As I'm thinking this, she smiles. It's a very small Mona Lisa smile. "You are not, and have never been, a mistake. Do you really think I was after *Boyd*, Echo?"

I blink. "What?"

"Boyd?" she says again. "Come on. Give me some credit. I wasn't after Boyd. Is Boyd here?" She pans her arms wide and pretends to look around the cave. "Do you see him anywhere?"

"What are you saying?"

"I was never after Boyd, Echo. It was you." She gives me a real smile now. "Poor, forgotten, used and abused Echo from Spokane. Do you know where Boyd is now?"

I lift up one shoulder, feigning indifference. Boyd and I were brought to the compound together, but everything up here was so… well, confusing, but exciting as well, that I just lost track of him. And there were so many other men to be distracted by. And Paul, of course.

Paul never took any notice of me until he came back up from the ground last New Year's Eve, but I sure as hell saw him.

I give Lucia my best guess. "Dead?"

"No." She purses her lips and shakes her head. "He was stupid, but he wasn't discarded. He had a family who cared about him, Echo. I can't turn people into halfbreeds if they've got family who will miss them. He left the very first day he got here."

My eyes narrow down. "No, he didn't."

"Name one time, after you came up here to the lodge, that you saw Boyd."

"Well, I can't remember right now—"

"You can't remember because I sent him home. He's married now, you know. Two kids. Both boys. He married into a large ranching family. He lives a simple, but good life, in Boise. Wears a cowboy hat and everything."

"Married with kids?" I scoff. "What the hell are you talking about? I haven't even been up here long enough—" But as soon as this sentence starts spilling out of my mouth, I know it's a lie. When Paul came back on New Year's Eve, he had been gone for two years. And I've been through several Paul disappearances. I blink at Lucia. "How long have I been up here?"

"Twenty-one years."

"Twenty-one…" But I can't finish. I look down at myself. Naked now, but I look the same. Better, actually, after bathing in that magical hot spring after my death. I look back up at Lucia. "*What?*"

She nods. "Time slips when you're not really alive. I killed you, Echo. Decades back. I gave you the blood, and you drank it, and time just… slipped."

Of course I knew I was dead. I mean, I remember the way Josep carved me up. I remember the halfbreeds feeding on me and tearing me to shreds. I even remember the part where Josep brought me back down here and walked into the pool, holding me in his arms until I was healed.

I remember all of that.

But for some reason, it is the knowledge that I already died decades ago that shakes me to my core.

"That's what a halfbreed is, Echo. Something in between.

Not in between human and vampire—you're nothing like a vampire. Something in between Heaven and Hell, for lack of a better example. But this stage, like all stages, will end."

"And then what?" I'm afraid to ask, but feel compelled to at the same time.

"Then?" She shrugs up her shoulders. "That's up to you."

"Up to me, how?"

Her small smile is sad now. "You're doomed, just like I am. But we don't have to accept it. We're powerful, Echo. In our own way." She looks down at her fingernails, studying them. "I'm going to dreamwalk my way into the past." Her gaze once again finds mine. "To the beginning of time. Well, for witches, at least. I'm going to live in the ice castle and find the purple and… I dunno. Just soak it all in, I guess."

"I don't even know what you're talking about."

"Of course not. I haven't explained it yet."

"So why don't you get to the fucking point?" I'm angry now. I feel… not betrayed, exactly, just… *used*.

"Evil things like us have two choices in the end. We can accept our fate and join the Darkness for all eternity"—she pans a hand at the cave around us, indicating Josep, I guess—"or we can leave it behind and travel."

"Oh." Things are starting to make sense. "The way Josep travels? In the earth?"

"No. That's a purely vampire thing. But our way is just as good. We travel in the purple, and sometimes the gold too. In the mist, Echo. It's…" She hesitates. "Well, it's not real. You need to understand that. But it will get you out of the infinite eternity of Darkness. Not your soul, of course—that's doomed—but you can save your consciousness. What's left of it, anyway."

I think about all these words. Everything she has just told

me. Boyd, my death, the time, the halfbreeds. And I come to the conclusion that I am… fucked.

"No, Echo, you're not fucked. I just told you there's a way out."

"Way out *how*? You didn't tell me anything useful. I don't even know what the purple mist is."

"It's Paul's magic."

"So? What's that got to do with me? Obviously, Paul hasn't shared this magic with me because this is the first I've heard of it."

"He never shared it with me, either." And then she laughs. "Power, Echo, is something you steal. If you want the magic of the purple, you need to *steal it*."

I point to myself. "You want me to steal from Paul?"

"I don't care what you do. I'm just here to give you your options. Stay in the cave with Josep, your own personal incarnation of evil and everything that entails. Or find a way to harness the magic you have access to so while your soul rots in the Darkness of Josep's infinite emptiness, your consciousness can create whatever life you want."

The dream world. Josep already offered it to me and I said no. To be loved is a good thing. Even if it's a demon's love. I've never been loved, not once in my life, so I'm attracted to what Josep has to offer.

But he's not human. Never has been human. He doesn't have *feelings*. I think he wants to be loved, but he can't comprehend the actual concept. And if I stay with him, I will be part of this misunderstanding. I will have his demon baby, whatever that means, and we will be a family.

But is this what a family looks like?

And now I know why I've been thinking about my parents.

Josep is a pattern.

Josep is a trap.

And if I stay here with him, I'll be teenage me, stuck in that house, hiding in that bedroom, taking pills I don't understand to escape my reality while my parents manifest their roles as enemies, forced to play a game together that no one wins.

"How do I steal this magic?"

Lucia's grin is wild and wide. "I thought you'd never ask. How much do you know about mirrors?" And then she takes my hand and leads me over to the pool of lavender water.

I missed it?

The pink-haired girl stares back at me. I remember her from that night Paul first brought me to his compound. She was his… acolyte, or something. They had some kind of relationship, I do know that. Or least an understanding. None of the other people from the compound were there, just her.

So whoever she is, she is *someone*.

This feeling about her place in my world is confirmed when she smiles at me. She can see me.

She's not looking into a mirror—at least, not an upright one—because she appears to be kneeling down, gazing into something.

A pool of water, I realize. "Who are you?"

Her smile does not break. "I'm Echo. And you're Syrsee."

"You were there when Paul took me up to that room so they could all feed on me."

"Well…" She shrugs and has the decency to feel a little bad about this, because she turns her head for a moment, unable to meet my gaze. "I was present in the general vicinity." She looks back at me again, expression more stoic now that she has been called out. "But I wasn't in the room and I had no idea what was happening."

"Do you know what's happening now?"

She nods, but it comes with a frown. "He used me, you know."

"Who? Paul?"

"No. Well, maybe him too. But I'm talking about Josep."

"Josep." I sigh. "I don't even know him. But he fed on me. He was there when the Darkness raped me."

"Well, that makes sense because he *is* the Darkness, Syrsee. He's pure evil and he's infected us all."

"What are you talking about?"

"He's inside you right now. The baby inside you is the Darkness. You're going to give birth to a thousand years of evil."

I scoff. "Well, thanks for the encouragement."

"But you don't have to, ya know. It's a choice."

"I don't think that would work. If only it were as easy as a trip to a clinic."

"That's not what I'm talking about. The baby is… whatever." She waves a hand in the air. "It's here. You can't get *rid* of it."

"No, I didn't figure I could."

"But you don't have to *birth* it."

There's an irrational flare of hope inside me because that was one of the things I had decided. This baby cannot be born. But I am cautious enough to reign that hope in and not put it on display. So I squint my eyes at her to show her I'm suspicious. "What? What are you talking about?"

She hesitates for a moment. Kind of turns her head like she's listening for something.

I get nervous and start looking through the gold mist all around me. "Do you hear something? Is someone coming?"

She turns back to me, shaking her head. "No. I was just thinking about stasis. That's what it's called when you don't birth the baby. You suspend it. Like when people freeze their heads, or whatever, after they die? You keep it inside you forever and never let it out."

This idea is so repulsive to me, I have to force down a gag. "*What?*"

"Stasis, Syrsee. We need to get you into stasis. That way, we can fight Josep and there will be no reign of evil."

I take a step back, letting the mist come between this girl and me. "Who the hell are you?" Because something is wrong with her, I can feel it. "*Where* are you? How are you even talking to me? Why are you here?"

Again, she looks to the side, listening. And this is when I figure out what she's doing. Someone is talking to her, telling her what to say.

I back off even further.

"Syrsee! Wait! You need to listen to me!"

But I shake my head and retreat another step. The mist is thick now, and a few moments later, she disappears.

What the fuck was that?

Stasis? Keep this baby inside me forever? I fight the gag reflex again, forcing myself to calm down.

The dreamwalk to the Guild—if that's what it was—was enough for me to forget about the demon cooking up inside me. I was distracted. I didn't look pregnant, didn't feel pregnant, and all those Guild tests came back fine.

Which, I realize now, was just part of the illusion. But the illusion worked. That's the important part here.

It has now officially worn off.

I am pregnant with some kind of demon.

But there's more to it than that. Ryet is a demon. A full-fledged—literally *fledged*—demon. With wings, and blue-black skin, and claws, and fangs, and blood lust and all of it.

But this is something *else*.

"Paul!" I scream this into the mist. I need to find him. Not only so I can feed him, but I want answers and he's the only one who has them. *"Paul!"*

I start running through the mist, passing mirror after mirror after mirror. Dozens of them. Hundreds of them. There is no limit to the number of mirrors in this place and every time I look into one, I see the pink-haired girl.

She sees me too, because she's yelling things. "Stop! I have a plan! I can help you! We can help each other!" It goes on and on like that as I run.

Clearly, there is no escape from this place. Not while I'm here.

I stop, close my eyes, forcing them shut as the girl screams at me from the nearest mirror.

It's a dream, Syrsee. All you have to do is wake up. Wake up! Wake up!

But when I open my eyes, nothing has changed. So I keep running.

"Syrsee!" the pink-haired girl yells. "Please! Listen! We don't have a lot of time. I'm in Josep's cave. He sacrificed me to the Darkness under the compound. Then he fed me, filled my body up with his blood, and made the halfbreeds drink me until they all died. They ripped me to pieces, Syrsee."

I stop, close my eyes again, and look at my feet. *This is not real. This is not real. This is not real.*

But it is. So I open them back up and just let her talk.

"I was nothing but tattered skin and broken bones, Syrsee. Then he took me back down here to the cave, put me in this water"—she points at her mirror, which really is some kind of spring—"and brought me back as something..." She shakes her head. "Well, much worse off than you, that's for sure. Because I'm not magical, Syrsee. And if I want to win, I need magic."

I repeat all these words over in my head, trying to force it all to make sense. "You want *my* magic?"

She nods. "It comes from Paul, and he gave it to you, and I *need* it. But we can trade. I have something to offer."

"What do you have to offer? To put me into a perpetual state of pregnancy? Keep the evil inside me for all eternity?"

"Isn't that better than letting it out?"

"Well…" I scoff. "From this girl's POV, *no*. Not really."

She laughs here. A tiny chuckle, but it helps. Because I let out a breath and so does she. "Trust me. I get it. I was given to the Darkness and torn to pieces. But I'm still here." She points to the ground.

"Are you in the mist too?"

"No. I told you. I don't have magic, Syrsee. I'm a wraith." She looks to the side again. "Shut up, Lucia. You're making things worse."

"Lucia!"

"She's here," Echo says. "She's telling me what to do. She doesn't want me to tell you that because she thinks you won't believe me if you know it's coming from her. But please," Echo begs with praying hands, "please give me a chance to tell you what's happening and what we can do about it. Because Ryet is caught up in it too, ya know. He's going to *be* the Darkness."

"You just said earlier that Josep is the Darkness."

"He is, for now. But why do you think they made Ryet?"

"So Paul could rule the world like a king?"

This throws Echo for a moment, but obviously, Lucia is filling her in because she comes back with an answer. "Paul is the enemy of the Darkness. He was made for that purpose only." She hesitates, looking to the side again. At Lucia, I guess. Her tone changes. *"That's* his *purpose?* How?" There's a pause here, where Lucia must be talking. "No. I want to know, Lucia Who the hell is he? What the hell is going on?"

"Yeah," I say. "I want to know too. Tell us, Lucia. Or I won't even listen to your stupid plan."

Echo's head juts back as if in surprise. "No fucking way!" Then she laughs as she looks at me. "You're not gonna believe this."

And when she tells me, she's right.

I don't.

"Listen," I tell her, "I need to go."

"Go? Go where?"

"I… I made a promise and I need to at least try to see it through. But I'll be back."

Obviously, Lucia is objecting offscreen, for lack of a better word, because Echo has turned her head to the side and is listening. When she looks back at me, her words are more urgent. "There's no time, Syrsee. They're here. And if we don't get a handle on this magic—"

"We?" I ask, suddenly angry. Because I don't even know this girl. She has no right to ask me for a favor, let alone try and guilt me into doing her one. "It's not about 'we,' Echo. This is my magic and what I choose to use it on, or how I choose to use it, is none of your fucking business. *I'll be back.*"

Then I turn away from all the mirrors, close my eyes, take in the mist all around me, feel the purple and the gold, and *press* into it.

I know it worked this time because when I open my eyes, the gold is so bright, I have to shield my eyes for a few moments.

"Syrsee?" Paul says. His voice is smooth and comforting, how I know it best.

"Paul!" I say his name with excitement, pushing my hand farther and farther away from my face until I can see him backlit against the... sun? I think? "I found you! I'm so sorry it took me so long, the mirrors were—"

"It's over, Syrsee. It doesn't matter anymore. It's... just... over."

And then, before I can even ask him what the fuck that means, I'm back where I was—trapped in the maze of mirrors—and no amount of shouting his name or pressing myself into the mist changes this.

I replay his words in my head, panicking.

I missed it?

"No!" I scream. "It's not over! It *can't* be over! I didn't win yet! I didn't do anything yet!"

"It's not!"

I whirl around and find Echo staring back at me from the mist. And then I look around and realize I'm not trapped in the maze.

I'm in a cave.

"Where am I?"

Lucia steps into view, smiling at me. "Welcome to Josep's lair, little witch. It's not over yet. Nothing is over yet. The battle is just beginning. But his scions are awake now and they will be here soon, so let's get to work. Where did you leave your mirror?"

For a moment I think she's talking about the maze of mirrors I just came from, so this question doesn't really make sense. "*What?*"

"The mirror Tristin brought you? The Coyrah mirror?"

"Oh." I take a breath, feeling very out of sorts. "I… think it's back at Ryet's cabin in West Virginia? I don't know, actually. I don't even know if that place is real."

"Doesn't matter," Lucia says. "Doesn't need to be real. Because you're gonna take us there in a dreamwalk."

It's blood lust

"Syrsee?" I shake her a little. "Are you hungry?" I cringe at this question. "For food, I mean." When she doesn't open her eyes, I shake her again. "Syrsee? Wake up."

No response. Not even an eye twitch.

But it's OK. She was tired. She's been through a lot—*I ate her*—but she got my blood and she's fine.

She is. I'm sure she is. But I just want to be sure. So I prod her again. "Syrsee. Syrsee, you need to wake up. Just for a moment. Just open your eyes for me and then you can go right back to sleep." I shake her a little harder this time. "*Syrsee.*" Her head lolls to the side and her long, dark hair falls over her face.

The panic comes, but I trap it inside me. I'm screaming in my own head. What did he do? What did he feed me that I fed her? *What did he do?*

But it wasn't him. It was me. *I ate her.*

Calm, Ryet. Stay calm. She woke up, she talked to you. And then Paul—

"Oh, fuck." He gave me a vial of blood. Blood I drank and then fed to her. Without even getting an explanation.

In my defense, Paul did walk out and promise to talk later.

And anyway, Paul doesn't want to kill Syrsee. Paul made her for *me*. She's mine. Whatever he gave me to feed her, it's not going to kill her.

And now my mind is spinning with all the things in this world that are worse than dying.

Being a vampire is at the top of my list at the moment.

Being a blood slave to a vampire is at the top of Syrsee's, I'm sure.

I look down at sleeping Syrsee and an ache fills my chest. An overwhelming ache that, mine or not, I've already lost her. That she will never love me. That our love never had a chance to begin with. That I will never love or be loved again.

Which isn't even true because I have Paul.

He's just… not the one I want. I don't want to spend eternity with *him*. I want Syrsee.

"Syrsee?" I say her name quietly, not expecting an answer.

Whatever I fed her, it's working now and I'll just have to wait until the process is over.

Paul won't kill her. Whatever was in that vial, it won't hurt her.

She needs this sleep. That's all. She needs to rest so her body can catch up. Hell, so her mind can catch up. So that means I have two options—stay here, waiting for her to wake up, or go looking for Paul and start asking questions.

Where did he say he was going?

He didn't.

I've got things to do, he said. *We're on a schedule.*

Which implies, at least through my reasoning, that he's here on the compound somewhere. If not, one of those scions downstairs will know where he is.

I slide Syrsee's body off of me and put her head on the pillow. Then I kiss her cheek. "I'll be back, OK? Don't go anywhere. Because I'm coming back and you're gonna be just fine."

It comes out with much more conviction than I'm feeling right now, but she doesn't stir.

Reluctantly, I turn away and leave the apartment, muttering, "I'll be right back," as I travel the hallway.

The enclosed hallway becomes open on the right side as I approach the main lobby and this is where the wall turns into a railing that leads to the stairs. I pause here, looking down at the stained floor below.

Blood and… I'm not sure. Remnants of body parts, I think.

Something really bad happened here. Something I didn't notice when I brought Syrsee in last night because we came from the pool out back.

I look around. The whole place is eerily quiet.

Where is everyone?

I stay completely still, using my vampire ears to pick up anything—any kind of sound. But there is no one in this house except for Syrsee and me. Not only can I hear the silence, I can feel it.

Now what?

I have to find Paul, but where do I start?

The dreamwalk seems like a logical place, but I don't really know how to do that. It's never been me controlling those things. It was Paul or Syrsee.

I'm sure I could do it, but the silent lodge is creeping me out and I don't like the idea of closing my eyes and turning my back on reality.

Sniffing the air, I catch Paul's scent. Tracking must be one of my new vampire superpowers because suddenly, I can smell them all—every single one of his scions. But even though the one guy told me his name was Jeff, I can't discern his scent from any of the others so it doesn't mean much to me.

Then there is an odd one. One that does not seem familiar at all, except it reminds me of Syrsee. It's not her, though. I definitely smell Syrsee and she is distinct from this scent. So I don't know what to do with that information either.

Paul's scent, though, is something I can follow.

Maybe.

I did track Syrsee using her scent when I was a scion. That was literally my job. But I have never been able to track Paul. He came and he went, usually in my dreams.

Everything about today seems about as far removed from those days last winter as they can get. I don't even feel like the same person.

I am not, in fact, the same person.

Hell, I'm not actually a person.

I'm a… I look down at myself and shake my head. I'm a demon. I look like a demon. This is the longest I've gone in this form so far and it feels pretty final. Like there's no going back now. That other guy, the one with the nice body and attractive face, he's gone.

It's not true. This is me, no matter what, but I don't have to stay in this form. Paul didn't. So one day, if I make it that far, I'll know how to control it the way he did.

But today is not that day. Today there is no illusion to cover up what I am.

Everything I've been through over the last ninety-three years has finally caught up to me. The bill always comes due.

"Enough," I say out loud, mostly to shake myself out of this creeping feeling that something is about to go terribly wrong. "You're a fucking vampire, Ryet. A *real* vampire. You've got wings, for fuck's sake."

So I let out a breath and continue my walk down the hallway, my fingertips sliding across the wooden railing as I approach the stairs.

I go down the stairs and walk over to the stain on the floor. Which is not really a stain, but leftover blood and... whatever that other stuff is. Body parts, I'm pretty sure.

But it's days old. Dried and cracking since this is the entrance to the lodge and there's a whole wall of cathedral windows allowing in sunshine.

The mess is lit up with this sunshine right now. And when I look out the window to check the sun's position, it feels like late morning.

How long has it been since the three of us fed on Syrsee? It feels like years—months, maybe. But it has to be weeks, at least, because winter was still hanging about and it doesn't feel like winter anymore.

I can't reconcile this timeline. There is no way I can put it all together because while I know that Syrsee and I really did go to my cabin in West Virginia, I don't know how many days passed while we were there and I have no fucking clue at all how many days have passed since I turned into the Darkness and got her pregnant.

I have a bad feeling about all that time between then and now. Like something was happening but I was too fucked up to realize it.

"Lied to, as well," I absently say, mainly focused on looking around.

In the dining room I find evidence of... well. I'm not really sure. I walk the length of the table, looking at all the bloodstains on the surface, then stop in front of the two golden wingback chairs at the top of the room. I didn't make these, they were purchased. Not by me, but they've been here for decades.

I've walked by them literally hundreds of times and never

taken a second look, but today they don't look like chairs in an intimate seating arrangement.

They look like thrones.

I glance over my shoulder, looking at the table. Then back at the chairs.

Even if I couldn't smell them, I would know that Paul and Josep sat here while something happened on that dining table.

Then it hits me.

They *fed*.

The scions fed while Paul and Josep watched.

And now it all makes sense.

Because I know, with one hundred percent certainty, that they fed on *me*.

No, not me.

Us.

Paul fed Syrsee and me to his scions.

Why?

But as soon as I ask myself this question, the answer is on my lips. "To turn them."

Turn them into what, though?

Not into vampires. If Paul could turn a horde of scions into vampires simply by feeding them my blood, then why wouldn't he be able to turn them by feeding them *his* blood?

No. That's not what happened here.

And now all those jars and vials in the cabin root cellar make sense. He did something to us. Something that would… what? What would it do to the scions who drank us off this table?

I don't know. But I suddenly remember that Jeff said he and the rest of them who saw me in the pool *didn't* get to feed.

So Paul didn't do it to all of them. Just some.

Why?

There's only one way to get that question answered. Find Paul.

I walk back down the length of the dining table and turn right, heading for the back of the house where the pool is. Paul is here on the property. Even if I didn't have his scent in the air, I would know this. The lodge is the final scene of whatever act of theater Paul is producing.

I step outside, the air chilly even though it's spring, and stop in front of the pool as a wave of scents hit me.

I lose Paul's for a moment because there are so many.

I'm not good at this scent tracking stuff, but this new ability is good enough for me to come to a conclusion.

There were three groups of people: The scions in the dining room who drank. The scions out here, who didn't. And...

I look around. Like take a *good* look around. Because this place has never been empty.

And... the halfbreeds.

That's the bloody mess on the floor of the lobby. Something happened there. Something that doesn't have anything to do with me.

I'm still trying to put all these pieces together when I sense a weird vibrational change.

I slowly turn my head to the left where the woods are and immediately feel adrift. Like the floor has fallen away beneath my feet. It takes me a moment to realize I have risen up in the air. My wings aren't even spread out, I just... rose up.

It's an instinct, I realize. A response to a threat. Because coming out of the woods are... they are... I don't have a word ready for what they are.

Because they are *not* scions.

They are not vampires, either.

They are… *dead*.

Every zombie movie I've ever seen flashes though my mind. And this is the same moment when they see me, because their arms reach out for me, and they begin to run as a horde.

My eyebrows go up, that's how confused I am.

What the hell do they think they're doing? Are they going to *attack* me?

I actually laugh.

But then Josep appears between the trees and some of the puzzle pieces start slipping into place.

Paul's little vials and puddings.

Splitting his scions in half.

Sending Syrsee and me to live in a dreamwalk while some of the scions drank us and some of them didn't.

This isn't the birth of the American Vampire, this is a *war*.

Josep versus Paul.

The Darkness versus… well, that's where my understanding ends and I don't have any more time to think about it because Josep is here. He is tall, and muscular, and beautiful. His skin is blue-black and as he exits the trees his wings stretch out and rise up so far on either side of his body, they block out the sun. And as this shadow falls over me, three things happen at the same time:

One, he smiles and his eyes light up with blood lust.

Two, my wings rise up as I bare my fangs and growl.

And three, the horde is here. Right below me. Reaching up with half-decomposed hands, trying to pull me out of the air. They look like they've been buried in the ground for decades, clothing tattered and dirty, faces contorted into expressions I don't even have words to describe—but the most noticeable thing is their scent.

That's not earth. It's not dirt or death, either.

It's blood lust.

I've never attached a smell to this longing to feed, but this is what it smells like.

And in their eyes is a singular look. A focus so intense, there's no way to miss it.

They are hungry for *me*.

And now I have to choose

"What was that?"

I ignore Tristin. My eyes are closed. I'm tired from feeding the scions and there are still three to go. If I open my eyes, I'll see them looking back at me with the blood lust and I'm just not in the mood.

"_Paul?_"

"What?"

"What was that noise?"

"What noise?"

"Don't you hear it? Listen."

"All I hear is the disgusting slurping of the scion latched on to my wrist."

The scion's eyes open. Well, try to. He's gone. So while he might hear the irritation in my voice, he's in no condition to care about it.

"Listen _closer_," Tristin snaps.

So I do. I tune out the scion's irritating mouth noises and let out a breath. After a few moments I do hear something. "What is that?"

Tristin is so done with me. "That's what I just asked _you_."

"Sounds like..." I listen again. "Battle?"

"Fuck. They're up. It's starting. We have to go _right now_."

I push this feeder off me, stand up, and look over at my scions—not the hungry ones, but the fed ones. Every single one of them is sleeping.

Even the one I just fed is about to go unconscious.

I point to the mass of bodies on the floor. "Do they look like they're ready for a battle of the ages? I have three conscious scions, Tristin, and they're starving." When I look over at them now, they are using every ounce of self-control they have not to attack me for my blood.

Not that they would get far. These three are no match for me.

But they're no match for Josep's army, either.

"How far away are they? How soon will they find him?" There's real panic in Tristin's voice now. But it's understandable. He's not a vampire, he's a worthless rogue. Though he does excel at logistics, which came in handy.

I listen again, trying to determine where they are. Then there is a great screech that vibrates the whole valley.

Tristin and I look at each other. "Ryet," we say at the same time.

"I thought you said you drugged him?" Tristin's panic has turned into full-blown horror.

"I did."

"Then why is he awake?"

It didn't work.

I look at my tiny, slumbering scion army. All oblivious to the chaos that is coming. None in any condition to help me.

Once again, the inhuman screaming from across the compound beckons me. "I have to go."

Tristin is shaking his head. "No, Paul. You don't. This is why you made him. He's doing his job, now you need to do yours."

In past times I might've ripped Tristin's head off for talking to me this way. For disagreeing with me. Rather, for assuming he has any idea at all about what motivates me. But that's just it. He doesn't. Because he has no idea what I'm actually doing.

"Tristin," I say, stepping forward to place a hand on his head. "You've been loyal. And I appreciate that." Even as I speak, I'm fading, slipping backwards into the purple.

Tristin's eyes go wide when he realizes I'm leaving. "Wait! No! We can *win* this, Paul! They are enough!" He points to my scions.

But he's wrong. We could win this, he's right about that. But winning was never my goal. Not even in the first days. Losing was the best I could ever hope for.

Losing everything to save *him*.

So I'm shaking my head as I sink into the dirt feet first and let the Darkness take me across the compound. The cool, damp earth is like a mist as I travel through it.

Even before I return to the world above, I can hear him screaming.

Ryet.

The scions we buried with us have returned and Ryet is in the middle of them. They are attacking from all sides—dozens of them, all trying to feed.

For a moment I'm disoriented. Some leftover insanity from the change, maybe. Or I might just be so distracted by the beauty of him, I can't think straight. My world stops and goes silent so I can just... *stare at him*.

Ryet.

His transformation is nearly complete and he is magnificent. His blue skin is so dark, it's nearly black. His fangs are glistening with saliva as he snaps at the air, an unholy scream charging the air around him with crackling bits of electricity. His eyes are blood red and lit up with fire as his wings expand and contract as he desperately tries to open them to their full span of what must surely be twenty feet or more.

I am struck dumb from his beauty, unable to move until I realize that time didn't slow down and my first true creation is fighting for his very survival.

Again, I am confused. Because the horde of scions is attacking him and it's not supposed to be this way. I poisoned Ryet's blood back in his cabin when I fed him all those jars. That's why Syrsee got so sick. That's why it's taken so long for him to change.

"Confused, Paul?"

Even above the screeching and wailing of scions and newborn vampire alike, Josep's voice booms through the air. It's midday, I think. Sunny, blue skies. But with Josep's announcement comes clouds. Dark, stormy things that look heavy enough to flood the entire Earth.

"What did you do?" My voice is low and deep and words slightly muffled because they have to get past my fangs. If I could see myself in the mirror, I'd be Ryet's twin. My skin, my eyes, my wings.

But I don't have to see myself in the mirror because I'm looking at Josep and he's in his unnatural Dark form as well. We stand on opposite sides of the massive lodge pool, glaring at each other.

Josep smiles first, his lips sticking to his formidable fangs until that smile is so big, he's grinning. "Did you really think I didn't know who you were?"

For a split second, I panic. My muscles tense up, ready for the fight I know is coming. But in the next moment that fear is gone and I relax so completely, my wings droop down at my sides. "Did you really think I didn't know who *you* were, Josep?"

I'm looking at him—my blood brother, my only friend, my one true enemy—but most of my mind is preoccupied with

Ryet's screaming as he futilely flings the scions off of him, only to have the group behind latch on. Big chunks of his skin are missing. Blood is pouring out of him in rivers because these scions are hungry for *him* and no matter how many times he snatches them up in his claws and throws them aside, they just get back up and come again.

They were made this way. To feed at any cost. One mission, one mind, one purpose.

To become more of us.

Ryet is losing and it is happening fast.

Which was always the plan, of course.

The official one, anyway.

We made him together, Josep and I. Our first-born. But we were never in agreement with what to do with him afterward.

Josep doesn't react to my taunt, just licks his lips. "Did you really think I didn't know what you were doing?"

He doesn't say he's referring to Ryet, and he could actually be talking about my mission, but I know he's not. Because I was never going to sacrifice Ryet for this lot of disposable carcasses and he knew this from the day Ryet was born. "Did you really think I haven't prepared him for your betrayal?"

Josep bellows out a laugh, guffawing at the noontime sky that looks like midnight, his eyes truly shining with amusement. But just as quickly as those red hellhound eyes widened, they narrow back down and he leans forward, his body growing taller as his true evil reveals itself in the reflection of the pool water.

Darkness.

He wasn't the favorite.

He is *it*.

He *is* evil.

The one thing cast down by the hand of God himself. An unnatural mistake that was thrown away like a piece of trash. Left here on this forsaken planet to rot, or rule, or do whatever the hell it wanted.

Because this place doesn't belong to *us*.

There is no amount of sacrifice that will change that.

Not even mine. Because Earth isn't the *home* of Darkness, it's Darkness itself. Made in its likeness. And Josep is but one teeny tiny piece of it.

"Forsaken?" Josep asks, reading my mind, I guess. He's towering over me now, still on the other side of the pool, but his body is gone and in its place is what he really is, the trickery stripped away so that nothing is left but a set of hellfire eyes and an elongated cylinder of wicked, black sand. "This realm is mine and it was never forsaken. *You* are the one who was forsaken."

Despite the constant barrage of screams bellowing out a looming assurance of defeat, I shrug up a shoulder. "And yet here I am."

He slithers now, nothing left of his body at all. He is black sand above the water, slowly moving across the pool in my direction.

It is evil, yes.

But so am I.

And even though the Darkness never blessed me, I have the blessing of something else. So I too become a cloud of sand. I too become pure evil. It was the deal I made and even though thousands of years have passed since I signed up and I *really* made the most of my time here, I never *truly* forgot.

Not *truly*.

Just… conveniently.

The only way to fight evil is with evil.

And now I have to choose.

The Darkness knows this.

One the one hand, the salvation of an entire planet.

And on the other… well. There's no way to hide which side I'm on.

I don't even bother trying.

Josep knows exactly where my loyalty lies.

Which is why he doesn't attack *me*.

He attacks Ryet.

Fantasy

Paul and I break for Ryet in the same moment. I am Darkness. I am ruler of this realm. I am king, not him.

I reach the horde just a fraction before Paul, morph back into my vampire body, and start tearing at my scions. Ryet is still conscious, still trying to fight, but he's weak. There is a lot of blood on the ground, not to mention inside the bellies of my beasts, and the few minutes that Paul wasted bantering with me will cost Ryet.

Maybe his life.

But I don't count on it. I am the geneticist who created Ryet, but Paul has been dipping his fingers into my magic the whole time. A little pudding here, a little vial of blood there.

Paul, no longer the black cloud of Darkness, crashes into me. I let go of Ryet, content to let my scions continue to feed while I end Paul's quest once and for all.

I swipe a claw across his throat. He opens up my ribcage from shoulder to groin. I twist in the air, pulling the wings in, then extending them out so I can fly. I bring Paul with me, dragging him through the air like a doll.

He spins, breaks free, and then we are facing each other.

I grin. Because no matter what, I've won. His Little Baby is dying at the fangs of the scions made, in part, by his own hand.

The irony is more than satisfying, it's nourishing.

Still, he smirks at me. Fake. Not even the Vampire Paul can pull off indifference at this point. "Smile all you want," I snarl. "It's over for Ryet." We're hovering in the air, teeth bared, claws out, bleeding like the sacrifices we are. "And I have to admit, I'm a little bit disappointed." I pause here to smile. "I overestimated you, Paul."

He lowers his head and has the nerve to check his fingernails. "How so?" But then his eyes slide upward, meeting my gaze. A sly look that in no way implies submission. It's a threat.

I've missed something. Something important. But my voice stays deep and confident. "The hedge. Against them." I nod to the scions below us. Ryet is on the ground now, dying as they feed. "The leftovers. I thought you'd wanted them to keep for yourself. Your own little army."

"Like your own Little Baby?" My face must betray my surprise because he chuckles. "Come on, Josep. How predictable. Why do you think I chose her in the first place? Why do you think she was waiting for you when you came up from the bunker?" His head is no longer bowed, his gaze is directed right at me. "Tell me, how did she turn out? To your liking?"

Paul pans his hands wide, as if he is the actual king of this earthly realm and he has just bestowed on me a gift. "You're welcome. Enjoy it while you can because she won't be keeping you company in the infinite emptiness. You're going to live in the eternal darkness alone, Josep. Because she's down there in your cave plotting against you right now. She has the power of the Coyrah. That water in your cave? How it keeps everything so cool? That nice lavender mist you've been enjoying since my heir built that place for you? Did you think… what, that I had Ryet out in your cave there for your comfort? You thought… what? That I had no idea who and what you were?" Paul laughs. *"Fantasy."*

No.

"Oh, it's true, blood brother. How many times have you looked into that water to gaze upon your fair face? Hundreds? Thousands?" He cackles now. "It's a mirror, you idiot. And who, exactly, controls the nightmare in the mirror?" There's a pause here, like I might actually answer him. But he doesn't wait. "The Coyrah controls the other side of reality. You, of all people, know this. And yet you didn't see it coming."

His smirk fills me with rage, but I control it. Because no matter what he did, Ryet is mine and the blood mother is mine as well. I *live* inside Syrsee. She is carrying *me*.

Echo was but a dream. A substitute I never needed in the first place. She is but a halfbreed revenant. Nothing but a toy.

"You're forgetting something," I say, my voice calm. "Your man down there, the one you pinned all your hopes on, invited me *inside him*. We shared the drink. And then, when it was over, he put *me* inside *her*. The little Black witch is eating her own tail as we speak. Water, mist, mirror—none of that matters now. The baby will be born and I will take Heaven just as I took Earth."

Paul winks at me and whispers, "*Fantasy.*"

We clash.

We clash like titans fighting for the sky.

Swirling clouds of Darkness one moment, twisted bodies of demons the next.

And all the while Ryet is dying.

Paul knows this. He knows he can't kill me. He knows he can't save Ryet now. He knows—

A chorus of screams makes me pause and look down. It's a mistake. And a moment later Paul attacks, biting me in the neck.

I morph out of the body of Josep and become the cloud of

Darkness. Something he can't get a hold of. Something he can't get inside of. Something he can't take unless I give.

But he's not even trying now, he's laughing. He's hovering in the air, backlit by a crack of lightning, laughing at me.

The screams. They are the wailings of something dying. And it's not coming from Ryet.

It's coming from the scions. They are stumbling away, passing out as they go. Falling face first and—

"Dead," Paul says. But he's not laughing now. "You fucked with me first, old man. You wanted more than your share."

I don't even wait for the explanation. Clearly, Paul has poisoned Ryet's blood in such a way that it kills my scions when they ingest his blood. And my only chance now is to get Ryet, if only so Paul can't save him.

I swoop down in the shape of Darkness, scoop Ryet up in my arms, and then retreat into the lodge, expecting a fight.

Morphing back into Josep, I hold Ryet in my arms like a baby, waiting for Paul's attack.

But Paul doesn't follow me.

And when I look outside, he's gone.

22 - Echo

Bad Little Baby

I'm looking down into the pool of water in Josep's cave, watching Syrsee as she thinks about what Lucia just said. None of it made any sense to me. Dreamwalk? I mean, I guess I can draw a conclusion. It's what we've been doing ever since I woke up. I'm not sure a real moment of reality has passed, that's how dreamlike this whole experience feels.

But I don't understand the technical details of this dream stuff, and Syrsee obviously does, because she's frowning. "What?" Her word comes out as a hiss.

Lucia doesn't skip a beat. "We're going to dreamwalk there, Syrsee. The mirror is—"

"The mirror," Syrsee interrupts, "is what got me into this mess in the first place." And now she's growling. "Ryet and I looked into it and it took me straight to Paul. The next thing I knew I was in a bedroom being raped by evil."

I shudder when these last few words come out of her mouth. Not for her, but for *me*. Because that's how I feel too. Since the night Paul came back on New Year's Eve, everything has changed. All of it for the worse. All my friends are gone. And I get it, they were just halfbreeds. Homeless drug addicts and worthless throwaways. But they were still my friends. We were like a family.

And then Josep poisoned my blood and fed me to them so they would die.

Lucia, unlike me, has not been deterred by Syrsee's bluntness because she chuckles. "Come on, Syrsee. You're not really blaming the mirror for your lack of knowledge on how to use it? That's ridiculous."

"Well, you know what's not ridiculous?" Syrsee retorts. "The power of that thing."

"I'll show you what to do," Lucia counters.

"Why would I trust you, Lucia? You told me to kill myself when this all started."

I gasp. "Oh, my God." Then I look up at Lucia, who is standing behind me in the cave—if she's really here at all—and meet her eyes in the pool of water. "Lucia, that's despicable. That's like… I dunno. It's just… the worst thing ever."

Lucia rolls her eyes at me. "The worst thing *ever*? Please. Look at yourselves. The two of you are living examples of worst-case scenarios. You're a dead remnant wraith and she's a…" It takes her a moment to find a word for Syrsee. "An… evil baby maker, to put it gently."

Syrsee and I both pull a face. But she's the one who asks. "To put it *gently*?"

Lucia shrugs up a shoulder. "Trust me, Syrsee, it can get far worse than this. Now are the two of you done complaining? Because the war has begun." She points upward and even though Syrsee isn't here in the cave with us, she looks up when I do. "Do you hear that? That's Paul and Josep fighting. Ryet has already been taken out of the game."

Syrsee gasps. "What?"

"Don't worry," Lucia says, putting a hand up as if to preemptively ward off an overreaction. "He's not dead. I doubt he can ever die now. But Josep has him and soon as he can get away from Paul, he's going to bring him back down here to do… something horrible, I'm sure. Milk him for magic, probably."

Again, Syrsee and I make the same face into the pool of

water, both of us grossed out by that prospect. Even though I doubt either of us know exactly what it entails, we can take a good guess.

And this, I think, is what pushes Syrsee over the edge. "Fine." She sighs. "What do I have to do?"

In the pool of water, I see Lucia let out a breath of relief. I don't know what she's up to—she could be setting us up. But things are going spectacularly badly and at this point, neither Syrsee or I really have a choice. We have to trust her.

"Bring us over," Lucia says. "Quick."

"Bring you over *how*?"

"Look at her, Echo," Lucia says. "Stare into Syrsee's eyes."

Syrsee and I look at each other, wondering what the hell good this is going to do. But the next thing I know, the mist around me begins to collect on my skin. Within moments, the fine droplets have turned into rivulets of water and the next thing I know, I'm sliding into the pool.

Not my body, but my essence. Because when I look over my shoulder, or what used to be my shoulder, I see myself kneeling down in front of the pool, staring intently in to it.

Then I'm somewhere else. In a dark place with a swirling purple and gold mist. And when I look down to see what has happened to me, I'm… well, *me* again. Echo from days gone by. Wearing a tattered Offspring t-shirt, and my black velvet bell-bottoms, and my Docs on my feet. When I glance in the mirror that Syrsee was using to see us across the mist, I have pink hair.

And even though I know it's all fake—it's my imagination, or magic, or a delusion—none of that matters because I feel like me again. For the first time in years.

Twenty-one, if Lucia is to be believed.

For the first time in two decades, I am *me*.

Syrsee looks me up and down before meeting my gaze. "Cute pants."

I beam. They were always my favorite too. "Thanks."

She nods, then looks at Lucia, who didn't get pulled through with me, but is here nonetheless. "Now what?"

Lucia looks around, taking in the space. She seems a bit awed by where we are, so she doesn't answer Syrsee immediately, but allows herself a moment. Then she tugs on her long dress, as if to put it back into place, and lets out a breath that is surely unnecessary, since she's a ghost or something. Once she's collected herself, her gaze comes up to meet Syrsee's. "Now… well… now you bring Josep into the nightmare and trap him there."

"What are you talking about?" This question is on my mind too, but Syrsee is the one who asks it out loud. "What nightmare?"

Lucia doesn't look as confident as she did on the other side of things. In fact, she seems very distracted by the space we're in. Because it's kind of like a hall of mirrors in a funhouse. Something you'd walk through in a cheap traveling carnival. But it's not all cramped and seedy. It's actually rather beautiful. The mist alone is something worth gawking at. The gold and purple swirls give off a fairy-tale atmosphere. And the mirrors are surrounded by thick, gold frames.

I walk over to one and peek in, only to see a woman with long dark hair doing something on the other side. "Who's that?" It comes out automatically as I point. But the answer to my own question hits me as soon as I'm done speaking.

Syrsee comes over, looks into the mirror, and gasps. "Holy shit. That's me?"

We both look over at Lucia, but her confidence has not reappeared. She looks a little lost.

"Lucia?" Syrsee growls. "What is going on here? What are these mirrors and what the hell is the nightmare?"

Once again, Lucia attempts to collect herself. "Sorry. It's just…" She kind of laughs here. "It's just, I've never seen it before. After hundreds of years of reading about it, and being told about it, and hoping it was real—I never actually believed it was."

I finally find my voice. "What was real?"

Lucia smiles. "The Coyrah." She points to Syrsee. "But here you are. And there you are too." She points to the mirror we're looking at. And now she's really laughing.

Syrsee lets out a long breath. "I guess I didn't believe it either. But there's no denying, that's *me* in there."

I stomp my foot, tired of being the last to know everything. "What the fuck are you two talking about!"

"Sorry," Syrsee says. "I'm some kind of ancient witch that has been split into many, many pieces. And that's how the Black blood is propagated to feed vampires." She pans a hand to the mirror, then indicates the hundreds of others all around us. "All my pieces are in these mirrors."

This is so crazy, my head is spinning.

Syrsee looks at Lucia. "OK. So now what? Why do we need that other mirror? The one Tristin gave me?"

Lucia hesitates and it's very clear she doesn't really know what comes next. But she rallies and takes a good guess. "I think these mirrors are just glimpses into what your other pieces are doing. The other mirror, the real one, the ancient one—that mirror is where the magic lives."

"Fine," Syrsee says. "But that doesn't tell me what to *do*."

Lucia frowns, then throws up her hands. "I don't know what to do. All I know is—"

But that's as far as she gets, at least from my perspective. Because suddenly I am yanked back through the water, and then next thing I know I'm in the cave and Josep the Vampire is staring down at me.

He is… angry.

Terrifying.

Evil personified.

He smiles. "You have been a bad, bad, *bad* Little Baby."

And then he attacks me.

What a trick he is

There is a scream, the likes of which I've never heard before. And in this scream comes understanding.

I have always known the vampire Paul. He's been a part of my life for as long as I can remember. But it is in this moment here, when Echo is viciously yanked out of the mist and back into her reality, that I finally *understand* who and what he really is.

A demon.

Evil incarnate.

And the funny thing is, it's not even Paul who forces this awareness.

It's Josep. Who is Paul, but worse. Because he's the one who just pulled Echo out of my mist and as Lucia and I stand in front of the mirror and watch, our mouths open in complete horror, he rips an arm right off her body.

I scream and Lucia slaps a hand over my mouth, leaning in to my ear. "Shhh."

But it's too late. The monster called Josep turns towards us, looking down into what must be a pool of water inside his lair, and he is snarling.

In one hand he holds Echo's bloody limb and in the other, he's got Ryet by his leg. Thankfully, still attached.

I put a hand over Lucia's hand over my mouth, just to make double sure I don't scream. *My Ryet.* Josep's got him and he looks dead. He's not moving, he's covered in bite marks, and the only reason I don't freak out about all this is because I don't think he can die.

Surely, though, there are things worse than death. Even I understand this.

But as I think those thoughts, Josep is in my head, laughing. It's the most sinister laugh I've ever heard. Could ever even imagine. And then he's got a hold of me somehow.

Not my body, which is somewhere else in the lodge right now, but my mind that is here in the purple and gold mist.

Then we are somewhere else. All the gold is gone and there's nothing left but the purple.

The magic of vampires.

Josep has given up all his beautiful pretenses. His long, pointed fangs are dripping blood and his eyes are dark, black, empty pits. His muscular blue-black body with fully outstretched wings looms large over me.

It's not real. He's not real. At least not here. We're dreamwalking, Syrsee. It's not real.

No matter how many times I try and convince myself of this, it doesn't work. I'm shocked still with fear. I don't do anything but stare at him, wondering how the hell I got here.

"The truth," Josep says, his voice deep and rumbly. "That's how you got here. You started asking questions. Which is a very stupid thing to do if you don't want to know the answers." He pauses here to laugh and smile. "Do you want to ask questions, Syrsee? Do you want answers?"

"I want you to leave Ryet alone," I blurt. "Let him go or else!"

He laughs again, this time louder. "Or else what?"

"Or else... I'll stop you. I'll stop everything you're doing and—"

"I don't need you!" His response cuts me off and it's so loud, it shakes the space we're in like an earthquake. "I don't need *you!*" And now he's growling at me. "I don't need Ryet either. Paul does. And so…" He lets out a breath, like he's collecting himself. Pulling back his anger. "And so, Ryet has to go."

"Go where?" But as soon as the words come out, I *know* where.

"The endless, eternal nothingness of infinite Darkness."

And then we're there.

Or, rather, we're nowhere. It's an absolute sucking away of everything. No air to breathe. No lungs to breathe it. No light, no eyes, no sound, no ears.

Just nothing.

I can't scream, I can't talk, I can't *move.*

It's like being trapped inside… evil.

That's the only way to describe it. I'm trapped inside evil.

"*No,*" Josep bellows. "You are evil, Syrsee. Just like me. Just like Paul. Just like Ryet. You. Live. *Here.* Inside the nothingness. For all eternity. And there is no way back."

A vision appears in front of me. Like a movie, but I'm inside it. And I suddenly know *everything.* All the truth I ever wanted plays out around me. It's like I read every book in the Guild library, and understood all the meanings of every word, all at once. I see the Darkness, and Josep, and Paul, and Lucia, and Ryet, and me. I see everything about all of them.

Josep spits words at me. "Oh, we're just getting started, little Black witch. Keep watching!"

Time, or whatever it is, starts moving forward and I see everything that comes next. The end of Paul. The end of Ryet. The end of me.

But not the end, of course. Not really. Just the end of us as we know it.

Because what happens next when the Darkness takes over is a thousand years of Hell on Earth. Volcanoes, earthquakes, and floods. Blizzards, and wildfires, and heatwaves. Dust bowls and sandstorms. Landslides and sinkholes. Starvation and death.

This is what's coming.

And as soon as I realize it, I understand that I am the cause.

Josep is laughing. "You," he says through this laughter. "You feed us, Syrsee. You feed evil because you are evil. Without you, little witch, my reign here on Earth would not be possible." His laughter dies and now he's growling. Snarling out his words at me. "But make no mistake, without you, evil still exists. Because this world was made evil. It belongs to *me*."

There's a bright flash now. Orange, and red, and yellow. It's like being inside a nuclear explosion. And this is when I see the truth. In this flash, everything is revealed. And it's just like he said.

I am perpetual magic. I don't control anything, I just feed the Darkness so I can make more evil. The horse and rider eating its own tail.

Eating my own magic to make more, and more, and more.

That is my only purpose.

I am not evil, I am just the source.

The flash ends and I slump to the floor of the misty place with all my mirrors. Lucia is bending over me as she screams words that I cannot hear.

No. The only thing I hear is my own voice inside my head telling me that I should've killed myself when I had the chance.

Because this is worse than death.

Maybe it wouldn't have worked, but then again… maybe it would've?

For the first time I fully understand what's at stake here.

It's not about me and Ryet. It's not even about Paul and Josep. It's about good and evil.

It's the black emptiness. The endless infinity of nothing.

I'm looking at the closest mirror as I think this and inside it is Josep's beautiful face. His perfectly symmetrical face with the strong, square jaw. His black eyes go red, then blue, then purple and they start to glow.

I thought Ryet was handsome. I thought Paul was beautiful. No. Josep is the most exquisite man I've ever seen. He's like an angel. Not made of light, though, made of Darkness itself. He speaks, and his voice is soothing now. "Would you like me to save him, Syrsee?"

Who? But I don't even bother saying it. Because I already know. And anyway, Josep tosses Echo's arm aside and reaches over to grab Ryet's leg. He holds his body up like a prize. Ryet is upside down, limp and lifeless, his wings spread out across the cave floor, just a bunch of worthless feathers.

"Do I want you to save him?" I ask, repeating his question to me.

Josep smiles. Because he already knows the answer. But just in case I'm wavering, he adds, "You are part of me. You already know this. And that emptiness I took you to? That nothingness? That is not where you will go, Syrsee. That is what you *are*."

He's right. That is the truth I was looking for. And right now, I'm very, very sorry I ever started asking questions. I would give anything to be ignorant again.

As if he's reading my mind, Josep says, "I can make that

happen." He holds Ryet up by the leg again. "I can give you ignorance, Syrsee. Give me your blood. All of it. And I, in return, will set you free. And as a bonus, I'll set him free too. You and Ryet, living out eternity together. How does that sound? Good? Would you like that? To be ignorant? To go back to that day in White River when you were standing in front of the hardware store, plotting a runaway adventure?"

"How do you know about that?"

He laughs. "I know *everything*, Syrsee. I am Darkness and this is my realm. I can give you and Ryet that dream. I can put your minds back in that moment. I can trick you into believing it's real, and the best part is, it can last forever!" He smiles, and wow. What a trick he is. So beautiful.

Magnificent promises. My grandma's words fill my head. *Be very sure about the man you give your heart to, my love. Because he will be your downfall. He will steal your soul.*

But she wasn't talking about Ryet. Or Paul.

She knew. *I* knew, because I am her. I knew that we'd get here eventually. And that I would have to make a choice.

I understand what Josep is offering. An eternal dreamwalk where all the things I could ever want are mine. Where all my desires become real.

What I don't understand is what he's getting out of it.

Because it's not my soul. If I ever had one, that's not it.

It's something else.

Suddenly, there is a fluttering in my stomach. And for a moment I think it's fear.

But then I know it's not.

And this is what Josep wants.

The baby.

The *new* Darkness.

Something real. Not a cloud of black sand, or nanoparticles, or whatever the hell this creature is, but something with a *body*.

Which, circular thinking proves, is the essence of me and him. This thing standing in front of me. I hold a piece of it. If he could take it for himself, he would, and he hasn't, so he *can't*.

It's mine.

The horse and rider.

Eating its own tail.

Power infinite.

That's what I would be trading for his magnificent promise.

I hold up a hand and then slowly raise my middle finger. "Fuck. You."

Josep swipes a clawed hand through the water, breaking the image into nothing but an endless series of ripples. And at the same time, he screeches at us. This noise is not anything I've ever heard before. It's some kind of frequency and suddenly the mirror we are looking through shatters, exploding all around us.

Lucia and I recoil backwards, hands over our faces even though we both know this isn't real and she's not even alive. It's just instinct. We end up on the ground, nearly drowning in the mist, as the glass settles around us.

Echo is gone and so is the doorway to Josep's lair.

We just sit there for a few moments, breathing hard, trying to come to terms with what just happened. But even Lucia is at a loss. Because when she looks at me, she's frightened.

I shake my head. "No. No, no, no, Lucia. You do not get to be the scared one here. You're already dead!" I point at the empty frame that used to be a mirror. "That thing has Ryet! And he just ripped Echo's arm right off her body! So, no! Fuck you! You do not get to be the scared one here! You're the one who's been calling me to this moment! You better have a fucking plan or I swear to God, I will… I will… follow you into the mist, or wherever the fuck you're going, and I will ruin your happily ever after! *Do you hear me! Tell me the fucking plan!*"

Let it shine

*"**You're OK, blood lover**. You can open your eyes now."*

But I don't believe Paul. Because I am dead, or in some fantasy dreamwalk place so I don't have to face the horror of what's actually happening to me. I'm alive, and conscious, and have been torn to pieces by scions.

And anyway, why should I believe him? All he's ever done is lie to me.

"Come on now, Ryet. It was for your own good."

"I'm an adult, Paul. Have been this entire time. You don't get to say what's good for me."

Paul's response is a sigh of relief. Because I'm talking to him. Well, not talking out loud. He's not actually here in this cave where I'm existing as a half-eaten, half-dead monster because that's how he rolls. Be somewhere safe while all the bad shit happens. Show up in some misty cloud of magic where you know none of it can touch you.

Paul scoffs. "Is that really what you think I'm doing? *Hiding?*"

"Yes. That's what I think. I think you're a fucking coward who has been using me for almost a hundred years. But the kicker is, it wasn't what I thought. It wasn't to make me in your own image. It was to use me to make *others* in your image." I open my eyes. Look straight at him. Loathe the fact that he's beautiful and hate myself for loving him.

His smile is small as he pans a hand around the empty, dreamwalk cave. There are no scions eating me here.

"It doesn't matter, Paul. Back there, it's already been done.

I've been *eaten.*" I pause to glare at him, daring him to contradict me when the next part comes out. "And it isn't the first time, is it?"

That small smile disappears. "I'm playing a very complicated game."

I nearly guffaw. "I bet you are."

"I've taken every precaution."

"No, you haven't. If you'd taken every precaution, I would not be a half-eaten, half-dead monster."

"It was necessary. You'll see. One day, I'll have a chance to explain and—"

"Fuck you. Fuck. You, Paul. There is no 'one day.' This is it. You're not here, so you don't know. They ripped chunks of flesh off my bones!"

He winces. Then takes a breath. Then tries again. "It's not permanent. You're immortal."

"You say that like it's a good thing! It's not, Paul. 'And in those days shall men seek death, and shall not find it; and shall desire to die, and death shall flee from them.' This is what you did to me! I am nothing but a punishment in Revelation! I am stuck in this nightmare for all eternity and you, the man who claims to love me, the one who claims to think of me as a son, did this to me!"

He scoffs now. "I don't think of you as a son. That's kind of… *gross*, Ryet. We're lovers."

"That's your response to what I just said?"

"You're missing the point."

"No, I'm not. I get the point. You are playing a game and I'm your chess piece."

He sighs while rubbing his hands down his face, suddenly looking very tired. Then he tries again. "The game is important.

And trust me when I say this, I don't like it any more than you do. But it was"—he shrugs—"assigned to me."

"What was assigned to you?"

"This role I'm playing. I mean, no one wants to live forever, Ryet."

I'm gritting my teeth when my words come out. "No shit. That's what I just said."

But he doesn't respond to that, just keeps going. "And the vampire? Is there a more diabolical creature in existence? They are loathsome demons. Feeding off the life force of others. It's despicable."

For a moment I'm confused because in all the years I've known Paul the vampire, he's never come across as self-loathing. He's proud. He's boastful. He's the definition of a narcissist, for fuck's sake. But it's a ploy. I know it's a ploy because everything about Paul is a lie.

"Well"—he chuckles—"you're actually correct. Everything about me *is* a lie." His face is somber now, and again, I find myself disoriented. "There's no time to explain now"—which makes me laugh—"but it'll be over soon and the good news is…" His pause is short, but noteworthy. "The good news is that we always win." He ends this proclamation with a forced smile.

I just shake my head. "This doesn't feel like winning."

But he's gone, and the purple dreamwalk fades, and I am nothing but a half-eaten, half-dead monster again.

I scream. And it's not a human one, either. It's something animal. No. Worse than that. It's something demonic. Because that's what I am. It's time to face the truth. I am a fucking *demon*.

I am the opposite of everything I wanted to be as a young man and my whole life has been nothing but one, long failure.

"Oh, come on, Ryet. You can do better than that."

I open my eyes and I'm back in a dreamwalk, only it's not purple, it's *white*. And the person talking to me isn't Paul, it's… *Jane*.

"Jane?" And for a moment I think I might cry. I stand up and just stare at her. "Am I in a delusion? Am I seeing things? You're not really here. You can't be here. You're too good, Jane."

She smiles and walks towards me. She's wearing a white, short-sleeved cotton blouse and a pleated mint-green skirt that covers her knees. Her shoes are white with no heel. And I recognize this outfit as one she wore often. At least once a week I would come home from work and find her in the kitchen cooking dinner in these same clothes. If there's a classic image of Jane in my mind, this is it.

That's how I know it's not real. She's not here. I'm delusional.

"You know that's not true, Ryet."

I scoff. "You left me. And it was a one-way trip."

"I had to. I was told to. And…" She hesitates, unable to meet my gaze for a moment, but she quickly recovers and stares right into my eyes. "And I made a deal."

"Deal?" I laugh. "A deal? No, go away. I don't want to hear about your deal. This isn't real. You're dead, Paul killed you and the kids, and *none of this is real*!" I yell this last part. "You're Paul. You're fucking with my head. You're trying to get me to do something. And—"

"Shhh," she says, putting a finger to her lips. And it's such a Jane thing to do, to shush me like she used to shush our children in church, that I actually shut up. "I made a deal, Ryet. To save the souls of our children, but not only that. It's so much bigger than that. You see, I had a vision when we first got married. *He* came to me in a dream."

"Who?" I ask, my heart thumping. But it's a dumb question. I know who.

"Paul. He was…" She shakes her head. "My God, the man is—"

"Not a man," I growl at her. "He's not a *man*, Jane. He's a fucking *vampire*."

"Of course he is. But he *was* a man. Once. And then he got the call. So when he came to me—"

"Oh, no. No. No, no, please tell me you didn't fall for his lies, Jane! *Please!*"

"They weren't lies, Ryet. It was all true. And this is all so much bigger than just us. It's about so much more than just a married couple with children. It's about… *everything*. Once he explained it all in detail, I understood and I knew what I had to do. Paul asked me if I wanted to go with them or stay with you. And it was my choice."

"Oh, my God." I close my eyes and shake my head. "No. Please, don't tell me this. I don't want to hear any more."

But Jane is not interested in what I want—has anyone ever been interested in what I want? She just keeps talking. "I chose to go with them and it was the right choice. Not just for me and the kids, but for you. Because I would've just held you back."

I open my eyes and look at her again. "Held me back?" And now I'm angry. "Your death, the kids, the burning church—these are the reasons I said yes to him, Jane! If this is true, and I don't think it is, then you're… you're a fucking bitch! You ruined my life! I said yes because you were gone! I had nothing left to lose. So hey, why not, right? Why not let this demon kiss me and feed me his blood? Why not let him change me into this despicable creature?"

"You let him do it because you knew it was your path, Ryet."

"And stop calling me Ryet! That's not my name! You know it's not my name!"

"You're not listening."

"No, I'm not."

Her smile is kind and warm, but she sighs. "It was all in the plan."

I hear the truth. I know it's all true. Because why wouldn't the one person I thought was pure and good betray me in the end? Of course she did. They all do. But I can't deal.

So I turn my back on her. "Go away. Go away and never come back."

And when I turn around, finally, someone has done what I asked.

But as the white fades back to purple, I hear something.

A song sung by children. My children.

Let it shine, let it shine, let it shine.

But as I slip back into my own hellish reality, she gets the last word. "Find a way to shine, Ryet. That's all I have left to say and that's all you have left to do. Just find a way to *shine*."

A hedged bet

Lucia just stares at me, her mouth open in shock.

She doesn't have a plan. "You have no fucking clue, do you?"

"That's not true," she says, putting up a hand. "I know things, Syrsee."

"Then start talking! Because in case you can't tell, we're done here! This is it! The endgame! What do I do?"

She looks around the mist, her eyes darting here and there like she's in a frantic panic. "The mirrors!"

"What about them?" I hiss.

"Look!" She points to one nearby and I walk over.

"There's nothing in there, Lucia." I'm growling at her now, so angry. "I can see the fucking mirrors! What am I supposed to *do* with them?"

But her blank stare back is all the answer I need. She doesn't know.

"That's great." I throw up my hands. "That's just great. This was your big plan? Bring me here to the mist and… what? Hope that we'd figure it out?"

Her shoulder comes up in a shrug. "Maybe?"

"You are such a bitch."

Lucia lets out a breath. "Just calm down."

"Calm *down*? I'm carrying some kind of new evil creature inside me with the power of eternity, or whatever, and its father, the actual essence of evil, wants it back, Lucia. Wants me to give over all my power to it, in return for an eternal dreamwalk with Ryet! I'm not calm, OK? I'm fucking scared!"

"Just shut up and let me think!" Then she turns her back and starts walking.

"Where are you going?"

"Shut up!" Then she turns and walks towards me again, only to do an about-face and walk back the other way. Pacing. She's pacing. Thinking.

I take a deep breath, trying to take her advice. I need to calm down. I need to get a hold of myself and stop this fear. No one makes good decisions in a state of fear. So… I breathe and start walking towards her as she is walking towards me.

We pace like this, on opposite ends of the mist, trying our best to be rational people, even though in this state, neither of us even qualifies as people.

I don't even know where my body is. In the lodge somewhere, I guess. But who knows? It could be anywhere. I could be stuck like this forever.

Oh, my God, this fear, it's consuming me.

I stop and look down at my feet, trying to breathe myself into a state of calm. Trying to play back all the hints I've been given over the years. Through all the conversations with Paul, and Ryet, and my grandma, and Lucia, and Tristin, and Zusi, and all my years at the Guild.

I've been given pieces. Many, many pieces of this puzzle.

All I need to do is fit them all together.

Suddenly, there's a spark in my mind. And I look up to find Lucia looking at me.

"I know what to do!" We say this at the same time.

Then we laugh and she points at me. "Go! Tell me your idea."

"I need my pieces, of course! I need to pick up all the pieces of me that are scattered around the world and get my fucking magic back!"

She nods, blinking. "Yes. Of course! I mentioned that, remember?"

She did. And it wasn't even that long ago, but we both forgot. Which, I suppose, is fine for her because she's dead. Like really dead. Headless and everything. But I'm not. "I think I'm crazy. I think whatever is happening to my body, it's fucking with my head, Lucia. Because I can't think straight."

"In your defense, you've been through a lot."

"I think it's the blood. Ryet was feeding me magic that Paul made and…" But right in the middle of the sentence, I lose my train of thought.

"Wow. OK. I didn't know that," Lucia says. "But also, I mean… not to bring up trauma or anything, you did get raped by the Darkness, darling."

I frown. "I did. I'm a wreck."

Lucia brightens. "It's fine. I'm here. I'm here to…" But she's forgetting things too! She must read this thought on my face, because she puts up a hand. "I'm here to remind you." And even though this isn't at all helpful, she beams a smile at me.

"Remind me of…?"

She holds up a finger like she's about to tick off a list. "Scattered pieces."

I wait for the second finger, but that's all she's got. "Oh, my God. We're doomed."

"No. I'm here to… tell you… that… you're supposed to… Oh!" She brightens again. Like she just remembered. "The baby!"

"What about it?"

"It can't be born."

"No shit, Einstein! Even I can figure that out."

"No." She lets out a breath. "I mean, yes. It can't be born. But you are pregnant." I make a face of 'duh.' Which prompts her to raise a hand at me. "So you just… split yourself in two."

I scoff now. "I thought the whole point of this was to gather up my scattered pieces so I can get my power back? How does splitting me into more pieces help? And anyway, I don't know how to split myself. Paul did it. Or… maybe it was Josep. All I know is that it wasn't me."

"It wasn't Paul or Josep," Lucia says. "It was magic. Your magic. Not theirs."

"Well, then they used me. Which is pretty much the same thing. It's more than I know how to do, at least."

"I'm sure that will change."

But I'm not. "I don't feel very magical, Lucia. In fact, I don't feel magical at all. The only thing I know how to do is dreamwalk and that's definitely not going to fix this. That's just gonna make it worse because as far as I can tell, the dreamwalk is just a way to escape. It's not real. It feels very real when you're there, but it's not. It's just a trap."

Lucia is quiet for a moment, but then she starts looking at the mirrors. She points at the closest one. "I think that these mirrors are your pieces. And to gather up your pieces, you only need to walk through to the other side and take yourself back."

I look around at the mirrors because this actually makes sense. At least in this crazy, fucked-up world I'm not living in, it does. "And then what?"

"Well, if you get your pieces back, you'll be powerful again. And if you're powerful again, you can split in two. One to keep the baby inside you forever, and one to just be yourself."

"Sounds like something out of a nightmare, if you ask me."

Lucia holds up a finger. "Three! The nightmare! Of course!

One. Gather up all your pieces. Two. Get your power back and split in two. Three. Imprison the baby inside you forever. The nightmare."

"Gross."

"Yeah." She nods her head and sighs. "This whole thing is gross."

"What about Josep?"

She blows out a long breath. "I don't know. We'll have to hope that Paul can take care of that part. Let's focus on what we can control. Your mirrors."

I walk over to one, staring intently into it, but I can't see anything. "How do I make it work?"

"I feel strongly that you need the Coyrah mirror. We need to get that first."

"*We?*" I ask, feeling both hopeful and doubtful at the same time. Because it would be nice to have someone with me. It would be awesome, actually. I'm so tired of feeling alone.

"If you agree to take me," Lucia says, "I'll come with you."

Now, excited as I am at this prospect of a teammate, we're talking about Lucia here. I might not actually know her, but I feel like I've got a handle on her essence. So I ask, "What do you want in return? Because I know you're not doing this out of the goodness of your heart."

She's going to object here. Get offended or something. And she even starts to do this, but then she gives up. "Fine. I do want something. When you're done with it, of course, I want the Coyrah mirror."

I actually deflate a little. Because I really thought she was gonna help me. "You're lying."

"About what? I just told the truth."

"You want my mirror."

"That's what I said, Syrsee."

"But that's *all* you want. You don't even know how any of this works, do you? You're just guessing that the Coyrah mirror works these mirrors in the mist."

She's getting ready to lie, I can tell. But she stops herself. "Fine. I don't exactly know that for sure, but I do know this— that mirror is the source of your power. Why else would the Guild have had it all these years? Why else would Tristin bring it back to you?"

"I don't know."

"Because it's yours, Syrsee. And that means it has power. It's the only power, that I can think of, at least, that might help me avoid eternal nothingness. And I get it. Why should you care about my end? You shouldn't. But…" She shrugs here. "It would be nice if you did."

This might be the most truthful thing Lucia has ever said to me.

It would be *nice*, I have to agree there. I mean, if I were in her shoes. Or my own shoes, actually. It's about being alone. Lucia, like me, has probably been an outsider her whole life and 'nice' is the perfect word to describe what she is asking for. It would be *nice* to have someone show up in my moment of greatest need and give a fuck.

To help me get past it, just because they *care*.

"Fair," I say. Letting out a long breath. "But I want to know more. How did you find out about the mirror?"

"I've been in that Coyrah dreamwalk hundreds of times. In fact, that's the only dreamwalk I've ever taken. That's why I had so much control over it. I know that place. And while I have never seen that mirror in the dreamwalk, I noticed something about that moment the original Coyrah tamed the aquis equī. She looked into the water."

I shrug. "So?"

"The water is a mirror."

This feels weak, and I'm not convinced, but then again, that girl Echo was looking into a pool of water when we found her. "A mirror is a… door?"

Lucia makes a noncommittal shrug. "I think so. This idea didn't really come to me until I saw Tristin give you the Coyrah mirror. That's when all the pieces started falling into place. So there has to be something to the mirrors. Why else would they be part of the human vampire legend?"

"Hmmm. Maybe. But it's all we have to go on, so I guess we start there. One more question though. Why the ice castle? Why would you want to go there?"

"You said it yourself. The dreamwalk is a trap. My soul was sold a long time ago. I'm using you to hide from the Darkness right now, but if Josep wins it'll come to claim me. And it will get me. Even if it doesn't win, I won't get a reprieve. The ice castle is my only option."

"Because it's the only place you can go."

She nods. "Yes. And while it *is* a trap, it's a trap I can live with. I'm OK with a delusion if it means I won't be cast into the pit of eternal emptiness. And anyway, it's not like I have a lot of choices. So… what do you say? Is it a fair trade if I come with you for support and guidance?"

She doesn't know any more than I do. All she was ever after was my power. Typical these days. But I don't say no to her request. Because she *has* been helpful. I doubt I would've even gotten this far without her, so she deserves a reward if we win. "If I don't need it, then… fine. But I'm not promising anything. I might need it, Lucia." I shrug. "I might. So that's the best I can do."

She sucks in a deep breath and slowly lets it out. "Deal."

We shake on it and then we turn back to the mirrors and just look at them for a moment.

They all look the same and this worries me. On the other side of each mirror there is a gold and purple mist, but there has to be something specific about each of them. If not, I'm screwed. Because I don't know where all my shattered pieces are. Even knowing that Paul has a small child version up in some village by White River might not be enough, so if the mirrors depend on me knowing the specifics of where I'm going, I won't be able to find even one of them.

I turn away from the mirrors and look at Lucia. "OK. Let's go get my mirror. Are you ready?"

She nods. "I'm ready. What do we do? Hold hands or something?"

I have no clue, but I nod my head and take both her hands in mine anyway, if only for moral support. "Close your eyes and… I dunno, concentrate on me, I guess. I'll do the rest."

I think.

After she closes her eyes, I close mine too. And then I concentrate, thinking about where I last saw that mirror. It was in Ryet's cabin. Ryet had just told me the truth about what I was, a vampire baby maker. And I was sick from drinking those vials on the counter. Despair. Loneliness. Regret. Contempt. Estrangement. Fear. Shame. Guilt. I was in bed and Ryet was taking care of me. I showed Ryet the mirror and then we both looked in to it. That's how we traveled to Paul and Josep.

That was the day everything turned.

Suddenly I'm somewhere else. For a moment, it's just darkness and I'm sick all over again as the horror begins to manifest right in front of me.

I'm on the bed inside the tower room of Paul's lodge. Josep and Paul are on either side of me, drinking. Ryet is hovering over me in his demon form and we are…

But that's not him. It's the Darkness. And let's just call it what it is. It's evil. And the evil is putting a baby inside me.

When this was really happening I was in a library having a witty conversation with Ryet. It was his gift to me, I guess. So I would never have a memory of what happened.

But like everything else in my life, it was nothing but a trick.

I turn my back on the scene and look down at my hand. I'm holding the mirror because Ryet and I used it to fall into the bed with Paul and Josep, and that's what I came for, so I close my eyes again and wish myself away.

When I open them Lucia is staring back at me, her face the incarnation of horror. She places a hand on my cheek. "I'm sorry. I didn't know about that."

I pull my hands out of her grip and let out a breath. "Never mind that. I have this." And I hold up the mirror. "Let's go."

I turn towards the closest mirror. I have no idea what I'm doing, but I don't ask Lucia for help. She doesn't know either and I'm just tired of everything right now. I'm tired of being used. I'm tired of being food. I'm tired of all of it.

But no one is coming to save me. If I want to find a way out of this, I'm just gonna have to do it myself. I walk right up to the mirror and hold up my Coyrah mirror so that I'm looking into a vast illusion of infinity. A mirror, inside a mirror, inside a mirror *ad infinitum*.

And then something weird happens. My eyes lock with the eyes of the first mirror image of myself and suddenly I'm somewhere else…

Ryet is on the floor of the cave where Josep lives. His wings are nothing but tattered feathers and his body is covered in bite marks.

Josep is yelling and when I look over to the right, I see him throw Echo's limp and probably lifeless body against the cave wall. He's tearing her to pieces.

Then he stops and I hold my breath.

Can he feel me?

Can he see me?

When he turns his head and those black pits for eyes lock on mine, I know he can.

He rushes towards me, mouth open, like I'm the next meal on the menu here.

But I fall backwards, out of the mirror, and land on the misty ground.

Lucia is next to me and we look at each other in horror.

"We're too late," I say. My heart filling up with sadness. "I've failed him. Ryet's dead. He has to be dead. No one could survive that."

But Lucia is shaking her head as she gets to her feet and grabs my arm, pulling me up with her. "You're wrong. He's immortal, Syrsee. He's not dead. And if you don't find your pieces and get your power he's going to live in that state for all eternity. *Now let's go!*"

She drags me back towards the mirror, and I recoil. "No, I don't want to go back there."

"Then you had better find yourself. Because we're out of time." And then she pushes me and I fall into the mirror.

I panic and frantically search for… something that will take me to a piece of myself. And, of course, I end up in the bedroom of a little girl sleeping in a crib.

Of course this would be the first piece. *Of course*. And even though I didn't have a clue two seconds ago of how I would need to take this piece back, now that I'm here, looking down at the sleeping toddler, I absolutely understand.

I need her blood.

Because that's my blood and all my power is in the blood.

"Oh, God," Lucia says. And when I look over at her, she's got her hand covering her mouth in horror. Because she knows too.

As I am thinking this, my teeth begin to ache. And when I bring a fingertip up to check them, I realize I have grown fangs.

Lucia's eyes are big now. Obviously, she didn't see this coming.

I'm the nightmare.

I knew this. But I really never expected it to get this bad.

Sensing I might back out, Lucia grabs my arm. "That's not a child, Syrsee. That's *you*. And as long as she exists, you will be weak. This is not a pep talk, this is the truth. Now do what needs to be done."

This is what it comes down to. I have to feed on the girl. And when I'm done, I will have to go back, enter another mirror, and do it again. Maybe hundreds of times.

"It's either this or let Ryet suffer, Syrsee. Think about that. Think about Ryet in that cave. That's happening right now and whatever happens going forward, it's not going to get any better. And I know what you're thinking—you're thinking that Paul will save him. But did you see Paul? Where is he? If you hope for that outcome and it doesn't work out, then what? What happens to Ryet if you back out?"

"I'm not backing out. I'm just trying to get to used to the idea that I'll be feeding on people who are not Ryet. It feels very different."

"Well, you shouldn't be feeding on anyone, Syrsee. You're not a vampire. You're not like me, either. You're *food*." I shoot her a look, but she waves it off. "The fact that you've been feeding on anyone is a huge clue that you've been prepared for this."

My eyes narrow down. "What?"

"Obviously, this is part of the plan." She points at the little girl in the crib. "You were meant to take your pieces back. Why else would you have a blood tolerance?"

"What do you mean, blood tolerance?"

"People can't drink blood, Syrsee. It makes them violently ill. And I've never heard of a Black witch drinking blood. Not unless it was during the Long Drink. And that was just a way to kill a Black witch, not make her more powerful."

She's right. The blood drinking is wrong. Not just ethically, but physically. I shouldn't be able to do it. I shouldn't have the craving.

But Ryet and I, we aren't exactly normal representatives of our species, for lack of a better word. He was craving food back at his cabin while I was craving blood.

Paul did that. Something in his blood when we did that initial feeding with Josep probably got it started, but we also ate and drank those puddings and potions.

It changed us. It made Ryet more human, I think. But it made me more like them.

It turned me into a blood drinker.

Paul set me up. He set us both up.

Understanding suddenly fills me up as this new revelation

changes my perspective for what seems like the hundredth time since I said goodbye to my grandma in that cabin. This little girl, she isn't just a part of me, she's a reservoir of power. She's a backup plan. A hedged bet. Or maybe just the winning move of a very long game I didn't even know I was playing.

It's not my game, that's another thing I realize. It's Paul's game and I am but a chess piece.

I walk over to the crib and pick the girl up. But to my surprise, I don't hold a little girl in my arms. I'm holding a copy of her. Perhaps just the *essence* of her.

Without thinking further, I lean down, sink my new teeth into her soft neck, and take my blood back, immediately recognizing the power contained within. It's a warm feeling, but also a sense of strength.

When I'm done, the little girl in the crib is dead and the one in my arms is nothing but a shrunken husk of skin. I drop the husk and as it floats to the floor, it disintegrates mid-air.

There's no coming back from this, that's perfectly clear. But I can't think about the consequences now. I have a lot of drinking ahead of me.

Lucia and I walk back through the mirror, but instead of coming back out into the gold and purple mist, we enter another space, or time, or place. I'm not sure. But there's a woman there who looks like me. Same eyes, same body, same hair.

She doesn't notice us because Lucia and I aren't actually here. She's a ghost and I'm back in the mist. I walk over to this copy of me, place a hand on her shoulder, and the same thing happens. A copy of her slips away from her body. And after I drink this copy, the witch in the room is dead and her husk has disintegrated while falling to the floor.

This time, the power is more than just warm, it's hot. And the strength is in my mind as well as my body.

We leave and enter the next room and I do it all again.

Over, and over, and over.

I take back my power until I am whole.

A petty monster

I *stumble through the door* of the building where Tristin is babysitting my scions, trying to hold in all the feelings.

"Well?" Tristin asks excitedly. "What the hell happened? Where's Ryet?"

I'm looking down at my feet, which are bare, and clawed, and muddy, but my eyes slide up to meet Tristin's. "I left him."

Tristin shoots me a confused look. "Left him…? Where?"

The exhale that precedes my answer is long. "With Josep, of course."

"Why? What was the point of leaving here if you weren't gonna save Ryet?"

"I *am* saving Ryet." But I look away now, hedging. Because the ending I've been planning for nearly two thousand years now hinges on many loose ends.

Loose ends like Syrsee. Who is not the strongest of protagonists. She's rather impressionable, actually. Which is a good quality when you're trying to coerce someone into doing horrific things that are completely against their human nature, not to mention their inhuman one. But not ideal when you're relying on them for the final, dramatic ending.

Loose ends like Josep. Who must succumb to certain desires. And while I do know he has Echo, I'm not sure where things stand at the moment. Does he want her enough to save her? Or will he sacrifice her in the end?

Loose ends like Ryet himself. Will he embrace the Darkness? Or will he fight it?

And then, of course, there is an end that was never tight in the first place.

Me.

Before I was the vampire Paul, I was no one. Just a skeptic who spent all of his early adult years whoring around and being inebriated.

But then the miracle happened and there was this moment—a single fucking moment—when I became a believer.

What a mistake that was. What a prime example of wrong time, wrong place. Because this moment of belief caught the attention of my Maker. Which led to me being a scholar, which led to me being a teacher, which led to me being a threat to the Roman Empire itself. Which is where everything really went off the rails, of course. Though you won't find any of *that* in the history books.

A picture has been painted over the last two thousand years. Of things I have done, or didn't do. Good deeds, mostly. But the records of these deeds, like almost everything in this world, are a combination of superstition, outright lies, and good storytelling, to be honest.

For sure, I did the things they say, but it was never with a committed heart.

I was forced. All of this was forced on me. I never wanted to be the Vampire Paul, let alone the harbinger of the Antichrist. Who the hell would want that job?

No one. Not even me.

And yet here I am.

I reach into my pocket, half-expecting it to be gone. But the little glass vial is still there. I pull it out and hold it up to the window, taking advantage of the fading light.

"What's that?" Tristin asks.

My smile is crooked when I look at him. "Dead Black blood."

He offers up another look of confusion. "Where did you get it?"

"I took it from the last Black witch I killed. Actually, I threw it up." I laugh here. It's a loud one too. And I'm still laughing when the rest of my words come out. "I was giving her the Long Drink and she tricked me into drinking her blood after she died. I got violently ill. Threw it all up over the course of a week." I chuckle again, thinking of that week that was only a few months ago, but feels like centuries. I tilt the vial back and forth in the dying sunlight, making it sparkle and take on a purple sheen. "I had given up on this, you know that?" Tristin stares blankly back at me. "I looked for it. For hundreds of years, I looked for the little bottle of dead Black blood that I gave Josep when made this little deal."

Tristin shrugs. "OK."

"But it's like he knew or something. He disposed of it. Or maybe just hid it well, because I never could find it. That's the only way to kill a vampire, you know. Dead Black blood." I eye Tristin now, who is very much confused. "It was the only way, really, to make this all work."

"So why did you give it away?"

"It was the only thing of value I had when it came time to talk Josep into accompanying me across the ocean. I mean, I had the lie, of course. 'We're gonna steal the Darkness, Josep. We're gonna take its power and make it ours.'" I chuckle again. "The American Vampires."

"That was a lie?"

"No, you idiot. It was the truth, of course. You can't lie to the Darkness. Not when it's inside you. And all vampires have the Darkness inside us, even me."

"I'm not following."

"Of course not. You're, what, a hundred and twenty-eight years old? You don't even have wings, Tristin. How could you know anything?"

"Ya know, for a guy who only got this far because of me, you're sure being a dick about it. It's not my fault I don't know what you're doing."

"Sorry," I say, rolling my neck until it cracks. "I do appreciate your help and I didn't mean to be so blunt." I rock the vial between my fingers again. "This is the only way to complete the final step of my mission. The fact that I had to give it away in the first place is just… well, divine irony, I suppose. A way to build character, perhaps."

"So you're gonna poison Josep with that?"

I shake my head, frowning. "No, Tristin. I'm going to poison *myself*." And then I pop the cork on the vial with my thumb and tip all the Black blood into my mouth.

"Wait!" Tristin comes over to me, trying to grab the bottle out of my hand. I let him do this, because it's too late. It's empty, save for a thick coating on the sides of the glass. "What are you doing, Paul? Why did you just drink that?"

"Because"—I smile at him now—"it's the only way."

Tristin is panicking now, probably imagining how he'll get out of this mess if I'm not around to save his ass. "The way to what?"

"To give all my Darkness to Ryet. Because, you see, when a maker dies, his protégé inherits all his power by default. And in this case, that would be Ryet. He's the real hero of this story, not me. I'm certainly not going to be stuck here on Earth acting out the role of the fucking Antichrist for the next seven years. That's ridiculous. Regardless of how many corners I've cut, my mission ends tonight and that means I have an appointment with my own Maker and I'm gonna get the last word here no matter what."

Tristin is shaking his head. "This is about… *spite?*"

I shrug. "Call it spite, call it revenge, call it petty, if you like. This is what two thousand years of character-building has turned me into. A petty monster. It is what it is."

Across the room, the scions begin to wake, moaning a little as they struggle to open their eyes and get to their feet.

I throw up my hands and grow bigger, my skin turning blue-black, my wings popping out of my back, my clothing ripping into shreds as I become the demon I was always meant to be. "Rise, scions!" I bellow.

They look up at me, still half-drunk off the blood, but struggling or not, they all get to their feet with a great expectation.

"It is time to end this now." I turn to Tristin and make a little bow. "You will stay here. You'll be safe. Thank you. I sincerely mean that, Tristin. If any of this gets into a history book, I hope they turn you into the unsung hero you are."

"But… what? Wait!"

But I'm already slipping into the floor. I'm already on the highway to Hell.

And all my scions follow me down into the earth.

You will live in the hell of my choosing.

I watch the ripples across the pool of water in my cave until the surface is calm again, but me? No. I am not calm. I am not calm at all.

Slowly I turn my head until I'm looking down on Ryet. There are hundreds of bite marks on his body. But it was a trick. His blood was poisoned and my army, small as it was, is dead now.

The anger builds inside me until I'm absolutely certain that I will explode if I don't release it somehow.

My first instinct is to get this release by torturing Ryet, but he's not in there. I know he's not in there because he's not making any noise and he should be screaming in pain.

So he's in the purple somewhere.

And if he can't feel my torture, then what good is it?

I spy a trail of blood on the cave floor and allow my gaze to follow it back to the body of Little Baby, minus one arm.

I smile, then laugh. Because she is making noises. Terrible noises. Groaning, and moaning, and sobbing. Which normally would piss me off enough to push the mute button.

But right now, it pacifies me because I need her pain. I need to hear her suffering. In fact, I need to make her suffer more.

I walk over to her, pick up the arm that's left, rip it off, and throw it across the cave. It crashes into a wall and the tattered remains fall to the floor.

Little Baby has stopped screaming, but only because she's in shock and not because she's dying. She can't die when she's already dead. Though her continued existence is something new that I don't fully understand, what I do know is that even if this incarnation of Echo could die another death, I would not let it happen. Why should she get to escape this hell while I must stay behind?

That wouldn't be fair.

I kneel down, slit my wrist, and let my blood drip into her mouth, which is open in a silent scream.

A few minutes of this and she starts coughing. The new blood has cauterized her arms and they start to make a sort of scab. Given enough time, they will grow back. But that's not going to happen.

"Little Baby," I say, leaning down into her neck so I can whisper this in her ear. "You will live in the hell of my choosing for all eternity for your betrayal." Her eyes are open and she can see me. And even though she doesn't reply or move, I know she can hear me too. "I will torture you until the end of time. And then, and only then, will I let you make it up to me."

I grab her hair, lift her head up, and then slam it down on the ground, cracking open her skull.

Given enough time, and a reprieve from my well-deserved punishments, that too will heal.

But I doubt I have that much self-control, so it will never happen.

Now I have to make a decision because Dark Baby has been corrupted. The girl called Echo was a poor choice for an incubator. She was a throwaway halfbreed. And I should've known better than to be lured with the promise of a family.

I kick her body, making it roll away. "You bitch. You lied to me! You made me love you and then you betrayed me. You don't deserve my Dark Baby."

I walk over to what's left of her body, push her with my foot until she rolls over on her back, and then swipe a claw down her torso from throat to belly.

The Darkness seeps out of her like smoke made of sand, whirling and twirling in the air, homeless and looking for a new vessel.

I open my mouth, ready to direct it back inside me, when a hand clamps around my ankle and when I look down, I see Ryet's blood-red eyes looking back at me.

He doesn't even wave

***Let it shine**, let it shine, let it shine...*

My eyes open and I realize I've got Josep by the ankle. I don't know where I am, I don't know what I'm doing, and I don't want anything to do with this fight.

You have to, Ryet. You have to fight for us until I can get there!

"Syrsee?" Suddenly, I'm in the mist again, but it's all gold now, and I am standing in between two full-length mirrors and no matter where I look, it's an illusion of infinity. Me, in a mirror, inside a mirror, inside a mirror for all eternity.

This is the definition of Darkness.

You have to fight, Ryet. Because I'm busy! I'll be there soon, but I can't come until I finish!

"Syrsee! Where are you?"

But the mist fades and then I'm back in the cave, staring up at the Darkness himself.

He snarls at me, raising one arm up above his head like he's about to attack. His claws are long and sharp and I am certain, without a doubt, that if he touches me, it's over.

I probably won't die, but there are worse things than death.

He swipes and I roll, getting to my feet like I'm committed to this fight. Like I'm going to do what Syrsee asked of me because I know I'll be saved in the end.

Josep missed me, but he's in far, far better shape than I am and when he raises his hand to try again, I force myself to stay still. If I move, I will collapse so I wait for it.

His attack is thwarted by a rumbling under the ground and

we both go tilting sideways as the rock floor of the cave splits open and Paul comes up from the stony earth, his eyes red, his skin blue-black, and his wings slowly opening like he's a god.

I stare at him, stunned, trying to make sense of what is happening. But I'm slow, and dizzy, and confused.

But Josep isn't. Barely a fraction of a second passes before he is flying at Paul in a full-on attack.

The two gods of Darkness clash in mid-air. Levitating, not flying, because while this cave is big, it's not big enough to contain the full wingspan of two demons.

They part, breathing heavy, and circle each other. Josep tips his head up, looking at the ceiling, and this is when I notice that there's a black cloud of sorts flying around above him. It looks like sand, not smoke, and it's long like a snake. It twirls in the air, flipping and turning. And for a moment I think that Paul brought this with him, because it looks like it's attacking Josep.

But it's not.

It's not attacking Paul, either, it's just... I don't know. I don't know what it's doing.

Paul swipes a claw across Josep's face and Josep responds by slamming Paul against the side of the cave so hard, a sickening gasp comes roaring out from his chest. I'm so stunned by the realization that Paul is *losing*, I can't move.

I can't even think.

This is when the earth rumbles again, but this time scions come up from the abyss Paul created. Scions I recognize as the ones who wanted me to feed them the last time we met.

They rush Josep, but he swats them away like they're flies.

They get up, rush him again, and Josep starts tearing off their limbs.

It's a distraction, I realize. A way for Paul to recover.

But when I look over there, he's not moving. He's still slumped against the wall, retching, blood seeping out of his mouth. He catches the blood in his open palms, greedily drinking it back down.

"What are you doing?" I yell. "Get up! *Get up!*"

Paul looks me straight in the eyes and laughs. "It's up to you now, Ryet. I poured it all into you."

"Me? I can't do anything! Get up! Get the fuck up!"

Suddenly Josep has me by the neck. He squeezes it so hard, I immediately start choking. Using every last bit of energy, I look around, hoping that Paul has recovered.

But he's still slumped on the ground, his head lolling back against the cave wall, smiling.

I crash against some rocks on the other side of the cave, and Josep stares down at me for a moment, trying to see if I'm still a threat. When I don't try and get up, he smiles at me. But nothing like the one I just saw on Paul.

It's evil.

"I am the Darkness," he says. "And you are *my* son now." He bares his teeth at me. "I'm going to take you into the endless infinity and torture you until the end of time. You will watch as I drink your blood lover dry and I will keep him forever, just like I will keep you, locked up in eternal emptiness. And while the two of you are suffering in the pits of Hell of my making, I will be drinking your little Black witch until she is old and smells of death and decay."

Then he turns and flies across the cave to Paul. He grabs him by the hair, lifts him up, and then sinks his teeth into his neck and drinks.

Paul's head lolls to the side, but his eyes are open and he's staring up at the ceiling, laughing.

I look up and see that sand serpent again, twisting and winding above Josep's head.

It's not trying to attack him, I realize. It's… part of him.

It's the Darkness. Not a little bit of Darkness, either, like what we get out of the blood, but an actual incarnation of it.

Time stops for me here. Because I am *thinking*. I'm thinking about that snake thing, and Josep, and how he's the Darkness.

But if that thing above his head is the *actual* Darkness, the incarnation of Darkness, then… it's not inside Josep right now.

It's trying to get back in.

Paul is making terrible noises across the cave, but I tune him out and slowly get to my feet.

It's trying to get back in.

I limp my way across the cave, past moaning and dying scions who have been scattered across the ground, and stand right behind Josep, looking up at the monster.

All you have to do is shine, Ryet.

Find your shine.

I open my mouth as wide as it can go, just like Josep did right before Paul attacked him, and this thing—this evil, horrible, revolting thing—accepts my invitation and the next thing I know, it's sliding down my throat.

I explode.

I explode with bright, red light and it seeps out of the hundreds of wounds on my body like blood-colored sunshine exploding through clouds.

This red light illuminates the whole cave and I levitate and begin to spin in mid-air as the shine pours out of my body.

Let it shine, let it shine, let it shine.

Everything really does slow down now because all kinds of things are happening at once.

Josep lets go of Paul, Paul slumps to the ground, laughing, Syrsee appears as a purple mist, her eyes wide and mouth open, aghast. And then…Josep begins to retch.

He bends over, looking at me, as I levitate above him.

"No!" he bellows, his deep voice making the whole cave rumble. And then he and I both look at Paul at the same time. Him because this had to have been planned, and that plan came from the vampire Paul.

And me because I know without even checking that Paul is dead.

Really, *really* dead.

His eyes are black pits, but they are utterly and completely empty.

Dead? But how? How could he be dead? Ten seconds ago Josep was bragging that he was going to sentence us both to empty darkness.

How could he be *dead*?

Josep falls to his knees, then face first on the ground.

And it hits me.

There is only one way to kill a vampire.

Josep didn't kill Paul.

Paul killed himself and he took Josep with him on the way out.

Everything stops now.

I crash to the ground, all the light gone, and in its place is nothing but Darkness.

"Oh, shit, Ryet! Oh, fucking shit! What did you do?" And that's the last thing I hear—Syrsee freaking out before everything fades to purple.

* * *

To no one's surprise I find myself in a wintery forest. Paul is sitting on a log in the middle of a clearing, wearing fur, and holding a baby.

"Nice coat," I say.

He smiles at me. "Yeah. Wolf pelts, not some stupid sheep."

I don't even know what to say to that. "OK."

"Well." He sighs. "This is it."

"This is… what?"

"The end."

I sigh too, then walk over and take a seat next to him. I look down at the baby, then recoil. "Holy fuck. Is that what I looked like when I was born?"

Paul laughs. "No. Of course not. I don't make ugly things."

"Then what are you doin' with it? Because that's…" I shake my head. "Gross."

"Come on now, Ryet. It's a face only a mother could love." He looks at me. "Or a father."

I grimace. "Oh, fuck. *That's* my baby?"

"Well, he's part mine too. I was there."

"And Josep."

"Yeah." Paul exhales. Like this was an unavoidable necessity. "But he's mostly yours. He's inside Syrsee right now. He can't be born, you know that, right?"

I nod, pressing my lips together. "Yeah, well, I don't know what to tell you. I'm not gonna kill Syrsee, no matter how evil that thing is."

"No, of course not. She already has a plan for it. That's not why I'm here. It's you we need to talk about."

"Me? You're the one who died. Hey, hold on. If you're here in the mist, then you're not dead!"

"Oh, no. I'm dead. I'm not here and neither are you. You've been taken over, Ryet. You don't actually exist anymore."

"Fun."

"Don't worry. Syrsee's resourceful and has a lot of magic at the moment. She'll come up with something. So that's why I'm here. You're going to live, Ryet. And, unfortunately, you're…"

I bow my head, so tired. "I'm what?"

"Well, I was going to say the Antichrist, but it's such a specific title. You're…"

I look up again. "Evil?"

"Yes." He points at me. "That's a given. But it's more than that. You're in *charge*, Ryet. The Earth is your dominion now."

"What's that mean?"

"You… rule the whole planet. Which is why I'm here."

"Hold on, back up."

"I don't have time to back up. Syrsee is very busy trying to work her new magic on you, and in a few moments, she'll succeed and I'll be gone forever."

"Wait, what? No. I can find you in the dreamwalk."

"I'm afraid not. You see, in order to kill Josep, I drank the Black blood. I wanted him to drink me afterward so that he would die. Of course, that's not enough because the Darkness was inside him. But that was rectified with Echo. Poor girl. But anyway, it all worked out. He gave the Darkness to her to make his own Dark Baby and then he cut it out of her inside that cave—"

"Oh, that was the black sand thing?"

Paul nods.

"Fuck. I ate it."

"Yes. You did." Then he smiles. "The part I need to explain is… well." He looks sad for a moment. "Well, obviously, I could've drunk the Black blood at any point in time and ended my existence here on Earth. But I didn't because I was on a mission. And if I gave up before I succeeded, then I would be damned to Hell."

"How are you *not* damned to Hell? I mean, come on. If anyone deserves Hell, it's you."

"True. But it's not my vibe, Ryet. You understand, right?"

"Uhhh, no. I have no clue what you're talking about."

"See…" He falters here, trying to find the right words. "That black sand thing you ate, it's the Darkness. And so, now, well, *you're* the Darkness."

I point to myself.

Paul nods. "Yep. You. And, honestly, it's not a great gig. I mean, I do enjoy the title. I like that. Ruler of the whole Earth is so much better than King of the American Vampires. And I also enjoy the part where I might've saved humanity—question mark? But the waiting, Ryet. It's been so *boring*. I knew once World War II was over that it was coming soon. Which is why I made you. I would've failed my mission, utterly, if I had let Josep become the Antichrist. Luckily, I figured out the whole feeder thing and you worked out. And even though it has taken forever to arrive here on the edge of Tribulation, here we are, nonetheless. As exciting as that all is, it's just not enough to give away my shot, ya know? Which is why I didn't want the job."

"Wait a minute. Hold on. Are you telling me this was *your* mission?" I point to myself. "You are supposed to be the Darkness and rule the world?"

"That's exactly what I'm saying."

"And instead of being… oh, I dunno, a fucking *man* about it, you turned me into the Darkness so you could… what? *Escape*?"

"That brain of yours always did catch on eventually."

"I cannot fucking believe you. Ya know what? I actually can. This is such a Paul the Vampire thing to do, I don't even know what to say about it. You sacrificed me to save yourself."

"In my defense, I have an appointment with my Maker. I have questions, OK? And that fucker's gonna answer them. Otherwise, I'd stay and we could rule together. You and I would be in love, and Syrsee would feed us, and it would be like… the best time ever. But I need my answers, Ryet. Because I didn't sign up for this any more than you did."

"You used me. Just when I was starting to like you."

"I did leave you a gift though."

I scoff. "What gift?"

"Syrsee, of course." He smiles. And, as always, I am enamored by his beauty. "I made her for you so you could be with the one you really love."

"That's not even true. You literally just said you made her so I would live and take your place as the harbinger of evil."

"It's the same thing. She's the Whore of Babylon so the two of you can be immortal together. It's practically fate. And don't worry too much about the whole Antichrist thing, it's just a title, Ryet. You two kids will make it work, I'm sure of it."

I'm slack-jawed as I run all those words through my head over and over again. Finally, I say, "I'm actually the Antichrist? You turned me into the Antichrist so you can have a Q&A with God?"

Paul grins here, like he couldn't be happier about how this turned out. "The good news is, you can make it yours. Rule any way you want. Of course, the prophecy is now in motion, there's the nasty Tribulations and all that other shit, and you lose in the end. Don't forget that part. But you're resourceful. It's gonna be amazing. And the even better news is, it ends. It's only seven years. We'll see each other again. Probably. My chances of getting past those pearly gates are slim to none, but if I *do* get in, Ryet, I will most definitely put in a good word for you."

Then he leans into my space and for a moment, I think he's gonna kiss me or something. But he doesn't. He hands off the monster baby. I take it out of instinct, but I'm instantly sorry. "What the hell am I supposed to do with this thing?"

Paul stands up and adjusts his wolf-pelt coat. "Syrsee has worked it out. See her for details."

And then… he just… fades away.

He doesn't even wave.

EPILOGUE – ECHO

My eyes are not even open yet when I hear them fighting. But instead of cringing and putting the pillow over my head, I smile.

It's like… music, this fight.

It's birdsong.

It's a church choir on Sunday mornings.

It's beautiful and I'm not gonna waste a single fuckin' minute of it. So I swing my legs out of bed and go into my bathroom.

I'm expecting to see someone different looking back at me in the mirror. After all, I'm not the same girl who left this house twenty-one years ago to join a vampire cult up in the Rocky Mountains.

But to my surprise, I am exactly the same. Short pink bob, bright blue eyes, and a face that has always been a little too round. This puts me squarely in the 'cute' department, especially since I'm only five foot two.

I'm wearing underwear and a black Offspring t-shirt promoting their newest album, but nothing else.

Inside the medicine cabinet I find the clippers, then I shave my head as best I can by looking in the mirror and feeling around with my hand. It's probably a mess, but it doesn't matter. The only thing that matters is that the pink-haired girl no longer exists.

Once that's done, I take the t-shirt off. The last thing I need is to be reminded of what I am thanks to the name of this band. Besides, I'm so over black.

I toss the t-shirt into the trash and walk over to my closet, picking through what I have, looking for something white. There is one dress that fits this description and it's slutty, has a shark-tooth hem, and is made of fake silk and cheap lace. I wear it to concerts sometimes. But it's all I have, so I put it on.

I have two pairs of white shoes. Pumps and Chucks.

I go with the Chucks.

Then I take one last look around my room, and leave.

Downstairs my parents are still fighting. They are so invested in this fight, they don't even see me, so I just slip out the door and turn right, heading towards one of the main roads that runs through Spokane.

At first, there's no one out here but me and it's kinda creepy. But then I realize that if I want this world to be real, then I have to create the people in it. So I do.

Cars appear. Just a few, at first. But as I continue walking there are more.

At the end of the next block there is a purple mist waiting for me. This is the end of my fiction, I guess.

But only until I think up something to put in its place.

So I do that, and the street continues.

For now, I just populate my personal version of the infinite emptiness with what I remember being here.

A gas station. A dry cleaner's. A strip mall.

One day, when I'm comfortable with my new existence, I'll try making brand-new worlds. Maybe even brand-new species of people. Fun animals and cool places.

Because even though I'm not magical, Josep gave me… something. I'm not sure what it is, but that power, in combination with the knowledge of how vampires travel, was enough to get this world started.

It took me a lot of tries before I had the house right. Took hundreds of mistakes before I had a realistic representation of my worthless parents. My bedroom was a little easier, but that's because it was all mine.

It was worth the effort though. Because this is it for me. This is my eternity and I'm going to make the most of it.

I'm getting a do-over.

Yes, I know it's fake.

Yes, I know where I really am.

Yes, I'm damned and there's no way to change that.

But it's not going to feel new forever.

One day I'll wake up and a new person will enter my life. Someone I made, obviously, but forgot about. So this new person will be my beginning and after that I'll start forgetting about other things too.

And once you forget you're not real, well… then you *are* real.

If you have no memory of your real self, it doesn't exist.

The sun breaks through a long bank of thick clouds, shining rays of light down on me.

And it feels like a blessing.

I am blessed.

EPILOGUE – SYRSEE

"Are you ready?" Ryet and I are standing in the mist between worlds, ready to do what needs to be done so we can carve out some semblance of normalcy for the next seven years. Not that that's something I'm excited about. It sounds like a pretty shit deal, if you ask me. But it could be worse. It can always get worse, so I am thankful for every extra minute Ryet and I get together.

Is it paradise? No. From what I've read, it's literally going to turn into Hell on Earth. But that hasn't started yet and I have decided that I will cherish every moment.

A few things have changed since I picked up all my pieces. The first is the color of the mist, which is still purple, but all the gold has turned scarlet, the color of blood. Which makes sense, I guess. The second is Ryet.

"I'm ready," he says. He's been stuck in his true vampire form since everything happened down in Josep's cave and he looks like Darkness. Which also makes sense, because he is.

He's more than that, though. He's... well, the actual incarnation of evil.

Except he's not. He's really not. I know this man and he's good. He was tricked. Paul said it was fate, but fate doesn't need to trick people. That's what monsters do.

So we've decided that we are in charge of our fates and we can do something about this. That's why we're here in the mist.

After picking up all my pieces, I immediately split myself in two and gave that other Syrsee the demon baby. I'm so grossed out by that whole thing. But I've felt a hundred times better since leaving it with my other half inside the dreamwalk, and

I'm sure Ryet will be back to his old self once we get rid of his Darkness too.

"OK." I blow out a breath.

I hold up the Coyrah mirror. This, I've learned, is the secret to my power. It's how I made myself whole and it's the only way I can split myself in half. Or, in this case, split Ryet. How the Obscurati did it, I have no idea. Blood magic, I'm sure. Which probably involves summoning the Darkness, but they can't do that anymore because Ryet and I control it.

Every bit of it, from what we know.

I have half inside the baby, which is now tucked away in a scarlet dreamwalk, and Ryet has half inside himself.

But not for long.

"Look into the mirror, Ryet. Stare at yourself." He does this, not even blinking. "Now close your eyes and imagine the good part of you. The light, the part that holds your soul."

Ryet, Lucia, and I had a long discussion about the wording of our spell. Which is what this is, which makes it evil in and of itself and I hate that, but why split hairs now? I'm a witch, that's all there is to it.

We don't think we have souls, but we *feel* like we do. And we're gonna hold on to that feeling. That's how I split myself in half and I guess I can thank Paul for that idea because that's the lie he told us so we would go into the Guild dreamwalk while those scions fed on us.

And it worked. At least I believe it did. And belief is a big part of magic, so Lucia has told me. I am the keeper of my soul. That other me, the one I sent into the endless scarlet mist with the baby, she's just a husk with the evil inside her.

I am good, and pure, and filled with light.

I got that part from Ryet because he filled up with light

when he ate the Darkness, which has to mean something, we're just not sure what.

"Did you find it?"

Ryet nods. "Yeah."

"OK. Now find the ugly, evil, dark part and push it away."

I look into the mirror now, and I watch as the reflection of Ryet steps backwards. "Keep sending it," I say. "Make it keep going." And then I continue watching as that other Ryet steps back, and back, and back until it's hidden in the blood-colored magic.

Ryet, the one on this side of the mirror, lets out a breath. "That's it?"

I shrug. "I guess."

"How do we know it won't come back?"

I extend the mirror out towards Lucia, who is waiting off to my right. "Because it's trapped in there now. On the other side of things. And Lucia is gonna take this mirror with her when she leaves, so…" I look at Lucia. "It's your problem now."

I say it kind of jokingly, but she's looking at me with a very serious expression. "Thank you."

"For giving you all the evil in existence? You're most welcome."

"I'll take good care of it. I promise. And if you ever need it back—"

I put up a hand. "I won't. Trust me. I'm here for the duration and I won't be splitting myself apart ever again." I slip my arms around Ryet's waist and lean up onto my tiptoes. "Whatever happens now, it's us against them." Then I kiss him. We linger in this kiss for a little bit, but my work is not done, so I pull back first. "I'll see you in bed in a few minutes."

"You're sure you don't want me to stay?"

I shake my head. "No. This is just a place for Lucia and me."

"OK. See you at home." He still looks like demon Ryet, but we're in the mist so it kinda makes sense.

I watch as he fades away, and then Lucia and I are alone. I turn to her and smile. "Your turn now. Are you ready?"

She is. I know she is, but she looks uncharacteristically nervous. And I completely understand how she feels. It's that second-guessing you get when you make a really big, life-changing decision and you're just about to go through with it when you start doubting yourself.

I've felt this way more times than I can count.

"It's the right move," I say, smiling at her.

Lucia doesn't look convinced. "But I'm not you."

"Nope. But I still think they'll love you. I mean, look at it this way, Lucia. You've got all the dirt. All the tea, girl. You've got all the latest news. And they know nothing. They've been living in their little dreamwalk ice castle for thousands of years. They're starving for outside information. They have to be. How could they not?"

Lucia shrugs up a shoulder. "They've evolved past petty gossip and the corrupt human consciousness?"

I scoff. "They wish." Which makes her smile. "They're dying for news. And you were *there*. First-person account. And how could they not want news of me? I mean, I get it. I've been gone for thousands of years. Maybe they don't remember how they got there, but if I were them, I'd keep that story alive. You're the epilogue they've been waiting for. They'll probably worship you before all the excitement's over."

Lucia spits out a laugh. "Great. That's all I need. Pseudo-god status."

But she smiles and I know that all my encouragement

helped. So I extend my hand and she takes it. Then she holds up the mirror and we both gaze into it.

The next thing I know, we're there. Back in that same dreamwalk she took me to. But thousands of years in the future.

The ice castle is still there, bigger and better than ever. Sunshine bounces off the walls, making it glitter and shimmer like it's something out of a storybook.

Like it's something right out of a dream.

I give her hand a squeeze, and I take a step back.

And when I blink, she's gone and I'm in bed with Ryet. His arms around me. His *human* arms around me. I turn and laugh and I know, whatever happens now, it's gonna be OK.

We'll get through it, because we're together.

Maybe we only get seven years and maybe all those years will be a living hell…

But then again, maybe they won't.

EPILOGUE – RYET

The Tribulation begins without any help from me. That's not my role and I take no part in it at all. I've been reading up on this whole Antichrist thing and it appears that I have to charm the world into giving me power if I want the prophecy to actually play out.

And I'm not gonna do it.

I'm just not gonna do it.

Syrsee and I decided to stay at the Montana lodge. It's mine, anyway. Plus there's a lot of weird secret shit up here on this property, not to mention cool tunnels, an underground garage, and a doomsday bunker that was the former home of one Dark Josep. So it's really the best place to sit out the plagues and shit that are coming our way.

And it's quiet.

A few of the scions Paul gave blood to at the end made it through. Jeff being one of them. They won't live long, but I'll take their friendship as long as they're around.

Tristin is still here too. He's more Syrsee's friend than mine, but it's nice to have another vampire around, even if this one was pinioned and is magicless.

He's got contacts with the Guild and the Obscurati. So even though news is slow—the power grids went out worldwide back when the first seal was broken—we still do get it. Some kind of Obscurati Pony Express, I guess. Letter-writing is back in style and Tristin leaves to gather news every couple of days. Syrsee says there are Guild Lounges in all the airports and bus stations, so I guess he goes there to get filled in.

They are still alive, all those vampires across the ocean. They don't need the Black blood like I do, so they're not really missing their Syrsee copies yet.

But they will. One day. Maybe they'll be here for the duration and I'll have to deal with them at some point, or maybe they won't.

I don't actually care either way.

I'm me again.

Like… *me* again. Ryet. Human Ryet. Handsome, and strong, and rich, and powerful. It's weird, but much better than the alternative for sure.

My only part in this whole Antichrist thing is a book I'm writing.

My story. My point of view. Me.

Because no one knows what's real anymore. The whole world has gone crazy. And if I'm gonna get blamed for all this shit, well, I'm gonna get my say before it's over.

I feel a little kinship with Paul over this, but not enough to forgive him for fucking me over.

All that talk of love. Such bullshit. He used me to get a meeting with God.

What an asshole.

But honestly, I really can't complain. My life is better than ever. I'm in my home. A place I actually built. And it's beautiful. The mountains, the sunsets, the pool.

I go hunting, and fishing, and every night I get in bed with the woman I love.

The Whore of Babylon, Paul said.

I didn't tell her that and it's not going into the book.

No. The Apocalypse can go fuck itself.

We're just gonna sit up here and live the dream…

I'm standing in a mist of gold so thick, I can barely see what's in front of me. But I know what's there and I know what it means to walk through.

If I get that far.

Technically, I cheated.

Will this be held against me at the Final Judgment?

Maybe. And if that happens the last two thousand years was all for nothing.

But it would be a waste to cast me aside at this point.

Did I not complete the mission?

Did I not unleash the Apocalypse?

Were you not entertained?

Only a petty, spiteful God would condemn me for imaginative logistics.

So I let out a breath, take another in, and step forward—

Suddenly, there is a flash of bright light. And I think to myself, *Fuck, yes! I did it! I'm in!*

But the light is coming from behind me, so I turn and find a shadow peeking through the curtain of gold. I squint. "Syrsee?"

"Paul!" She exclaims my name as she holds up a hand to make a shadow over her eyes. "I found you! I'm so sorry it took me so long, the mirrors were—"

But I interrupt her. "It's over, Syrsee. It doesn't matter anymore. It's… just… over." Poor thing. She's traveling through time. And not doing it very well, at that.

She opens her mouth to say more, but the mist takes her away.

She tried her best, though. She did come back for me.

Several times. Though, after this visit, I'm starting to suspect that she hasn't actually made those trips yet.

Which means they are some time in the future.

Hmmmm. I ponder this, then smile, satisfied. Because this little visit of hers tells me two things. One, she tried really hard to help me. And two, she doesn't hold my betrayal of Ryet against me. So she's thinking about me.

Hopefully for not all the wrong reasons. Reasons like Ryet isn't around anymore.

But it's all out of my control now, so I turn back to the waiting gates.

All I have to do is pass through.

If I do that—if I am allowed to do that—all my questions will be answered.

So I take another breath and step forward into my dubious future…

End of Book Shit

Welcome to the End of Book Shit. This is the part of the book where I get to vomit up my feelings about what you just read or listened to. It's not edited and will most likely have some typos.

And I'm going to be brutally honest. My opinion of vampires has changed forever since I started writing this book. When I first got the idea to write a vampire series the one thing I didn't want to do was tell the same old 'stupid story'.

Think Buffy, think Vampire Diaries, think True Blood.

Those are all good stories about vampires. I never got in to Buffy but I watched every single episode of Vampire Diaries and True Blood. I was a really big Anne Rice fan—still am. And I love what she did with the genre. Totally changing it up and going back in history the way she did. Lestat was revolutionary for the vampire genre.

I wanted to do what Anne did—tell an original story. I know, I know, I know… readers love their tropes. They like same-same, they love the repeat story, all they want is for their expectations to be met.

I get it. That's what I want too. As a reader.

But as a writer… well, I'm just gonna say it. Writing books is a hard thing to do. It not only takes a lot out of you, it takes a lot of time. And time is something you can't buy. No one gets more time. It's a finite thing. So that's my number one rule for everything in life – I will not waste my time.

And writing books about same-same shit is, in my singular opinion, a waste of time.

I said in my last EOBS that I was unsure what the message

was in this series. The message for ME, the writer, and not YOU, the reader.

Because—again—I don't do any of this for the reader.

I don't write books for other people. I write books for me. So the message that I'm looking for in every story is for me. And that is often what I pass on to you in the EOBS.

And that's why this series took so long. Even when I gave in and had the audiobook scheduled—I think that was last summer, maybe? Yeah, I think so. Even at that moment, I didn't have the message. I just knew it was time to put some attention here on this story again, and so I did.

The message came to me slowly over a period of months as the world unfolded in the lead up and aftermath of the US elections.

I'm just going to tell you up front right now, I don't vote. I didn't vote for anyone.

I don't know if you're aware where the word 'vote' comes from, but it's from the Latin, *votum*.

If you look up the meaning of this root it gives you "a promise to a god" as the standard definition. But this is a good thousand years after the origin of the word.

Because it actually goes back to ancient times and means a 'sacrifice to a god for a favor'.

And by god, I don't mean God. Because if one is a God, one does not dwell, or deal with, the lives of humans. If one is a God, one has no need for devotees, or sacrifices, or pledges of any kind. If one is a God, one is above—and apart—from everything else.

I was put in this world—arguably—against my will, and I have been forced to deal with situations that I have almost no control over. And that's all I'm doing. That's all I can do, just control my reactions.

I don't have to condone this world, I don't have to accept it, and I most certainly do not have to participate in it. So I don't.

But it became pretty clear over the past several years—and culminated to a final conclusion during this past election season —that the root of all evil is liars.

Liars.

Like Paul.

He's easy to hate, but he's also easy to like. That's the problem with evil. It's true in just enough ways to fool you.

Liars who know exactly what they're doing, and do it anyway. That is true evil.

They've invented a fun new word for it—gas-lighting.

Gas-lighting. How quirky. How trendy.

Gas-lighting describes a pathological liar. Someone who gets off one telling you something false just to see if you'll fall for it. Just to see if they can drive you crazy. Just to see if they can hurt you.

We have fun names for these gas-lighters too. Trolls. Spammers. Scammers. But that's not what they are. Gas-lighters are sociopaths. They are mentally ill. They are disgusting examples of human beings. And this world we live in—this 'modern marvel of wireless communication' is a breeding ground for them. It's the perfect warm, moist environment for disease to grow and flourish.

This is evil. You live in in. You're like a goldfish in a bag of water set inside a new tank to be acclimated to the change in temperature. You've been watching a propaganda machine your entire life—a box in your living room that told you to trust it— and you did.

We all did. Who would think that the only purpose of that box in your living room was to lie? I mean, normal people think this idea is crazy because normal people aren't sociopathic liars. Normal people aren't evil. And thus, normal people cannot relate. They cannot find a motive, so they cannot believe it's true.

I get it. It took me a long time to unravel this mystery of liars. Why do they do it? What do they get out of it? And why do they want this reward? Why are people evil?

I doubt most people will ever ask those questions, let alone do the work necessary to find and understand the answers. But this was my message in this series. MY message. Not my message to you. You can do whatever you want with this story, but me? I've found the take home.

And while it is a very simple message, it's also sad and frightening at the same time.

Because the message is… Paul exists. A beautiful thing with selfish intentions. A creature that will lie to your face, tell you it loves you, and then sentence you to hell in the same breath.

But that's not even the worst part. The worst part is that this evil has a direct line of communication to everyone. It's like the dreamwalk, this telephone line. A way to be in your space, without really being there.

It's in the TV, it's in your phone, it's in your car, and on your wrist, and in the air all around you. Everywhere you hang out, there are psychopaths. Gas-lighters. Trolls. Scammers, griefers, spammers, and sock-puppets.

And the saddest thing is, these days people think… this is all normal.

It's not.

Evil has never had such a captive audience.

That was my message from the muse that fuels me. And that's it. There are no answers coming, you guys.

Just warnings. "And in those days shall men seek death, and shall not find it; and shall desire to die, and death shall flee from them."

That is what the vampire truly is.

A liar who will live forever.

Thank you for reading, thank you for reviewing, and I'll see you in the next book.

Julie
JA Huss
May 4, 2025

ABOUT THE AUTHOR

JA Huss is a New York Times Bestselling author and has been on the USA Today Bestseller's list 21 times. She writes characters with heart, plots with twists, and perfect endings.

Her books have sold millions of copies all over the world. Her book, Eighteen, was nominated for a Voice Arts Award and an Audie Award in 2016 and 2017 respectively. Her audiobook, Mr. Perfect, was nominated for a Voice Arts Award in 2017. Her audiobook, Taking Turns, was nominated for an Audie Award in 2018. Her book, Total Exposure, was nominated for a RITA Award in 2019.

She lives on a ranch in Colorado with her family.

9 781957 277363